CARAVAN OF DEMONS

"Look!" Irith called from above. She pointed. Kelder looked.

A man in a black robe had climbed atop one of the big wagons and was rising to his feet, standing on the wagon's roof. He was shouting aloud, and his words were like nothing Kelder had ever heard.

The bandits were almost to the row of wagons now. The battle was just about to be joined when the first black thing popped out of the ground. Then, like water from a fountain, they came from beneath the wagon where the man in black still stood.

The creatures' faces were truly hideous. Great staring white eyes, noses like blades or blobs, mouths that gaped in enormous yawning grins . . . Kelder was very glad he was no closer.

"Demons!" Irith called. "The man in black's a demonologist."

Kelder felt a shudder run through him . . .

By Lawrence Watt-Evans
Published by Ballantine Books:

THE LORDS OF DÛS
The Lure of the Basilisk
The Seven Altars of Dûsarra
The Sword of Bheleu
The Book of Silence

The Misenchanted Sword
With a Single Spell
The Unwilling Warlord
The Blood of A Dragon
Taking Flight
The Spell of the Black Dagger*

The Cyborg and the Sorcerers
The Wizard and the War Machine

Nightside City

Crosstime Traffic

*Forthcoming

TAKING FLIGHT

Lawrence Watt-Evans

A Del Rey Book
BALLANTINE BOOKS • NEW YORK

A Del Rey Book
Published by Ballantine Books

Library of Congress Catalog Card Number: 92–97054

ISBN 0–345–37715–X

Manufactured in the United States of America

First Edition: March 1993

Dedicated to
Charlotte and Mark
and Laura and Arthur

TAKING
FLIGHT

PROLOGUE

The girl squirmed on her seat, and the old woman cast her a quick, angry glance. She quieted, and the woman turned back to her customer.

"Well, lad," she said, "what would you have of me?"

The boy hesitated.

"I'm . . . I'm Kelder of Shulara," he said.

"I know," she replied, nodding.

It was a lie, of course; she hadn't known anything of the sort. In fact, it struck her suddenly that the name might be false, and instead of looking omniscient she might look foolish if she believed it. "Kelder of Shulara"—well, really, that probably *was* a lie! And not a very original one, at that. Smoothly, so that the boy saw no pause, she winked at him and continued, in a mysterious tone, "I know all I *need* to know."

The lad looked suitably confused and impressed. Behind him, the little girl rolled her eyes upward and mouthed something—it looked like "Oh, come *on*, Grandma!"

"So, Kelder of Shulara," the woman went on, a bit hurriedly, "you have come to Zindré the Seer to learn your future—and I see it laid out before me, vast and shining. There is too much to tell you all of it, my child, for your life will be long and rich; you must ask me specific questions, and I shall answer them all . . ."

The girl cleared her throat. Her grandmother glared at her and continued, " . . . at the cost of merely three bits apiece."

Kelder, fortunately, didn't notice any of the byplay between Zindré and her granddaughter; he was staring intently at the

1

crystal bowl on the table before him, as if he expected to see something in it himself.

That was an uncomfortable thought; Zindré did not like the idea of a customer who had *real* magic.

But surely the boy couldn't have any magic; he was just a peasant.

He cleared his own throat and asked, "Will I *ever* get out of Shulara?"

That was an easy one. "Oh, yes," Zindré said. "You shall go, and you shall go far, beyond the hills and into strange lands, and you shall return safely." He probably wouldn't, but she knew what he wanted to hear.

"Return? I'll come back?"

Zindré suppressed a frown and silently cursed herself for not listening more carefully to the boy's tone and phrasing. "Oh, yes," she said, "you will return, covered in glory, to tell those who remained behind of the wonders you saw."

"To stay?" Kelder asked; then something registered, and without waiting for an answer he asked, "Wonders? What wonders?"

"Many wonders," Zindré said quickly, hoping to distract the boy from the question of exactly where he was going to wind up. "Great cities and vast plains, strange beasts and beautiful women, and much mighty magic." She usually threw in something about mountains rather than plains, but in a place as hilly as Shulara she thought that plains would be more exotic and intriguing.

"Magic? But what will I do? Where will I go?"

Zindré gestured broadly and stared into the bowl before replying. "The magic is strange, of a kind I have never seen, and that neither wizards nor witches know. It will both be yours and not be yours. You will roam free, unfettered, and you will be a champion of the lost and forlorn, honored by the dead and those yet unborn." That should sound vague and mysterious enough to suit anyone.

From the corner of her eye she saw her granddaughter clearly signing to ease up a little; Zindré reviewed what she had just said and decided the girl was right, she had been getting carried away. "As for where," she said, "I see a long road stretching before me, but just which road it might be I cannot say."

Kelder's disappointment showed on his face. The granddaughter broke in.

"Excuse me," she said, "but that makes fifteen bits, and you only paid a single round; I'll need another before you ask my grandmother any more questions."

Kelder turned, startled, and stared at her, open-mouthed.

She held out a hand.

Abashed, Kelder dug in the purse at his belt and pulled out another copper round. "That's all I have," he said.

"That leaves one bit," the girl said. "Do you want change or one more question? My grandmother will answer one more at discount."

"Another question," Kelder said immediately.

"Think well before you speak, then, Kelder of Shulara," Zindré intoned.

Kelder thought.

"Tell me about the girl I'll marry," he said at last.

Zindré nodded. "She will be bright and beautiful, with a laugh like birdsong," she said. "With a magic all her own. You will bring her to your home in pride and delight and spend your life with her in joy." That one was easy; it was a standard question, and she had used that standard reply a hundred times, at least.

"Children?" Kelder asked.

"Money?" the granddaughter demanded.

Woebegone, Kelder admitted, "I don't have any more."

"It matters not," Zindré said quickly. "The vision dims; the spell is fading away. I could tell you little more in any case." She picked up a green cloth and dropped it neatly over the crystal bowl.

"Oh," Kelder said. Reluctantly, he stood.

The granddaughter gestured toward the door of the hut, and Kelder, with a polite little bow, departed. The girl escorted him out and closed the door behind him.

When the door was shut the girl said, "I guess he believed it."

"Of course he did!" Zindré said, bustling about, adjusting the hangings on the walls and straightening candles that had slumped as the wax melted unevenly. "Are there any more?"

"No," the girl said. "You know, Grandma, I still don't understand how we can get away with this—can't *anybody* tell real magic from lies?"

"Those that can," Zindré said complacently, "don't come to us in the first place."

Outside, in the gathering dusk, Kelder found two of his sisters chattering with the smith's daughter, near the forge. "Where have *you* been?" Salla demanded, as her little brother ran up.

"Talking to the seer," he said.

All three girls turned to stare at him. "Oh, Kelder, you didn't," Edara said.

"Didn't what?" Kelder asked defensively.

"You didn't spend all your money on that charlatan!"

"No, I didn't!" Kelder replied angrily.

"How much *did* you spend?" Salla asked.

"Not that much," he said.

"*How* much?"

"Two rounds," he admitted.

"Oh, Kelder!" Edara sighed.

"Magic is expensive!" he protested.

"Kelder," Salla told him, "she doesn't have any more magic than *I* do! She's an old fake! A liar!"

"No, she isn't!"

"Yes, she is! She's here every year, and none of her predictions have ever come true."

"Not *yet*, maybe," Kelder said.

"*Never*, Kelder. She's a fake. None of what she told you is going to come true."

"Yes, it will," Kelder said. "You just wait and see!" He turned away, hurt and angry, and muttered to himself, "It *will* come true."

A moment later he added, "I'll *make* it come true."

CHAPTER 1

*K*elder sat down on the grassy hilltop and set his pack down beside him. The gods were pouring darkness across the sky, now that the sun was below the horizon, and it was, in his considered opinion, time to stop for the night.

This would be the third night since he had left home—and by the feel of it, the coldest yet. It was quite unfair; this was spring, after all, and the days were supposed to be getting warmer, not colder.

He looked down the slope at the road below, still faintly visible in the gathering gloom as a pale strip of bare dirt between the dark expanses of grass on either side. On the near side that grass was at the foot of the hill he sat upon, while on the opposite side, the north, the land flattened out remarkably.

He was beyond the hills, at any rate.

This was cattle country, so there were no tilled fields to be seen, and at this hour all the livestock had gone home, wherever home might be. The road below was the only work of human origin anywhere in sight.

Kelder was pretty sure that that road was the Great Highway. He stared at it in disappointment.

It was not at all what he had expected.

He had imagined that he would find it bustling with travelers, with caravans and wandering minstrels, escaping slaves and marching armies, as busy as a village square on market day. He had thought it would be lined with inns and shops, that he would be able to trot on down and find jolly company in some tavern, where he could spend his scrupulously hoarded coins on ale and oranges, then win more coins from careless strangers who dared to dice with him—and the fact that he had never played dice before did not trouble his fantasies at all. He had envisioned himself watching a wizard perform wonders, then escorting a comely wench up the stairs, flinging a few bits to a minstrel by the hearth as he passed, making clever remarks in half a dozen languages. Everyone would admire his wit and bravery, and he would be well on his way to fulfilling the seer's prophecy.

Instead he saw nothing but a long, barren strip of hard-packed dirt, winding its way between the hills on either side, and utterly empty of life.

He sighed and pulled open the flap of his pack.

He should have known better, he told himself as he pulled out his blanket. Life was not what the seers and storytellers made it out to be. Much as he hated to admit it, it looked just about as drab and dreary as his sisters had always said it was. It wasn't just the family farm that was tedious, as he had always thought it was, it now appeared, the entire World.

And he should have guessed that, he told himself, from his previous expeditions.

The first time he had run away had been the week after his visit to Zindré the Seer at the village market. He had only been twelve.

That had been rash, and he had been young; Zindré had never implied that he would begin his journey so young.

Kelder had had reasons, though. His father, determined to keep the family farm in the family and having let all three of Kelder's older sisters arrange to marry away, had adamantly refused to arrange an apprenticeship or a marriage for Kelder; Kelder was going to inherit the farm, whether he wanted it or not, and settling the legacy on him meant no apprenticeship, no arranged marriage.

It had meant that Kelder was expected to spend the rest of his life on that same piece of ground, seeing nothing of the World, learning nothing of interest, doing no good for anyone, but only carrying on the family traditions. That was hardly roaming "free and unfettered," as the seer had promised, or being "a champion of the lost and forlorn."

Kelder had not *wanted* to spend the rest of his life on that same piece of ground carrying on the family traditions.

So, frustrated and furious, he had left, convinced excitement and adventure must surely wait just across the ridge. He had wandered off that first time without so much as a stale biscuit in the way of supplies, and had crossed the ridge, only to find more dismal little farms much like his own family's.

He had stayed away a single night, but his hunger the following morning had driven him back to his mother's arms.

The next time he left, when he was thirteen, he had packed a lunch and stuffed a dozen bits in iron into his belt purse and had marched over not just one ridge but a dozen or more—four or five miles, at least, and maybe farther. He had known that soldiers were said to march twenty or thirty miles a day, but he had been satisfied; he hadn't hurried, had rested often, and the hills had slowed him down.

And when darkness had come spilling over the sky, he had spent the night huddled under a haystack. He had continued the following day—but around noon, when his lunch was long gone and he had still seen nothing but more ridges and more little farms, he had decided that the time of the prophecy's fulfillment had not yet come, and he had turned back.

The spring after that, at fourteen, he had plotted and planned for a month before he set out to seek his fortune. He had carried sensible foods, a good blanket, three copper bits and a dozen iron, and a sharp knife.

He had made it to his intended destination, Shulara Keep, by noon of the second day, and he had done so without much difficulty. But then, after the initial thrill of seeing a genuine castle had faded somewhat, and the excitement of the crowds in the market square had dimmed, he had found himself unsure what to do next. He had not dared to speak to anyone—they were all strangers.

Finally, when the castle guard had shooed him out at sunset, he had given up and again headed home.

At fifteen he had decided to try again. He had again gone

to Shulara Keep, then continued to the west, until on the morning of the third day he had come to Elankora Castle. Elankora was "beyond the hills," and while it wasn't anyplace particularly interesting, it was a "strange land" in that it wasn't Shulara, so it was a step in the right direction.

There he had encountered a problem that had never occurred to him. Most of the people of Elankora spoke no Shularan, and he, for his own part, knew only a dozen words in Elankoran. Realizing his mistake, and frustrated by the language barrier, he had turned homeward once more.

That was last year. This time he had prepared for that. He had found tutors—which had not been easy—and had learned a smattering of several dialects, judging that he could pick up more with practice when the need arose.

Old Chanden had taught him some Aryomoric and a few words of Uramoric. Tikri Tikri's son, across the valley, had turned out to speak Trader's Tongue, and Kelder had learned as much of that as he could—it was said that throughout the World, merchants who spoke Trader's Tongue could be found in every land.

Several neighbors spoke Elankoran and Ressamoric, but he could not find anyone willing to waste time teaching him; he had to settle for picking up a few bits and pieces.

Most amazing of all, though, Luralla the Inquisitive, that bane of his childhood, spoke Ethsharitic! Her grandmother had taught her—though why her recently deceased grandmother had spoken it no one seemed to know.

It had even been worth putting up with Luralla's teasing to learn *that*! After all, it was said that the Hegemony of Ethshar was bigger than all the Small Kingdoms put together—so it was said, and he had never heard it contradicted, so he judged it to be the truth.

And if he was to see great cities and vast plains, that could well mean Ethshar.

Kelder had discovered, to his pleased surprise, that each language he attempted was easier than the one before. He had feared that his brain would fill up with words until he could fit no more, but instead he had found patterns, similarities between the different tongues, so that learning a third language was easier than a second, and the fourth was easier still.

Even so, a year's spare time, given the distractions caused by all his chores on the farm, was not enough to really become fluent in any of them. He felt he could get by well enough in Trader's Tongue, and knew enough Ethsharitic to avoid disaster in the event no other tongue would serve. In Aryomoric he was, he judged, about on a par with a three-year-old, while in Uramoric and Ressamoric and Elankoran he knew only scattered phrases.

But then, he didn't intend to need Uramoric or Ressamoric or Elankoran, or even Aryomoric. He had decided to strike out to the north, all the way to the Great Highway, where his Trader's Tongue and Ethsharitic could be put to use—to the Great Highway that ran between the legendary bazaars of Shan on the Desert to the east and the huge, crowded complexity of the Hegemony of Ethshar, with its ancient capital, Ethshar of the Spices, to the west. The seer had said she saw a road stretching before her that he would travel—what other road could it be but the Great Highway?

So he had set out, his pack on his shoulder, and for three days he had marched north, through pastures and meadows, past farms and villages, through most of Shulara into Sevmor, and then from one end of Sevmor to the other.

At least, he thought he had passed beyond Sevmor, because he had never heard of any highways that ran through Sevmor. The Great Highway ran through Hlimora, and he therefore now believed himself to be in Hlimora.

What else could that road be, but the Great Highway?

And what was it but a long strip of dirt?

Three days of thirst, sore feet, and backache had taken much of the glamor out of his plans, and the sight of that empty road was the pebble that sank the barge. This trip, like the others, was a failure.

Maybe his sisters had been right all along, and Zindré the Seer was nothing but a lying old woman. He would never see the great cities she had promised him, the strange beasts and beautiful women, the mighty magic.

He wrapped the blanket around his shoulders, then plumped up the pack to serve as a pillow. His food was gone; he had eaten the last at midday. He would need to use his precious handful of coins to buy food from now on, whether he went on or turned back.

And in the morning, he promised himself as he lay down, in the morning he would turn back. He would go home to the family farm, to boring old Shulara, and he would stay there, dismal as that prospect was. He would listen to his family and give up his belief in the seer's prophecy.

After all, what need did he have of the wonders she had promised? He had a safe, secure position. With all three of his sisters married he would one day own the farm himself, the green pastures and the rich cornfields and the thirty head of cattle. He would undoubtedly marry someone—probably not the magical beauty the seer had predicted, but someone boring, like Inza of the Blue Eyes from across the valley. They would settle down and have children. That was just what his family had always said would happen, and they were right after all. He wouldn't see any wonders, wouldn't be an honored champion—all he would do would be to keep his parents happy by working the farm.

How horribly dull!

He opened his eyes and peered down through the darkness at the highway. The greater moon was rising, casting a pale-yellow glow, so he could still see the road, faintly.

It looked horribly dull, too—that was the problem. All of life, all the World, seemed to be horribly dull, with no wonders or beauty anywhere.

Maybe he was just tired, he thought. Maybe everything would look better in the morning.

Even if it did, though, he would go home—not covered in glory at all.

He sighed, closed his eyes, and slept.

CHAPTER 2

He awoke twice during the night, shivering with the cold; each time he curled himself up into a tighter ball, pulled the blanket more closely about him, and went back to sleep. The third time he awoke the sun was squeezing up out of the ground, far to the east, and he blinked at it unhappily.

With a sigh, he rubbed his eyes and sat up, remembering just where he was.

He was facing north atop a low hill, and below him lay the legendary and very disappointing Great Highway. To his left both moons were low in the west, and to his right the sun was just rising, and the combination cast long, distorted, and colored shadows across the hills. The sky was streaked with pink and gold and feathered with bits of cloud. The morning air was cold and sharp in his nostrils, carrying the smells of wet grass and morning mist.

A dawn like this was a sort of wonder, at any rate, but no more so than he might have seen back home.

He got to his feet and stretched, trying to work some of the stiffness out of his joints, and stared down at that disappointing strip of dirt below.

At the very least, he told himself, he should go down and walk a few paces on it, just so he could honestly say, when he got home, that he had traveled on the Great Highway. After all, wasn't that part of the point? Wasn't he trying to do things that he could brag about when he got home? He didn't really think he had ever seriously wanted to stay away forever, and the seer had said he would return. He couldn't quite imagine not going back home sooner or later.

11

He just hadn't intended it to be quite so soon.

He had learned years ago, in the face of his sisters' mockery, to keep his mouth shut about Zindré's predictions; still, he had secretly harbored hopes of someday making them all come true.

Now he was finally convinced it would never happen. The World was just not an exciting place. There were no wonders to be seen.

He would just go home and be a farmer.

Something moved in the corner of his eye; he looked up, startled. The movement had been off to the left; he turned and looked, trying to spot it again.

At first, of course, he looked at the highway, and then at the fields to the far side, and then along the row of low hills along the near side. Only when the sparkle of something bright catching the morning sunlight drew his gaze upward did he spot it.

It was pale and gleaming and more or less cross-shaped, flying along above the highway, and initially he took it for a huge and unfamiliar bird. It swooped closer as he watched, gleaming in the dawn as he had never seen a bird gleam. He stared, trying to make it out, and realized that it was no bird.

It was a *person*, a person with wings, and it was coming toward him.

He hesitated, unsure whether to run or stand his ground. A person flying meant magic, and magic, much as he wanted to see it, could be dangerous.

The World might not be quite so dull as he had feared, but, he told himself, it might be more dangerous than he had thought.

Then the flying figure drew close enough for him to see the curve of breast and hip and the long sweeping flow of golden hair, and he knew it was a woman, a young woman, and like any lad of sixteen he wanted to see more of her. He stood his ground.

The figure drew closer and closer, her wings spread wide to catch the gentle morning breeze; they flapped occasionally, but she was gliding more than actually flying. Sunlight gleamed brilliantly from the wings, sparkling and iridescent; rainbows seemed to flicker across their silvery-white surfaces. She was wearing a white tunic with colored trim, though he could not yet make out the details; below the tunic were fawn-colored breeches, rather than the skirt a woman should be wearing—Kelder supposed a skirt would be impractical in flight. Her dangling feet were bare.

He held his breath, expecting her to veer away or vanish at any moment, but she came closer and closer. He could see her face now, the high cheekbones and turned-up nose, the large eyes and mouth. She was *very* young, not so much a woman as a girl, his own age or even a year or two younger. The trim on her tunic was green and blue embroidery, depicting leaves and flowers.

He stared, utterly astonished, as with a final swoop she settled gently to the earth not ten feet away from him.

She was the most beautiful thing he had ever seen. Her face was heart-shaped and perfect, her eyes a deep, pure blue, her hair a flowing stream of gold. Kelder had heard of blondes and had even seen pictures, but he had never seen one in person before.

The wings that grew from her upper back were sleek and white, with every curve gleaming polychrome; the back of her tunic was slit on either side and hemmed to allow them through. In front her breasts filled the tunic out nicely.

As she landed her wings, which had spread at least five yards from tip to tip, folded about her sides, like a cape. The embroidery at her neckline and on her cuffs, he noticed, showed morning glory vines in full bloom. A bloodstone as big as the top joint of his thumb glowed at the base of her throat, catching the morning sun.

She was four or five inches shorter that he was, though he was scarcely a giant—a shade below average height, in fact. She looked up at him with those deep blue eyes.

"Hello," she said, speaking the single Ethsharitic word in a soft and velvety voice.

"Hello," Kelder replied, when he had caught his breath. He

was suddenly very, very glad that Luralla's grandmother had known Ethsharitic.

Who *was* this miraculous creature? And why was she speaking to *him*? Had Zindré told the truth after all? Was this one of the prophesied wonders?

Was she perhaps even more?

"I'm Irith the Flyer," she said. "Who are you?"

"I'm ... I'm ..." he gulped and tried again. "I'm Kelder of Shulara."

She studied him thoughtfully for a moment, then pointed to the south. "Shulara's *that* way, isn't it?" she asked, cocking her head prettily to one side.

Kelder nodded, staring down at her. She was unbelievably beautiful.

"Then what are you doing *here*?" she asked, blinking up at him.

"I ... I wanted to see the Great Highway," Kelder replied, horribly aware that his answer sounded stupid.

She turned to look down at the road. "Well, there it is," she said. "It's not really much to look at, around here." She turned back and smiled at him. "Of course, this is one of the dull parts," she said. "The best parts are at the ends."

That was a fascinating bit of information, and Kelder was very pleased to have it. "You have traveled on the highway?" he asked. The Ethsharitic words came to his tongue with difficulty; he feared that if the conversation went on he would soon be lost.

Irith grinned at him. "Oh, I've been back and forth along it a *hundred* times!" she said. "What about you?"

"I came here last night," he admitted. "From Shulara."

"Oh." She glanced southward. "They don't speak Ethsharitic there, do they?"

"No," Kelder admitted.

"I don't think I remember how to speak Shularan," she said apologetically. "Would you rather speak Trader's Tongue?"

"Ah ... it might be easier, yes," Kelder agreed, relieved. Trader's Tongue shared rather more vocabulary with Shularan than did Ethsharitic, and the grammar came more easily. Besides, Tikri Tikri's son had been a more knowledgeable and congenial teacher than Luralla the Inquisitive.

Irith nodded. "All right," she said in Trader's Tongue. "You came here cross-country all by yourself?"

Kelder needed a minute to switch languages; then he replied, "Well, there *aren't* any roads in Shulara, not really." Trader's Tongue was much easier, once he had made the adjustment.

"Oh, I know," she said. "I was there once, a long time ago. It's pretty, but not very exciting." She shrugged, then looked back up into his eyes. "Is that why you left?" she asked. "To find somewhere more exciting?"

"Something like that," he agreed, marveling at how she seemed to be equally fluent in both tongues. "I wanted to seek my fortune, you know, like in the stories. My father wants me to just stay home and be a farmer the way he did, and he . . . well, I didn't want to. Or at least, not yet." He made no mention of the prophecy, for fear she, like his sisters, would think it stupid and laugh at him.

She nodded. "Grown-ups can be so *boring*, can't they?" She giggled.

The sound, Kelder thought, was almost like birdsong.

Bright and beautiful, with a laugh like birdsong, with a magic all her own—*this* was the girl he was to marry! It had to be, beyond a doubt. He would bring her to his home in pride and delight, and spend his life with her in joy.

That was what the seer had said. Kelder swallowed.

Irith smiled at him, then abruptly sat down, cross-legged, on the grass. The movement exposed her ankles, and Kelder noticed something on one of them, several narrow bands encircling her leg.

Then she stretched her arms over her head and yawned, and Kelder stared at the display of curves elsewhere and forgot about her ankles. Wings aside, blond hair aside, Irith was still *far* more interesting than Inza of the Blue Eyes.

"I got up early this morning," she said casually, when the yawn was done. "I wanted to do a little early flying, before anybody else was up."

Kelder settled to the ground himself, far more slowly and carefully, a few feet away from her. He stared at her, at the great shining wings, and wondered where she had come from. If he was going to marry her, he wanted to know something about her background. Was there a whole nation of winged people somewhere?

That would be a wonder worth seeing!

"Do you live around here?" he asked.

"Oh, I don't live anywhere in particular," she said with a wave of her hand. "Just wherever I happen to land." She smiled at him again, an intoxicating smile. He smiled back without knowing why.

"What about your family?" he asked.

"Don't have any," she said. "They're all long gone."

"Oh, I'm sorry," he replied.

She turned up an empty palm in a shrug.

They sat silently for a minute, each contemplating the sunlight on the grassy hillside and the road below. The place that Kelder had found so dismal the night before somehow seemed to be sparkling with beauties and possibilities now that Irith had appeared. Kelder wanted to say something to her—he wanted to impress her, to sweep her off her feet, to hurry along the process of courtship and marriage. Zindré had told him he would marry this creature, but she had never said how long it would take.

But Kelder found himself tongue-tied, unable to think of a word. Irith's beauty was overwhelming.

Then Irith asked, "So, if you're off to seek your fortune, how old are you, anyway? The traditional age is still thirteen, right? You certainly don't *look* thirteen."

"I'm not," he admitted. "I'm sixteen."

She nodded. "I guess you left it a bit late, then?"

He nodded. "What about you?" he asked.

"I'm fifteen," she said.

He nodded again. That was just right, a year younger than himself.

Not that he would have minded if she wasn't.

After a moment's hesitation, he gathered his nerve and said, "I never saw anyone with wings before."

She giggled—definitely birdsong, he thought.

"As far as I know," she said, "there *isn't* anyone else with wings. Just me."

"Oh." That answered that, and disposed of any notion he might have had of finding a land of winged people, but left her background a complete mystery. Kelder tried to think of some clever way to phrase his next question, but couldn't. "How did you come to have wings, anyway?" he said. "Were you born with them?"

She giggled again. "No, silly, of course not!" She pushed playfully at his shoulder.

Startled and pleased by the unexpected familiarity, he asked, "Then where'd you get them?"

She blinked at him, then leaned over toward him as if she were confiding a secret. "Well," she said, "I was a wizard's apprentice once, a long time ago. And I think I was pretty good at it, too. But my master was an old grouch, really stuffy about all these stupid rules and regulations and his precious guild and all my obligations as a wizard in training, and all that stuff, and I just got really fed up with it all, you know? So one day when he'd been especially nasty to me, after I was done crying and while he was out at the market or somewhere, I borrowed his book of spells—or stole it, really, I guess, since he'd told me never to touch it, but I gave it back. Anyway, I took it and looked up a spell he'd told me about that would give me wings, and I used it, and it worked! See?" She preened slightly, flexing her wings so that they caught the sunlight and shimmered brightly.

"They're beautiful," Kelder said in honest admiration. He was tempted to reach out and touch them, but dared not.

He wondered what it would be like, taking a flying girl to bed. Would the wings get in the way?

She smiled as she peered over her shoulder at them. "Aren't they? And flying is such *fun!*"

He smiled back at her, sharing her delight, then asked, "What happened after that? Did the wizard catch you?"

She laughed. "No, silly," she said. "At least, not then. I just flew away and never came back. And the next time I saw him wasn't for *years*, and by then nobody cared anymore, and we just forgot about the whole thing."

Kelder nodded. "So you never finished your apprenticeship?"

"No. Why should I? I've got everything I need!" She spread her wings wide, and the breeze they made blew the hair back from Kelder's forehead. "See?" she said.

He stared in amazement. He wondered just what she meant when she said "years," though. She *couldn't* mean it literally. After all, she must have started her apprenticeship at age twelve—that tradition was so ancient and sacred that Kelder couldn't imagine it being violated—and it must have taken her at *least* a year before she learned enough magic to attempt something like a wing-making spell and got fed up enough with her master to use it. He had always heard how difficult wizardry was, and he would have thought it would take at least a journeyman wizard to do something like that; the magicians he'd seen mostly limited themselves to little stunts like lighting fires or making trees whistle. Nobody could have made journeyman before age eighteen, from what he'd heard—sixteen at the very least. And yet Irith claimed she'd gotten her wings and run away years ago, and she was only fifteen now.

Of course, the wizards Kelder had encountered in a quiet nowhere like Shulara weren't the best, but even so, she must have needed a year or two before she could have learned such a spell.

And she'd talked about visiting Shulara, and traveling back and forth on the Great Highway hundreds of times—she must just be prone to exaggerating, he decided.

Well, that was no big deal. Lots of the girls he knew liked to exaggerate—and not just girls, either, for that matter. So what if she twisted the chronology a little?

Of course, it did make it harder to know just what had really happened. She must have been a good pupil, he thought, to learn a way to conjure her wings so young. She probably ran away only a few months ago.

Part of the prophecy ran through his head—"The magic is strange, of a kind I have never seen, and that neither wizards nor witches know. It will both be yours and not be yours." His wife's magic would be his and yet not his—were Irith's wings the "strange magic" that had been referred to?

But according to Irith's story, this was a magic that wizards know, wasn't it?

Well, perhaps Zindré had gotten that one little detail wrong, or Irith had distorted something.

And the details didn't really matter, anyway, did they? He decided not to be nosy and asked no further questions. When they were married he would have plenty of time to find out.

"So where were you heading?" she asked him. "You said you came to see the Great Highway, right?"

"That's right," he agreed.

"Well, you've seen it; are you just going to go back home to your folks now?"

"Of course not!" he said.

Actually, he had been planning to do exactly that, but he was not about to admit that in front of the girl he was destined to marry. He didn't want to look like a coward, or a fool, walking all this way for nothing.

Besides, her very presence proved that Zindré the Seer had not lied.

He had traveled far, beyond the hills and into strange lands; he had seen the road stretching before him; he had found the girl he was to marry—but he had not yet seen great cities or vast plains or strange beasts, he had not seen beautiful women in the plural. Irith's magic might qualify as "mighty," or it might not, but the prophecy had said "*much* mighty magic." And he had not yet championed anyone lost or forlorn. It was not yet time to return safely home with his bride.

And he wasn't about to let Irith think he was a coward or a fool; if she spurned him, his entire destiny would be jeopardized.

"Where are you going, then?" Irith asked.

"Where are *you* going?" he countered.

"Oh, I haven't decided—and besides, I asked first!" She smiled brightly. "So where *are* you going?"

"That way," he said, choosing a direction more or less at random and pointing east along the highway.

"Oh, good!" She clapped her hands together in delight. "All the way to Shan on the Desert?"

He nodded. Why not? Why shouldn't he actually do it, go all the way to Shan on the Desert? It was a great city, wasn't it? The prophecy had said he would see great cities. And the Bazaar there was said to be *full* of wonders and magic.

"I haven't been there in the *longest* time," Irith said. "Could I come with you? We could get to know each other better—I get lonely sometimes, living by myself."

"Sure," Kelder said, trying to sound nonchalant. "I'd be glad of some company myself."

That, of course, was an understatement. Kelder thought she was the most beautiful thing he had ever seen, and given half a chance, he'd have followed her wherever she wanted to go. To have *her* following *him* was even better, since she couldn't very well consider him a nuisance in that case.

The prospects for a short courtship and swift marriage were looking better every moment.

There were obstacles, of course, like his limited funds, but he tried not to think about those.

"Let's go, then, shall we?" She got to her feet, and he caught another glimpse of the curious colored rings on her ankle as her breeches fell back into place. She started down the hillside.

He started to follow, then stopped. "Wait a minute," he said, flustered, "I need to pack up my things here!" He turned and quickly gathered up his belongings, stuffing them into his pack as fast as he could.

When he was sure he wasn't leaving anything important he got up, slung the pack on his shoulder, and trotted down the hill to where Irith waited, smiling. It was only as he came up beside her that he realized her wings were gone.

"*Hai!*" he said, startled.

"What is it?" she asked, looking about.

"Your wings," he said, feeling very foolish. "Where'd they go?"

The thought occurred to him that maybe she had never really had wings at all, maybe they'd been an illusion of some kind—but hadn't she said she had wings?

"Oh!" she said with a giggle. "Didn't I tell you that? It's part of the spell. I don't have wings all the time, only when I want to. And they're kind of a nuisance when I'm walking, so I got rid of them."

"But . . ." Kelder began, then stopped. He really didn't know how to express his puzzlement, especially not in Trader's Tongue.

"Oh, don't worry about it, silly!" Irith said. "Come on!"

She started walking, and he hurried to catch up. A moment later he asked, "But where do they *go?*"

She shrugged, a gesture he found wonderfully winsome. "*I* don't know," she said. "It's magic, of course."

"But when you want them back, where do you . . . I mean . . ."

She sighed. "Don't worry about it, all right? I'm a shapeshifter, that's all. That's what the spell really was. I can shift back and forth between being me with wings and me without wings, just the way some wizards can turn themselves into cats or birds or other things. *That's* all!"

"Oh," he said, trying to absorb this. Shape-changing or not, that something could exist sometimes and not at other times did not seem to make very much sense.

Then he decided not to worry about it. It was magic, and as far as he knew, magic didn't have to make sense, it just *was*. If she could shift her shape, she could do it, and there wasn't any point in trying to figure out how, any more than in trying to figure out how that wizard had made a tree whistle.

Figuring out more about Irith herself was far more interesting, anyway.

And at least it meant that he needn't worry that the wings would be in the way.

They walked on, chatting occasionally and simply enjoying each other's company the rest of the time, strolling on at a comfortable pace, eastward toward the rising sun and Shan on the Desert.

The question of just what Kelder was going to do in Shan, or anywhere else, of just how the rest of the prophecy would fulfill itself—or could be *made* to fulfill itself—lurked unheeded in the back of his mind.

CHAPTER 3

*A*s *they walked, a handful of people passed them* eastbound, riding horses or heavily loaded mules; one brown-clad man on foot ran past, panting. In the other direction they had as yet encountered only a single traveler, an old woman in a green robe who strode past at a pace belying her age. The two youths spoke to none of them, but Kelder was relieved to see that there actually were people using the Great Highway. They met no caravans, no marching armies, no minstrels or magicians—at least, not so far as Kelder could see—but at least the road was not deserted.

They had been walking for slightly less than an hour when they first came in sight of the forest. Kelder stared.

He had seen trees before, and groves, but the forest seemed to extend forever, all along the south side of the highway, while to the north there were only the familiar farms, a patchwork of cornfields and pastures, with occasional sheep and cattle scattered in the pastures.

"That's called the Forest of Amramion," Irith told him, "even though most of it's actually in Uramor, and this corner here is in Hlimora."

"It is?"

"Sure. It means we're getting close to the border between Hlimora and Amramion, but we haven't reached it yet."

"Oh," Kelder said. He stared at the forest for a moment more and then said, "It certainly is big."

"Oh, it's nothing special," Irith said offhandedly. "The forests in Derua are a lot more impressive—the trees are at least twice as tall."

23

"They are?" Kelder asked, turning to look at her face. It was more attractive than the forest anyway. For all the time they had been walking he had hoped she would speak, that she would say something that would give him an excuse to talk to her, a chance to develop a little more of a relationship. He wanted to get to know his future wife better.

He had thought that perhaps a traveler would greet them, or Irith would remark on something, or simply that some opportunity would occur to him to speak up—but now that he had that opportunity, he feared he was sounding like an idiot.

"Yes, they are," Irith said. "I've seen them. And I've heard that the woods in Lumeth of the Forest are even better, but I haven't been there, and some people say that way up north in Aldagmor and Sardiron there are forests that make anything *anywhere* in the Small Kingdoms look like nothing much."

"Really?" Kelder asked.

"*I* don't know," Irith said. "But that's what I've heard."

They walked on silently for a moment after that, Kelder trying to think of something to say to continue the conversation. Finally, prompted by an emptiness in his belly, he asked, "Have you had any breakfast?"

Irith glanced at him. "No," she said, "but that's okay, I'm not hungry."

"*I* am," Kelder said. "Do you think we can find something to eat around here?"

"Well," Irith said, a trifle reluctantly, "there are inns in the village of Amramion, where the king's castle is."

"How far is that?"

Irith looked up that highway, then back the way they had come. "Oh," she said, "about three leagues. Hlimora Castle's a lot closer, of course."

"It is?" Kelder asked, startled.

"Sure," Irith said. "That's where I stayed last night. Where did you think I came from?"

"I don't know," Kelder said, "I guess I thought you'd camped out somewhere, same as I did."

She looked at him as if convinced he was insane. "Why

would I do *that*?" she asked. "It's cold and wet and uncomfortable, sleeping outdoors."

"But ..." Kelder was flustered, unsure what question most needed asking now. It didn't help any that he still had some difficulty thinking in Trader's Tongue. Finally he managed, "How far is Hlimora Castle?"

"About a league, maybe a little more—just out of sight of where we met. But it's in the wrong direction, if you're going to Shan. And besides, it's boring."

"Oh." Kelder struggled to decide which was more important, going to Shan and not being boring, or getting something to eat. The three leagues to Amramion seemed like an awfully long distance to travel without his breakfast.

There were no other travelers in sight just now. Had there been, Kelder might have attempted to beg some food, but as it was he didn't have that option. He looked down the road ahead, where he could see nothing but cornfields and pasture and forest, and then he looked back toward Hlimora, where he could see nothing but hills and cornfields and pasture, and he thought about the difference between the hour or so it would take to reach Hlimora Castle and the three hours— more, really, as he'd need to stop and rest somewhere—it would take to reach the village of Amramion, and he thought about the emptiness in his stomach.

Then, when he thought he'd decided, he looked at Irith's face and forgot about food.

"Oh," he said, "I'll be fine." He glanced around and added, "But if you see anything to eat anywhere, tell me." He eyed the corn growing in the fields, but as yet there were only green stalks, not even unripe ears to eat.

"All right," she said.

They marched on, and the forest stretched on alongside. They met no other travelers on this stretch.

About twenty minutes later Irith pointed to a low plant growing by the roadside, almost in the shade of the forest. "Those are strawberries," she said, "but I don't know if any of them are ripe."

Kelder wasn't sure he *cared* if they were ripe; he picked a handful. After his first taste, however, he decided that ripening was important after all; he tossed the rest away. He and his stomach grumbled on.

An hour or so later, after silent encounters with two more horsemen and twice that number westbound afoot, they came to the border between Hlimora and Amramion, a border marked by a small tower of reddish stone. It looked deserted, but as they approached a man in a steel helmet leaned over a merlon atop the tower and shouted at them.

Neither could make out his words, but Irith waved cheerfully.

The two of them strolled on, Kelder growing nervous, Irith quite calm as they approached the watchtower.

The man shouted again, and this time Kelder understood him; he was speaking Trader's Tongue.

"Who goes there?" he called.

Kelder looked at Irith, unsure what to say. She just waved gaily and called, "Hello!"

The guard squinted down at her.

"Irith?" he called.

She nodded.

"Walking this time, are you?" the guard called. "What happened to your wings?"

She grinned and stepped back away from Kelder for a moment.

When she stepped away she was just a girl—a very beautiful one, but a girl. Then, suddenly, she had wings that unfolded behind her, those great glistening white wings he had seen before. Kelder revised his earlier estimate; her wingspan was more than fifteen feet, and might be a full twenty.

She folded her wings, and then they were gone again. Kelder started to ask something, then didn't bother.

"Magic," he muttered to himself, "wonders and magic."

"What about him?" the guard called, pointing to Kelder.

"I met him up the road," Irith called. "His name's Kelder."

"That right, boy?" the guard called.

"Yes, sir," Kelder replied. "Kelder of Shulara."

"You a trader?"

"No, sir."

"You of noble birth?"

"No."

"You armed?"

"No, just a belt knife."

"Doesn't count. You a magician?"

"No."

"You swear that you've told me the truth?"

"Yes, sir."

"Irith?"

"Oh, *I* don't know, I just met him," Irith replied, a bit flustered. "But I *think* it's all true. It's the same thing he told *me*!"

"All right, go on, then," the guard said. "And you, Kelder, you be careful of Irith."

Kelder blinked and nodded. The soldier waved them on, and they walked on.

Kelder puzzled over the guard's last sentence. His knowledge of Trader's Tongue was still far from perfect, and he wasn't sure whether the guard had meant that he should defend Irith or beware of Irith.

The latter didn't seem to make much sense. She might be a shapeshifter, but she was still just a girl. And the guard himself certainly didn't seem very worried about her; he'd greeted her as an old friend.

So he must have been asking him to look after her.

Well, that sounded fine to Kelder. He was very interested indeed in looking after Irith indefinitely.

And the guard knew who and what Irith was and had greeted her by name. He had seemed willing to take her word for Kelder's identity. That implied, at the very least, that she really had traveled the Great Highway before, probably more than once. Kelder looked at his companion again, wondering how she had managed it. She must have started *awfully* young!

Impressing her was going to be very difficult, he realized, if she had traveled so far and seen so much. He wished he knew more about her and more about women in general. All the other girls he had associated with much were people he had known since childhood; he had had no practice in getting to know females, in attracting their interest—and he needed Irith to be interested in him. She was so beautiful, so endearing, that just walking beside her was a constant blend of agony and delight—delight at her presence and agony at the frustration of doing nothing *but* walking beside her. He wanted to touch her, hold her—but he didn't have the nerve yet.

The mere fact that she was there meant she liked him, since, after all, she could fly away at any second—but he had no way to judge how *much* she liked him, or what she wanted from him.

Boiling with indecision, he walked on, watching her.

They reached the town of Amramion a little over two hours after crossing the border.

It was quite a pleasant and interesting town, as far as Kelder was concerned—the largest he had ever seen, though the village surrounding Elankora Castle had come close. The castle that stood at its center, atop a low hill just south of the Great Highway, was rather larger and more sprawling—and less fortified—than the ones he had seen back in Shulara and Elankora. It had four small towers and no keep that Kelder could spot; it had a dozen half-timbered gables and no curtain wall.

Around it were scattered scores and scores of houses and shops—the shops of wheelwrights, wainwrights, blacksmiths, poultrymen, and more. And all along the highway there were carts and stalls where the locals offered for sale all their best produce—fine dyed wool, and smoky-scented hams, and early vegetables of half a hundred varieties, most of which Kelder had never seen before. The earthy smell of fresh produce and the tang of the hams reached his nose and set his mouth watering.

Irith seemed unaffected.

At either end of the town were inns, standing close by the roadside and marking the ends of what was, in effect, a long, narrow open-air market. Four inns stood at the west end, where Kelder and Irith entered; Irith told him there were three more at the far eastern end.

Kelder, now ravenous, didn't care to walk that far for his breakfast. He strolled perhaps a hundred feet along the market, weaving through the crowd and looking over the merchandise. He bought himself a slightly underripe orange—obviously imported, as the Amramionic climate was clearly unsuitable for oranges—and headed for the nearest inn, hoping that the fantasies he had had about life along the highway might yet come true, at least in part.

Irith stopped him.

"Not that one," she said. "It's second rate. *This* one!"

She pointed to one of the others. The signboard depicted a robed man sitting cross-legged, holding a staff, and hanging his head heavily. "It's called the Weary Wanderer," Irith told Kelder. "They make the best biscuits on the entire Great Highway here."

Kelder followed her inside.

Ten minutes later he was glad he had, because if the biscuits were not the best on the Great Highway, then Kelder had spent his life with some very wrong ideas about biscuits. He had never encountered any so tasty. In fact, his entire breakfast was phenomenally good.

Of course, hunger makes the best sauce; he knew that. Even so, the food at the Weary Wanderer was exceptional.

Although Irith had insisted she wasn't hungry, she, too, ate and drank eagerly. Besides the famous biscuits, the specialty of the house was a thick, frothy lemonade that obviously contained more than just the usual water and lemons and honey, and Irith and Kelder each downed several mugs of the stuff.

Somehow, Kelder was not particularly surprised when the innkeeper greeted Irith by name. She didn't intrude on the meal, however; once she had delivered their breakfast she returned to the kitchen and left the travelers in peace.

The only drawback to the meal came at the end, when Kelder, who had offered to pay the bill, discovered that he owed about twice what he had expected. He had made the offer partly because to do so was the traditional male role when courting, and partly because he had seen no sign that Irith had any money. Now, though, he almost regretted it.

"That's a lot," he said.

Irith shrugged. "Only a fool sells the best for less," she quoted. "Besides, prices are always higher along the highway."

Kelder grimaced, but he paid.

Thus fortified, the two of them continued on their way, strolling onward through the town of Amramion and out into open farm country again. Traffic was heavier now; they encountered an occasional wagon and entire parties of travelers. One red-dressed woman had a dulcimer slung on her back, and Kelder brightened at this sight—a minstrel, surely, the first he had ever seen.

It was about noon when they passed another isolated guard tower. Irith identified this one as marking the border between Amramion and Yondra, and this time the guard let them pass without comment.

"They're Amramionic," Irith explained when Kelder asked why the guard had ignored them. "They monitor the traffic *into* Amramion, but not *out*. If it were a Yondran guard he'd have asked us questions, but Yondra doesn't post guards at the borders."

They walked on.

Irith seemed tireless, and after a time Kelder found himself trudging wearily along while she scampered ahead, looking at flowers and butterflies. Stones and dust didn't trouble her at all, even though she was barefoot, and he marveled at that. His feet ached, and his own half-boots, new a sixnight before, were visibly worn, yet she was scampering about like a squirrel, her feet in nothing but her own skin.

Kelder wondered again just who she was—and *what* she was. Her story about being a wizard's apprentice made sense enough on the surface, but no matter how he figured it, the times were all wrong. She was only fifteen; how could she possibly have done and seen everything she claimed?

There was a mystery here, and if Kelder was going to fulfill his destiny and marry Irith, he would have to unravel it.

How could a girl younger than himself have traveled so widely? Why was she roaming about by herself, with no family or friends, yet apparently known everywhere she went? How did she keep from tiring? Was that more magic, perhaps?

She was a marvel in many ways, certainly—her wings and her beauty were merely the most obvious. When he brought her back to Shulara as his bride, when his family and his friends saw her, that would surely put an end to any teasing about his desire to see more of the World and his belief in Zindré's predictions. If there were creatures like Irith to be found, then obviously the World was worth seeing.

He was tempted simply to ask her, right now, to turn back and go to Shulara with him and marry him, but he didn't dare.

For one thing, she would almost certainly say no; while she was friendly enough, he didn't think she was so carefree, or so fond of him, that she would abandon her own plans—whatever they might be—to accompany him. And surely, she would have more sense than to marry a stranger she had just met. She had no reason to do so save to please him, and she had no reason to care that much about pleasing him.

Better to wait and let their relationship grow naturally.

And he didn't really want to go back home yet, anyway—not while there were more wonders to be found and the rest of his destiny to find. Great cities, vast plains, strange beasts, more magic—they were all out there, still waiting for him.

And now he had a guide to show him the way. He would never have found the Weary Wanderer and its almost miraculous food without Irith, and she might show him other marvels, as well. He wasn't sure whether those biscuits qualified as a wonder, but they certainly came close.

So for now he resolved to carry on, to try to impress Irith in any way he could, and to learn whatever he could about the World.

Another hour or so brought them to Yondra Keep, a small, old, vine-grown and weather-battered castle atop a hill, with a quiet little village clustered about its walls. Irith looked up at it and a faintly worried expression crossed her face.

"Kelder," she said suddenly, "maybe we should stop here for the night."

"But it's scarcely midafternoon," he said, puzzled. "Why stop so early?"

"Well, it's a good four or five leagues yet to Castle Angarossa, that's why," she explained. "We couldn't possibly get there before dark, or at least *you* couldn't, and I don't want to fly on ahead without you, *that* wouldn't be any fun. And Angarossa isn't . . . well, there are other places I'd rather be after dark than on the road in Angarossa, let's just put it that way."

"Oh," Kelder said. "Ah . . . why? Are there dragons or something?"

"Dragons?" Irith asked, startled, turning to stare at him. "On the Great Highway?" She smiled, then giggled. "Oh, Kelder, you're so *silly*! No, of course there aren't any dragons." Her smile vanished, and she said, quite seriously, "But there *are* bandits."

"Oh," Kelder said again. While the prospect of meeting bandits might have seemed exciting once, right now, footsore as he was, it didn't have any appeal at all. He looked up at Yondra Keep and its surrounding village. "All right, let's stop here."

"Good!" Irith said, clapping her hands gleefully. "I know just the place!"

CHAPTER 4

The inn was not on the Great Highway itself, but tucked back in a corner of the village, behind a row of houses that was itself behind a row of shops. It was a very small inn, with only four rooms upstairs and one of those occupied by the innkeeper himself, and a dining room that held only a single large table, with seating for a dozen or so.

The food and accommodations were excellent, though. Kelder shuddered to think what the bill would be.

And of course, as he had half expected, everyone knew Irith by name—not just the innkeeper, but the steward and the scullery boy and the other guests, as well. Irith introduced Kelder to them all. He bowed and nodded politely, quite sure he wouldn't remember all the names and faces.

The other guests, half a dozen in all, were traveling merchants, which was, when one thought about it, hardly surprising. Kelder sat and listened to them swap stories about remarkable deals they had made; the merchants found this endlessly amusing, but Irith politely excused herself and spent the remainder of the afternoon playing with the kittens in the kitchen, instead.

Kelder thought that Irith had probably made the better choice; half the time he didn't even know what the merchants were talking about, with their markups and discounts and percentages.

At least everyone along the Great Highway seemed to speak Trader's Tongue. Kelder had heard other languages spoken, but only in the background; travelers and strangers always seemed to be addressed first in Trader's Tongue.

Which, of course, was why it was called Trader's Tongue, and why it was such an easy language to learn—this was what it was *for*.

It was after dinner that night—a good but unremarkable dinner—that Kelder discovered one great advantage of staying in so small an inn. With only three rooms, he and Irith had to share.

And with just the two of them, they were given the smallest room, with only one bed.

Kelder thought about making some noble gesture like sleeping out in the stable, or at least on the floor, but then he looked at Irith's smile and realized that she must have known, when she led him to this out-of-the-way inn, exactly what the situation was and what she was getting into.

It would seem that he had, indeed, been courting, and more successfully than he thought. He had not seriously anticipated so quick a conquest—if conquest it was. The question arose in Kelder's mind, and was immediately suppressed, as to just who had conquered whom.

It didn't really matter; they were, he knew, fated for each other.

They talked for a long time about nothing in particular—Kelder learned a great many new words in Trader's Tongue, and felt himself becoming more comfortable with the language—and in the end they did more than just talk.

It was wonderful.

It was very late indeed when Kelder finally fell asleep.

By the time they were up and dressed in the morning the other guests had eaten their breakfasts and departed. Kelder was in no hurry, but for once Irith seemed a little impatient, so they ate quickly and set out without dawdling.

At first he found himself wondering about little things he had noticed about Irith. She never removed the bloodstone choker, for example, not even when sleeping—but maybe the clasp was hard to work. He hadn't really gotten a good look at it, in the dimness of their shared room.

She also always wore six or seven narrow bands of some sort tight around her right ankle, none of them particularly attractive, and from what little he had seen Kelder was unsure if they were bangles, or bracelets, or possibly even tattoos. Three had designs involving feathers, and one gleamed like mother-of-pearl. He was determined to get a better look at them sometime.

There was no hurry, though.

After they had been walking for a while, Kelder's attention turned to the journey itself. They were meeting far fewer travelers now; traffic east of Yondra Keep was apparently less than traffic farther west. Also, the distance from the Keep to the Angarossan border was roughly three times as far as to the Keep from the Amramionic border, which seemed odd to him. Shouldn't the Keep be in the center of the kingdom?

Well, it obviously wasn't, so he trudged on and on, expecting every minute to cross the border into Angarossa.

"Tell me," he asked Irith around midmorning, as she danced on ahead of him, bare feet skipping lightly across the highway's stones, golden hair flashing in the sun, "what's the route, exactly?"

She turned and looked back, her hair settling to her shoulders like a flock of doves landing. "You mean where the Great Highway goes?"

He nodded, somewhat out of breath.

Irith pointed eastward. "Through Yondra, and then Angarossa, and Sinodita, and Dhwerra, and then out across the desert to Shan," she told him.

"And how far is that? To Shan on the Desert, I mean."

She looked ahead and considered.

"About fifteen leagues, I guess," she said at last.

"Oh," he said. He glanced back at empty roadway and then asked, "How far have we come? I'm not very good with distances."

"Oh, four or five leagues," she answered, with a vague wave indicating that her reply was little more than a guess.

He stopped and looked back, and then at the road stretching endlessly on ahead. They had covered no more than a fourth of the journey?

That was a depressing thought.

Of course, he'd come a good distance before even reaching the highway, and Irith wasn't counting that.

And in stories people journeyed for sixnights on end, or months, or even years.

And he wasn't really in any hurry to get to Shan, was he? He had no business there; it was just a convenient goal, an excuse for traveling. The real reason he was going to Shan, after all, was to fulfill the prophecy, and that spoke only of the journey itself. A longer journey also meant a chance to spend more time with Irith before proposing marriage, and that was a good thing, too.

So why hurry?

"*Hai*, slow down!" he called to Irith, who had not stopped when he did. "What's your rush?"

"I don't like bandits," she called back. "Come on!"

He sighed and hurried to catch up.

They passed an empty, crumbling watchtower just before midday.

"We're in Angarossa now," Irith said. "You don't see too many robbers in Yondra, though they'll cross the border sometimes to catch people off guard, but the hills of Angarossa are full of them." She peered warily to either side and spoke in a tone far more serious than her usual chirping, cheerful manner.

"Really?" Kelder asked, a little more skeptically than he had intended. For one thing, the gently rolling countryside hardly qualified as hills, by his standards—in Shulara or Sevmor such terrain would have been considered effectively flat.

"Yes, really," Irith snapped back.

He looked about, studying their surroundings, then stopped and pointed ahead. "Look!" he called, "What's that?"

Irith followed his finger and suddenly spread wings that, a second before, had not been there at all. She flapped, and Kelder was almost bowled over by the wind as she rose into the air.

"What is it?" he called. "What's the matter?"

"I'm getting a better look," she called down to him. "I'll be right back."

He stood, watching helplessly, as she rose into the air, propelled steadily upward by the great iridescent wings. Then he turned his attention back to the spot on the horizon that had attracted his attention.

He still couldn't make out details; whatever it was was big, and its color not very different from the color of the highway itself—probably, he supposed, because it was dusty. It was at the top of a rise and disappearing slowly over that rise even as he watched.

Then Irith was settling back to the earth beside him, her wings folding away into nothingness. "It's a caravan," she told him. "A big one."

"That?" he said, pointing at the distant object. "That's a caravan?"

She put her hands on her hips. "Well, all you could see from down *here*, silly, was the very last wagon!"

"Oh," he replied, feeling foolish.

"Come on," Irith said, starting to run, "if we can catch up with them, we can all travel together. It'll be safer."

"It will?" Kelder asked, breaking into a trot.

"Sure!" Irith said. "They'll have guards and everything!"

Kelder was still unsure just why, but he ran after Irith. The girl seemed as tireless as ever, but long before they reached the caravan Kelder was panting and stumbling.

"Wait," he called, "I have to catch my breath!"

With a worried glance at the caravan—its nature now plain, as they had crossed another low ridge—Irith slowed to a walk. She danced impatiently as Kelder trudged along.

When he had stopped gasping and was fully upright again, she called, "Come on!" and started running again.

"You go on," he said. "I'll catch up."

She frowned and then nodded, and there were wings on her back once again. She spread them and leaped upward, soaring into the air.

Kelder trudged on.

He could see the caravan for what it was now; he counted five wagons, and others were over the next hill, he was sure. There were people sitting in and on the wagons, and outriders on horses and oxen along either side, and a few people walking along on foot, as well. This was no casual grouping such as they had sometimes seen west of Yondra Keep; this was a serious expedition.

The wagons were big, solid things, brightly painted and almost the size of houses; the last in line was a saffron hue that happened to blend fairly well with the dust of the road, but the others were red and green and blue, with gilded or silvered trim that sparkled in the sun. They didn't bear much resemblance to the open farm wagons Kelder had seen back in Shulara, or the ox-carts the local merchants had used, or any of the other vehicles he had encountered previously. Each one was drawn by at least four oxen; two of the five he could see had six oxen apiece on their yokes.

With all those people and beasts the caravan, of necessity, moved at a slow walk. Kelder had no trouble in keeping up with it even while catching his breath and could gain any time he was willing to pick up his pace a little.

He didn't bother to catch up, however. He was in no hurry.

Irith, on the other hand, flew directly up to the caravan and over it. People looked up as her shadow passed over them, stared and pointed, and called to one another.

Kelder smiled. He couldn't hear what they were saying, but they probably all knew her by name. Maybe he and Irith would be able to ride on one of the wagons, or share a meal with the merchants.

Then someone walking alongside the third wagon from the end picked up a stone from the roadside and threw it at the winged girl. Someone else had drawn a sword; a third rummaged under the seat of the rearmost wagon and brought up a bow and arrow.

"Hai!" Kelder screamed, and broke into a run.

Irith veered off, away from the caravan, away from the highway. The stone had missed her completely. She flapped, turned, hovered for a second, and then turned again and came sailing back toward Kelder.

He slowed, and she landed before him, and he embraced her, hugging her tightly to him, relieved that she was unhurt.

Her wings had not vanished, which made the embrace somewhat awkward, so he released her quickly.

"Are you all right?" he asked.

"I'm fine," she said. "Are *you* all right?"

He nodded, then looked up. He had intended to ask why the caravan's people were so hostile to her, but the words died on his lips—a horseman was approaching them. The caravan itself was moving steadily onward as if nothing had happened, but one of the outriders had peeled away and was trotting toward them. Irith saw Kelder's face and turned to face the horseman.

They stood and waited as the man rode up.

"What do you want?" Kelder called in Trader's Tongue, in an angry attempt at bravado.

"To give you an apology, and a warning," the horseman replied in the same language.

Irith and Kelder glanced at each other and then back at the horseman. "Go on," Kelder said.

The horseman bobbed his head in acknowledgment. "First," he said, "the apology. If you are no more than the innocent travelers you appear to be, then we regret our actions toward you."

He paused, but neither Irith nor Kelder answered.

"And the warning," the horseman said. "There are bandits in these hills . . ."

"We *know* that," Irith interrupted. "That's why we wanted to join your caravan!"

The stranger nodded and continued, unperturbed. "There are bandits in these hills, and they have been known to use several tricks and ruses. Accordingly, we cannot trust *anyone* we meet here—and most particularly not a person like yourself, who clearly has great magic at her command. So while we mean no harm to anyone, if you approach again the guards will do their best to kill you."

"*Kill* me?" Irith squeaked. "But I'm Irith the Flyer! Everyone on the Great Highway knows me! And this is Kelder, and he's harmless!"

The horseman shrugged, palms up. "Perhaps you are what you say," he said, "but we will not risk it. I'm sorry."

Before Irith could say anything more, he turned and snapped the reins, sending his horse cantering back toward the departing wagons.

Irith blinked, then turned to Kelder, furious.

"They can't treat us like that!" she said.

Kelder shrugged. "Why not?" he asked. Almost immediately, however, he regretted the words—a reaction like that was not going to impress anyone. He didn't want Irith to consider him a coward.

"They don't own the highway!" Irith shouted. "We can pass them if we like!"

Kelder reluctantly shook his head—appearances or no, and even if it meant an accusation of cowardice, common sense was on the side of caution. "It's not right," he said, "nor fair, but I wouldn't try it. There are an awful lot of them."

Irith looked at the wagons for a moment, considering, and then stuck out her tongue. "Who needs them, anyway?" she said. "And did you notice that weird smell?"

"What smell?" Kelder asked, startled. The only odors he had detected were those of dust and horses.

"That sour smell," Irith said. "When the horseman rode up just now. The whole caravan smells like that. Didn't you notice?"

"I didn't smell anything," Kelder said, puzzled. "Except horse," he added, for the sake of accuracy, "and maybe sweaty leather."

"Well, then your nose doesn't work," Irith retorted, "because the whole caravan stinks."

"I didn't smell anything," Kelder repeated.

Irith considered for a moment, then announced, "They stink, anyway. Who needs them?"

Relieved, Kelder smiled, and she smiled back, and the two of them walked on, following the caravan at a safe distance of roughly two hundred yards.

CHAPTER 5

"*How* is it there are so many bandits in Anga-rossa?" Kelder asked as they trudged onward. They had been following the caravan for hours; it was still ahead of them, and in fact moving a little more slowly than they ordinarily did, but leaving the highway to pass it did not strike the pair as worth the effort. Instead, they had slowed down, giving Kelder more time to think. "Why here, and not other king-doms?"

"Because of King Caren, silly," Irith replied.

Kelder blinked. "Who?" he asked.

"King Caren," Irith repeated. "The King of Angarossa."

"Oh," Kelder said, trying to see if he was missing some obvious explanation. He didn't see that he was. "What does that have to do with it?" he asked. "Is he a bad king, or some-thing?"

"Not as far as the bandits are concerned," Irith said with a grin.

"I *mean*," Kelder said, slightly annoyed at the girl's atti-tude, "is he particularly bad at running the country?"

"And *I* mean," Irith replied, still grinning mockingly, "that it depends on whether you look at it from the point of view of a caravan master or a bandit."

"You're the one being silly, then," Kelder retorted. "It's part of a king's duties to stop banditry." He might not know as much of the World as Irith did, but he knew *that* much.

"Well, in that case," Irith answered, turning more or less serious, "King Caren's an absolutely rotten king, because he doesn't see it that way."

"He doesn't?" Kelder said, startled.

"No, he doesn't. As long as the bandits pay their taxes, King Caren doesn't bother them."

"Taxes?" This conversation was, in Kelder's opinion, becoming very strange indeed. He wondered if Irith was teasing him somehow, but that didn't seem likely. He didn't think she could lie that well. "Do bandits pay taxes?" he asked.

"In Angarossa they do," Irith explained. "If they don't want the king's men to hunt them down and kill them."

"They pay taxes?" The concept still didn't seem to make sense.

"One-eighth of everything they steal," Irith assured him.

"But . . ." He groped for an intelligent response and found none.

"Pretty rotten, isn't it?" Irith said with a grin.

"It's . . . it's . . ." It was plain that there were wonders in the World that had nothing to do with mysteries or magic, and were nothing he'd care to brag about seeing when he got home. He struggled for something to say.

"Yes, it is, isn't it?" Irith said, smiling.

Kelder stopped trying to find words to express his appalled amazement, and Irith explained.

"King Caren's greedy," she said. "I guess most kings are. Anyway, when he came to the throne, the kingdom was broke, so he tried to raise money. Angarossa hasn't got a lot going for it—it's not good farmland, the weather's pretty bad, there's nothing worth mining, and the army didn't amount to much. About the only thing in the kingdom that's worth anything is the Great Highway, so King Caren tried to impose tolls."

Kelder needed a moment to remember the word "toll" but did eventually figure it out. "That makes sense," he admitted.

"Yes," Irith agreed, "but only if people *pay* the tolls. The merchants wouldn't pay. They all traveled in big caravans, like the one up ahead, and when two or three guards tried to stop them at the border and collect a toll, the merchants would just laugh and march right on past, and if the soldiers tried to stop them, the caravan's own guards would beat the toll collectors to a pulp. So King Caren threatened to march his entire army out to the highway to collect the tolls."

"What happened?"

"The merchants sent a delegation to Castle Angarossa to negotiate and told King Caren that they'd never paid any tolls here before and didn't want to now, and they didn't pay any tolls in Yondra or Amramion or Sinodita, and why couldn't he make his money by taxing the innkeepers and farmers, like everybody else? And besides, at the time there was this bandit named Telar the Red who was causing trouble, and the merchants said that if they had to pay to use the highway, at the very least the king ought to make it safer to use and get rid of Telar."

The story was not particularly fascinating, but watching Irith was, and listening to her voice was, as well. Kelder nodded encouragement, and Irith continued.

"So King Caren got an agreement from the merchants that if he captured or killed Telar the Red and got rid of his bandits, then the merchants would pay a toll, a small one. And he sent out his army, and they tracked down Telar and caught him—and Telar offered them money to let him go again."

"Did they take it?" Kelder asked, since she seemed to expect a reaction.

"No," Irith said, "they were too scared of the king, because everybody knew he had a really nasty temper, and if the story got out he would probably have them all disemboweled. Instead they took Telar back to the king, and Telar offered King Caren the money—and the king thought about it, and saw that the money was more than he'd get in a year of collecting tolls from merchants, and that Telar was a lot easier to deal with than the merchants, so he took it. And other bandits heard about this, and it looked like a good deal." Irith shrugged, fingers spread. "So there still aren't any tolls in Angarossa, but there are plenty of bandits."

Kelder thought this over for a moment, then said, "That's ridiculous. Why do the merchants put up with it?"

"Well, some of them don't want to," Irith admitted. "They've been talking about building a new highway, south of Angarossa, through Shimillion and Omanon. It would be a lot longer, though, and so far most people settle for hiring guards or bringing magicians along."

"Couldn't they offer to pay tolls, if King Caren would get rid of the bandits?"

Irith shrugged. "*I* don't know," she said.

They walked on silently as Kelder considered the notion of a king who could be corrupted so easily by mere money. Kings were supposed to protect their people, weren't they?

But then, the merchants weren't really King Caren's people, were they? They were foreigners passing through, while the bandits lived in the country. Did that mean that other kings were actually betraying their people by stamping out banditry?

No, that was silly—but why was it silly?

He struggled with the whole question for some time, mulling it over as the afternoon wore on and the sun descended to the west, and he finally worked it out.

Banditry helped the *bandits*, in the short run, but it hurt the innkeepers and the local merchants by stealing money that the caravans might have spent in town. And in the long run, it might mean rerouting the highway, which would hurt *everybody*, Angarossan or otherwise.

Besides, how could the king be sure that the bandits would rob or kill only foreigners?

So King Caren ought to stop the bandits.

"There's that smell again," Irith said, interrupting his thought.

"What smell?" he asked, startled.

"That funny sour smell that the caravan has."

Kelder sniffed.

"I still don't smell anything," he said.

"It's there," Irith insisted.

"Maybe the wind shifted," Kelder suggested.

Irith abruptly had wings and flapped them tentatively.

"No," she said, "the wind's still from the northwest."

Her wings vanished again.

"You really don't smell it?" she asked.

"No," Kelder admitted, "I really don't."

"It's very strong now."

"I don't smell it. Maybe it's something magical? Something only girls can smell?"

Irith frowned, an expression that Kelder found comic and endearing; he resisted the temptation to grab her and forget all about mysterious odors, hostile caravans, deranged kings, and so forth.

"I don't know," she said, "I never heard of anything like that."

Kelder could think of nothing more to say; he could smell nothing but dust and grass and the leavings of the caravan's draft animals. He looked about, trying to think of another subject to take up and to distract himself from Irith's charms.

Something caught his eye, far out on the horizon.

"What's that?" he said, pointing.

Irith's gaze followed his outstretched finger, but she didn't need to answer; it was plain now what Kelder had spotted.

A line of horsemen was charging down over the low ridge to the north of the highway, sweeping down toward the caravan.

"Bandits!" Irith exclaimed, and her wings were back. Before Kelder could say anything to calm her she was aloft, flying up out of danger.

Kelder had no such convenient escape, but he saw no need for one. He was no more than a neutral observer, after all—neither the bandits nor the caravan had reason to harm him. He stood his ground and watched.

The idea of watching a battle was both alluring and repulsive—it would certainly be something to tell everyone back in Shulara, but at the same time, he didn't want to see anyone hurt or killed. They were going to be hurt or killed whether he watched or not, however, so he stared intently.

The horsemen had swords drawn, their blades glittering in the sun. They were shouting, though Kelder could make out no words. The caravan could hardly help but see them now, and the guards and merchants were running around madly, the horses whinnying in dismay at the excitement, the oxen plodding stolidly on undisturbed, or stopping if their drivers remembered to rein them in or if they came too close to the wagon in front.

It seemed to Kelder, from what he had heard of such affairs, that certain things should be happening. The caravan guards should be forming a defensive line, or a ring, or something, while the merchants and other noncombatants should be taking shelter—but that didn't seem to be what *was* happening. Instead, people were rushing back and forth along the line of wagons, while others, including most of the guards, were gathering along the south side of the wagons, away from the approaching riders.

"Look!" Irith called from above, her word barely discernible above the hubbub of shouting, babbling voices, rattling equipage, and drumming hooves. She pointed.

Kelder looked.

A man in a black robe had climbed atop one of the big wagons and was rising to his feet, standing on the wagon's roof. He was shouting aloud, and even over the general din his voice seemed to cut like a hard wind.

The words, though, were like nothing Kelder had ever heard before. They were no language he recognized—and no language he *wanted* to recognize. They were harsh, alien sounds that had no right to emerge from a human throat.

The bandits were almost to the row of wagons now; their original neat line had broken, as the faster horses pulled ahead and the slower ones lagged. The foremost attackers were reining in, rather than barreling straight on into the sides of the wagons or charging past their objective entirely.

The battle was about to be joined when the first black thing popped out of the ground.

At first Kelder wasn't sure what he had seen, but then others appeared, so fast that he couldn't say where the second or third had emerged; there were none, there was one, and then there were hundreds, faster than he could react, a sea of them springing up from under the caravan. Like water from a fountain, they came from beneath the wagon where the man in black stood, still chanting.

They were shorter than people, perhaps three or four feet tall, but as broad across the shoulders as most men. Their limbs were crooked, but clearly powerful. Their bare skin and shaggy, unkempt hair were black or dark gray. They wore no armor, and for that matter no clothing, but charged into the fray naked—but not unarmed. Axes, swords, knives, sticks, weapons of every kind were clutched in their misshapen hands, the blades as naked as the creatures that wielded them.

And the creatures' faces were truly hideous. Great staring white eyes, noses like blades or blobs or broken rock, mouths that gaped in enormous yawning grins, full of jagged yellow teeth—Kelder was very glad he was no closer and could not make out all the details. He had never seen anything so ghastly.

At least, not until the fighting began.

The creatures made no distinction between man and mount; it seemed they would gleefully hack at anything that moved that came within reach and was not a part of the caravan. Horses screamed in agony as the axes and knives chopped at their legs and flanks; they fell, and their riders' screams joined their own.

"Demons!" Irith called from overhead. "The man in black's a demonologist!"

That made sense to Kelder. It also sent a shudder through him, and he began backing away. He wanted to turn and run, but the idea of turning his back on those horrors was at least as bad as being this close to them.

Wasn't demonology illegal? Weren't all demons banished from the physical world hundreds of years ago, when the Great War ended? How could this be happening?

He watched in horrid fascination.

One of the demon-things spotted a new target, but this one happened to be one of the merchants who had accompanied the caravan; the creature leaped toward her, then stopped, as if in midjump, and turned away, holding its nose.

Enlightenment burst upon Kelder. The smell Irith had insisted she smelled—it was real, it was magical, and it protected the caravan from the demons!

But why could Irith smell it and not himself? Was it because she was a creature of magic, like the demons, while he was a merely ordinary human being?

That had to be it—but this was no time to worry about it, when the hideous spectacle before him yet continued.

Some of the bandits had tried to turn and flee, but none had gotten more than a few yards before dozens of the creatures were upon him. Then the last of the bandits was down, but the demon-things did not stop; they continued hacking and hacking, knives and axes rising and falling, as blood sprayed and spattered. They gibbered and shrieked in an inhuman chorus as they chopped and stabbed, until the caravan's own people were cowering in terror, retreating southward away from the highway, as the creatures reveled in the destruction they had wrought.

The entire battle had lasted only a few seconds. It had happened much too fast for the reality, the horror of it all to sink in.

"Eeeww," Irith said loudly, somewhere above Kelder's head. "Gross!"

Half a dozen of the demons heard that, turned toward her, and saw her.

And below her, they saw Kelder.

CHAPTER 6

Kelder *began to back away more quickly; above* him he heard a strangled squeak, and the beating of wings fading into the distance, and then nothing.

The demon-things were grinning at him and making weird whooping noises. Then one began to run toward him, ax raised, and a second followed, waving a short sword. The black-robed man atop the wagon was waving his arms and chanting again, and Kelder took an instant to wonder why before he turned and started running for his life.

The demons came shrieking after him as he fled, the noise growing closer with every step he took—until it abruptly stopped.

The total silence was so astonishing that he stumbled and fell. His arms came up instinctively, shielding his face; he curled into a ball and rolled in the dust of the highway, waiting for the first blade to cut him, and first club to batter him.

Nothing happened.

Carefully he opened his eyes and lifted an arm from his face.

There was the caravan; the man in black was climbing down from his perch, and the merchants and guards were returning to their places, preparing to move on.

There were no demons.

There was no sign of them anywhere.

The only evidence that any demons had ever existed was the mangled corpses of the bandits and their mounts.

Kelder slowly uncurled and got cautiously to his feet.

There were no demons. The demonologist had presumably

sent them back wherever they had come from, and they were completely, utterly gone.

One of the caravan guards on foot had drawn his sword and was whacking the heads off the corpses of the bandits. This was obviously not necessary to ensure that they were actually dead; even from this distance, Kelder had no doubt at all that they were all dead. The guard was presumably collecting trophies. The battle was undeniably over.

Kelder stood for a moment, considering, and then began stumbling toward the caravan. It was not that he particularly wanted a closer look at the corpses, or the wagons, or anything else, but he was afraid that if he turned and fled the demonologist might decide he was a bandit after all. Kelder looked up, seeking Irith, intending to urge her to join him.

She wasn't there. There was nothing above him but empty sky, clear and bright blue, with a few fluffy white clouds drifting here and there.

Kelder stopped dead in his tracks. Where had she gone?

He slowly turned, studying the heavens, and finally spotted her, far to the west; she was little more than a dark speck against the sun. For a moment he panicked; he didn't want to lose her. He *couldn't* lose her, that would destroy the entire prophecy! He waved and shouted, but then stopped, feeling foolish; she wouldn't be able to hear him from so far away.

He considered running after her, but the speck seemed to be growing; he stared and decided that yes, it was definitely getting larger. She was coming back.

He stood and waited for her while, three hundred yards to the east, the caravan regrouped and moved on, ignoring him and the flying figure. By the time Irith dropped to the earth beside him, the wagons were almost out of sight over a distant rise. Only by shading his eyes with his hand and staring hard could Kelder make out an upright pike at the back corner of the last wagon and a bloody head impaled upon it.

Irith's wings fluttered, stirring Kelder's hair, and he turned his gaze on her. "What *were* those things?" he asked.

Irith shrugged prettily. "*I* don't know," she said.

"You didn't learn about them when you were an apprentice?" said Kelder.

She stared at him as if he had said something exceptionally stupid; when it sank in that indeed he had, she replied haughtily, "I was a *wizard's* apprentice, not a demonologist's!"

Her disdain was actually painful, and Kelder tried to recover by asking "But didn't you learn about the other kinds of magic? To keep up with the competition, as it were?"

"No," Irith said. "Just learning wizardry was hard enough!" Her tone softened. "Besides, nobody around where I lived *knew* anything about demonology back then."

Kelder blinked. She was doing it again, speaking as if her apprenticeship had ended years ago, when it couldn't possibly have. "When was that?" he asked.

She glared at him, obviously annoyed, but he was unsure why.

"*Ages* ago," she said. Then she turned away and pointedly ignored him for a few seconds.

"Oh," he replied feebly, after a moment.

She turned back. "Let's get going," she said.

He nodded, and they began walking. Irith's wings vanished after a few paces.

Five minutes later they reached the first of the dead bandits. Blood had sprayed across the highway and the neighboring grass, but it was already dry and brown, no longer red. The corpse was absolutely ghastly—pieces were scattered about, while the main mass was unrecognizable.

And of course, the head was gone completely.

A score of other corpses, all equally mutilated, were scattered along the roadside ahead, interspersed with the carcasses of an equal number of horses. Flies were settling on them all, crawling across the faces.

Kelder's stomach cramped, and he fought to keep down his breakfast. He had seen death before—in farm animals and sick old people who died at home in bed. He had never seen anything at all like this carnage.

"Ick," Irith said, stepping carefully across one of the dried streaks of blood.

"Ick?" Kelder stared at her. "Is that all you have to say?"

She looked at him, startled. "What else should I say?" she asked.

"*I* don't know," Kelder snapped, irritated. "But something a bit more respectful than 'ick'!"

"Respectful?" She looked at him in honest puzzlement. "How is 'ick' disrespectful?"

"You don't think the dead deserve something a bit more . . . more . . ." Words failed him. He was unsure he could have found the right phrase even in his native Shularan, and in Trader's Tongue or Ethsharitic it was hopeless.

"Oh, the *dead*?" Irith said. "I thought you meant *you*!"

"Me?" Kelder was taken aback. He had expected to earn Irith's respect eventually, but had hardly presumed he had it already. "No, I didn't mean me, I meant the . . . the corpses."

"What do *they* care?" Irith asked. "They're dead, they don't care if I say 'ick.' And they're really yucky. I don't like blood."

"I don't, either," Kelder said without thinking. Then he caught himself and said, "Can't you be a little more . . . more compassionate? I mean, these were *people*, with homes and families, probably."

Kelder was struggling with an internal conflict; Irith was so incredibly beautiful, so obviously magical, and so widely knowledgeable, that he kept expecting her to be noble and pure and perfect in every way. Whenever she demonstrated that she wasn't, he balked at the incongruity.

Besides, he expected his *wife* to be caring and compassionate, and Irith was destined to be his wife.

Irith shrugged. "Well, *I* didn't kill them," she said.

"Doesn't it bother you, seeing them like this?" he asked, still hoping to restore her to her pedestal.

Her expression turned to outrage.

"Of *course* it bothers me!" she yelled. "That's why I said 'ick'!"

Kelder felt as if he were trapped, somehow, in a web of wrong words and misunderstandings. He didn't want to argue with her; quite the opposite. In fact, looking at her, he was overwhelmed anew by her beauty and found himself *unable* to argue with her.

Maybe it was *he* who was imperfect.

"I'm sorry," he said, surrendering. "I just never saw anything like this before. It's got me upset, and it seems as if you should be more upset than you are, too."

"Oh," Irith said, looking around at the corpses. "Oh, I guess I see what you mean, if this is your first time on a battlefield. But it's not the first time for *me*; I saw lots of dead people in the war, you know? I mean, this is really gross, but I used to see other stuff that was just about as bad."

"You did?" Kelder looked around and struggled to hold down his rising gorge.

"Oh, yes," she said. "There was one time when a spell backfired and these people got all ripped to pieces . . ." She saw Kelder's expression and concluded apologetically, "But I guess you don't want to hear about that."

"No," he agreed, "I don't think I do."

"Well, then," she said reasonably, "let's not talk about it, let's just get out of here."

Kelder nodded. When Irith did not immediately move he took the hint, turned away from her, and started walking.

Irith looked at the blood, the flies, the debris, and made a small noise of disgust. Then her wings reappeared, and she flew on ahead, avoiding the mess.

As Kelder stumbled past the last of the corpses, he found himself wondering what war Irith had seen. There were always border wars going on somewhere in the Small Kingdoms—wars were inevitable when you had two hundred and some separate governments jammed into an area the size of the Small Kingdoms—but he hadn't heard about any particularly bad ones recently. And the kingdoms along the Great Highway supposedly tried harder than most to avoid fighting, since it cut down on traffic and therefore hurt business. Reportedly, the kingdoms along the road were generally significantly smaller than the regional average because of this—rulers were slower to put down secessions or to go empire-building here than elsewhere.

So what war had Irith been talking about? Had she studied under a master wizard in Korosa or Trothluria or some other land that had recently fought a war? Had she been involved in the war somehow, that she saw the battlefields? Had that been part of why she fled?

But the Small Kingdoms didn't use magic in their wars—at least, most of them didn't, though there were stories about the new so-called Empire of Vond in the far south, where just last year some warlock had reportedly used his magic to conquer everything in sight. A wizard's apprentice wouldn't be allowed near the battlefields in Korosa or Trothluria.

Irith had said a spell had backfired, though. Where could *that* have happened? Vond?

Just where was she from? He still hadn't asked her directly; he suspected she wouldn't answer, would avoid the issue somehow. It was all very mysterious, and he wondered about it, but looking at Irith, who was waiting for him a hundred yards up the road, he decided not to ask her about it.

Not yet, at any rate.

And maybe, he admitted, never. She didn't look as if she wanted to talk about wars she had seen, and he wasn't sure that he did, either. He was interested in Irith's past, all right—but he was much more interested in her future. Forgetting about the dead bandits would probably be the best solution all around.

He trudged onward, intently not looking back—but then his steps slowed.

Had he heard something move? Did he feel someone watching him?

Irith had turned back and was watching him, waiting for him, tapping a foot impatiently, but even so he paused and glanced back over his shoulder.

Nothing was on the road behind him but dust and blood; nothing moved among the dead but flies. He glanced to either side and saw nothing but rolling grassland. He looked harder.

Was that someone, on the northern horizon, crouched in the tall grass?

No, it wasn't, he decided. He was just spooked. He turned east again and marched ahead, calling unnecessarily to Irith, telling her to wait.

CHAPTER 7

*C*astle *Angarossa was low and broad, spreading out* across the land; most of the market and town were actually inside the gates, making the community something midway between an ordinary castle and a walled city.

Kelder had had his first glimpse of it only minutes after leaving the battlefield where the slaughtered bandits lay. He had stopped to stare at its beauty, as the setting sun lit the walls a warm gold and the rooftops a deep, rich red, the lengthening shadows highlighting every graceful line. The caravan that had destroyed the bandits was at the castle gates, inching in; he could see a pike on each wagon, a severed head atop each pike.

"Come on," Irith had urged, and he had hurried on, eager to reach the place. Irith was clearly not *too* annoyed with him, Kelder thought, or she would have flown on ahead; wanting to keep it that way, he was careful not to offend her, and the easiest way to do that was to say nothing, so they did not speak again until they arrived at the gates an hour later.

By then the sun was down, the sky dimming, and most of the light came from lanterns and torches. The shadows had grown, spread, and turned ominous, their edges blurred and their hearts impenetrable. Kelder hesitated, wondering if it was safe to enter the castle of a king who openly permitted bandits to roam his lands, but Irith told him he was being foolish.

"This is the *one* place in Angarossa where you *don't* have to worry about bandits, silly!" she explained. "They know

57

better than to cause any trouble *here*, where they might get the king angry!"

"Oh," Kelder said. He was annoyed at himself; his ignorance and excessive caution were both showing far more than he liked. He was looking like a fool in front of Irith. Resolving to do better hereafter, he followed her meekly into the marketplace. "Do you know a good inn here?" he asked.

"Of course," Irith answered. "But I want to look around the market first."

Kelder acquiesced and trailed along as Irith looked over displays of fabrics and jewelry.

Most of the merchants were packing up for the night; people were reluctant to buy anything by torchlight, when flaws were so much harder to spot. Kelder was glad of that, as his feet were tired and sore. Irith would not be able to look much longer.

The caravan they had followed for most of the day was in town; he saw the wagons down a side alley, pulled into a yard, recognizable both by the bright designs painted on them and by the gory trophies adorning them.

He considered pointing this out to Irith, or going to talk to the people there, but decided against it. He saw no one near the wagons, and besides, he didn't really want anything to do with that demonologist. At the thought of the black-garbed magician he shuddered slightly.

"Is demonology legal?" he asked, interrupting Irith's perusal of a bolt of black brocade.

"Where?" she asked, startled.

"Anywhere," he said.

"Sure," she said. "Lots of places. All of Ethshar."

Hesitantly Kelder said, "I don't think it is in Shulara."

"Probably it isn't," Irith agreed. "Most of the Small Kingdoms aren't big on demons. *I'm* not."

"What about here?" He gestured at the castle market about them.

She turned up an empty palm. "Who knows?" she said.

"If it isn't legal, how could that caravan use it?"

"*Banditry* isn't exactly legal, either, Kelder," she said with exaggerated patience. "Even if the king doesn't stop it. Lots of people break laws."

That was hardly news, even to Kelder, but he persisted, his curiosity momentarily overcoming his desire to please Irith. "I thought that the gates to Hell were closed off at the end of the Great War, so how can demonology still work?"

Irith sighed and let the brocade drop. "Kelder," she said, "do I look like an expert on demonology to you?"

"No," Kelder admitted.

"Then don't ask me all these *questions* about it, all right?" She glared at him and then added, "But anyway, that just means demons can't enter the World unless they're properly summoned. Demonologists can still *call* them." She turned back to the display of fabrics.

"Oh," Kelder said, embarrassed.

He stood silently for a moment as Irith held the cloth up to the light, trying to see it properly; the merchant had already packed away most of her goods, but was waiting to see if this last customer might buy something.

As he stood, he felt, as he had on the battlefield, as if someone were watching him. He looked around the market.

He saw a handful of late customers, a score or so of merchants and farmers who had not yet departed, and a great deal of empty space. The castle wall curved along the far side of the square and a bored soldier stood on the ramparts, leaning on a merlon and yawning as he gazed out over the countryside. Three or four children were chasing each other back and forth through the open gates; another child, a thin barefoot girl in a ragged blue tunic, was standing to one side.

She was staring at him, Kelder thought, or at Irith, or at the cloth merchant whose wares Irith was fondling. Was that what he had sensed?

Well, there was nothing to be feared from a little girl. He wondered, though, why she was staring like that. It was hard to tell in the evening gloom, but she appeared to have been crying.

Maybe her mother had beaten her, Kelder thought to himself. Maybe she was out here wishing she didn't have to go home, envying Irith her age and beauty.

Maybe she even recognized Irith; after all, as Kelder had discovered, the Flyer was well known along the Great Highway. At the moment she had no wings, but how many white-clad blondes were there in Angarossa?

How many blondes were there in all the Small Kingdoms, for that matter?

It suddenly occurred to Kelder for the first time that Irith might not be from the Small Kingdoms at all. Perhaps she was from one of the distant, barbaric realms far to the north-west, beyond the Hegemony of Ethshar—Tintallion, or Kerroa, maybe. It was said blondes were slightly more common in the north.

Wasn't Tintallion in the middle of a civil war, at last report?

That might explain a great deal. It could explain her references to a war, and perhaps the rules were different there, and she had been able to apprentice at a younger age than twelve, which would explain why she seemed to have done so much for a girl of fifteen. If that was it, then she must have fled to the Small Kingdoms because they were about as far away from her angry master as she could possibly get.

It all hung together.

So Irith was Tintallionese? He looked at her speculatively, listened to her chatting with the merchant in Trader's Tongue, and wished he knew some Tintallionese himself.

He forgot all about the little girl by the gate and listened to Irith and the merchant, trying to spot clues to the Flyer's origin. Her accent didn't sound particularly northwestern to him, but then, he had never actually heard anyone from Ethshar or beyond, only local people imitating them. There was no reason to think that barbarians would have accents much like the people of the northwestern Small Kingdoms.

Irith didn't seem to have any noticeable accent of her own at all, really; she spoke Trader's Tongue with the sharp simplicity of an experienced traveler. She spoke Trader's

Tongue better than the merchant she was haggling with, in fact.

Kelder considered. He could just ask her where she was from, of course. Asking where a person came from was a harmless and natural thing to do.

He would wait until the appropriate time, though, when he had a chance to bring it up in the course of the conversation; she was annoyed enough by his questions about demonology, and asking her out of the blue would be rude.

Irith turned away; the cloth merchant called a "final" offer after her, but she just laughed and walked away, with Kelder close beside her.

"You never did plan to buy anything, did you?" he asked.

She smiled and winked. "Of course not," she said. "What would I do with a bolt of black brocade on the road to Shan, carry it over my shoulder?" She laughed again, then paused and added, "If I was staying in town it might be different. It's good fabric."

Kelder nodded.

"The inn is down this way," Irith told him, pointing at a narrow alleyway.

"Really?" he said dubiously.

"Really," she replied. "It's a shortcut, a back way. I'll show you."

She led the way, and he followed. A few feet into the passage—for it was little more than that, a corridor between buildings, not a street—he glanced back at the market.

That young girl who had been watching them from the gate was now standing near the cloth merchant's stall and still watching them. Something about her made him uneasy.

"That girl's watching us," he said to Irith.

She turned and looked, then shrugged and walked on. "People do that sometimes," she said.

He took another look, and then he, too, shrugged and walked on.

The alleyway opened out into a small kitchen yard; to one side a bantam cock stared at them through the slats of his coop, a well and windlass occupied a corner, and a big gray cat slept on the sill of a candelit window beside a heavy black door. Irith marched directly across and rapped on the door.

A sliding panel opened, and a nervous face peered out.

"Hello, Larsi," Irith said. "It's me."

"The Flyer?" a woman's voice asked.

Irith nodded.

The panel slid shut, and the latch rattled. The gray cat stirred slightly. Kelder took a look back up the alleyway.

The girl in the blue tunic was running down the passageway toward them.

The door opened, and Irith stepped up on the granite threshold. The person she had addressed as Larsi, a plump woman of forty or so, beckoned for her to enter. "I brought a friend," Irith said, gesturing at Kelder.

Kelder saw the expression on the little girl's face as it caught the light that spilled from the open door, and on a sudden impulse he said, "Two friends."

"You will be a champion of the lost and forlorn," Zindré had said, and that child certainly looked lost and forlorn.

Startled, Irith turned and looked as the little girl panted into the dooryard. The waif turned pleading eyes up toward the Flyer, and Irith corrected herself.

"Two friends," she said.

Kelder smiled with relief. Irith could be compassionate toward the living, however callous she might have appeared toward the dead bandits, and Kelder was very pleased to see it. Maybe he could use this miserable creature to draw himself and Irith closer, as well as fulfilling the prophecy.

"Well, come in then, both of you," Larsi said, beckoning. Kelder hastened to obey, and the girl scrambled after him.

They found themselves in a great stone-floored kitchen, surrounded by blackened oak and black iron and stone in a dozen shades of gray. A wooden cistern stood on an iron frame over a stone sink; stone-topped tables lined stone walls between wooden doors. Pale tallow candles shone from black iron sconces. The only touches of color in the entire place were the fire on the great hearth and the vegetables spread on a counter—orange carrots and pale-green leeks and fresh red-skinned potatoes.

"Go on, then, out with you," Larsi said, waving them toward one of the doors. "You've no business in my kitchen, and Irith, I wish I'd never shown you that back way!"

"I'd have found it anyway," Irith retorted, grinning. "You can see it from the air."

Larsi huffed and herded the three of them through the door into the main room.

This was brighter than the kitchen, but not much more colorful; here the dominant hues were black and brown, rather than black and gray. Brown wood tables and chairs, wood-paneled walls, a black slate hearth, and a wooden floor were illuminated by a dozen lanterns and in use by a dozen patrons.

"You'll have the stew," Larsi said, as she showed them to chairs at the near end of one of the two long tables that took up most of the space.

Irith nodded. "And that beer you make," she said.

Larsi threw a significant glance at the blue-clad girl, and Kelder said, "She'll drink water."

The girl nodded eagerly.

Larsi snorted, then turned back to the kitchen.

When the door was shut again Kelder commented, "Doesn't look like much." He looked around himself at the complete absence of paint, brass, or brightwork of any kind.

Irith shrugged. "It isn't," she admitted, "but it's the best food in Angarossa." Then she turned to stare at the girl.

Kelder turned his attention to her, as well. Here was his chance to show Irith that he could be kind and understanding and firm, all at once. "Now," he said, "who are you, and why were you following us?"

The girl blinked, hesitated, and then said, "My name is Asha of Amramion—and I think you killed my brother."

Kelder and Irith stared at the girl. That was not an answer they had expected.

She stared defiantly back.

"I've never killed anyone," Kelder informed her.

"I don't *think* I killed your brother," Irith said.

Something in the back of Kelder's mind took note of the fact that Irith hadn't said "Neither have I." He was not happy about the implications of that and fought down the entire subject, preferring to concentrate on Asha.

At least for the moment.

"Well, *somebody* killed him," Asha said, "and you were there."

"We were?" Kelder asked, startled.

Asha nodded.

"Where?" he inquired.

"On the road this afternoon, a league west of here," she replied.

"You mean your brother was one of those bandits?" Irith asked.

Asha, somewhat reluctantly, nodded.

For a moment nobody spoke. Then Kelder said, "We didn't kill anybody; some demons did."

Asha looked openly skeptical.

"No, really," Irith told her. "It was really gross, I mean, all these little goblin creatures popped up out of nowhere and started hacking away at everybody. It was really disgusting."

"Where did they come from?" Asha demanded, clearly not convinced.

"Just *pop*, right up out of the ground!" Irith said, gesturing broadly.

"A demonologist summoned them," Kelder explained.

"What demonologist?" Asha asked. "I didn't see any demonologist. Not unless it was one of you two."

Kelder grimaced, put a hand to his chest, and raised his eyebrows. "Do I look like a demonologist?" he asked.

Asha glared at him without answering, then pointed at Irith and said, "She was flying, I saw it."

"Sure," Irith said with a nod, "I was flying. I can have wings if I want to; I'm a shapeshifter. But that's wizardry, not demonology. I don't know anything about demons."

"Well, how do I know that it wasn't wizardry that killed my brother and all his friends?" Asha demanded. "All I have for it is your word!"

Kelder looked at Irith and shrugged.

"I don't know," he said. "I guess you'll just have to trust us."

"Why *should* I?"

Up until this point, Asha had spoken in a rational and fairly adult manner, despite her diminutive size and voice, but now her voice cracked, and she was obviously on the verge of tears.

"Because we didn't do it," Kelder told her. "Honestly, we didn't."

"Well, then, who *did*?" Asha demanded. "I was following Abden, but they were on their horses and I couldn't keep up, and when I got there they were all dead, and you two were standing there arguing right in the middle, and I watched and I followed and I never saw anybody there but you two . . ."

Her voice broke completely, and she began to sniffle.

Kelder tried to think of something comforting to say, but before he could, Irith asked, "What would you do if it *was* us?"

Asha's tears suddenly stopped, and her face twisted in anger. She reached down under the table and came up with a knife—an ordinary belt knife, not any sort of fighting knife, but quite capable of doing serious damage.

Kelder grabbed her wrists, both of them.

"We didn't kill *anybody*," he insisted. "We were walking behind a caravan, and the bandits attacked it and rode right into a trap—there was a demonologist there, and I don't know much about magic, but he had demons appearing out of nowhere in less than a minute, so it must have been all set up in advance, it can't be *that* easy to summon them."

Asha stared up at him and said nothing.

"The caravan went on, and so did we, and we must have just gotten to the . . . the dead when you got there, so you saw us there—but it wasn't us, we didn't kill anybody."

"What caravan?" Asha said, fighting back sobs. "I didn't see any caravan!"

"Drop the knife, girl," Larsi's voice said, and the tip of a sword suddenly thrust up against Asha's throat.

The three travelers looked up, startled.

Larsi was standing over them with a laden tray, and beside her stood a young man with a naked sword. The young man was thin and pimply and had his sword against Asha's neck.

Asha stared and refused to move; Kelder released one wrist and took the knife away from her. She didn't resist.

He threw the weapon on the table and told Larsi, "It's nothing, really. She's just upset."

Larsi glared, then gestured.

The sword was withdrawn from Asha's throat.

"Fine friends you bring in here, Irith," Larsi said in a voice that dripped scorn.

Irith shrugged and grinned. "Just a little harmless excitement," she said. "Traveling can be so *boring*!"

"I like it boring," Larsi said. She waved an arm at the other customers, and for the first time Kelder realized they were all staring at the little group at the end of the table. "My *customers* like it boring. They don't like kids screaming and people yelling and blades being drawn, any more than I do. Now, if you three can keep it boring, you can stay, but if there's any more excitement, *out*!"

"Yes, Larsi," Irith said, ducking her head in a sort of nod.

"Agreed, mistress," Kelder said.

Asha glared.

Larsi glared back, and at last the little girl broke and said, "All right, I promise."

"Good," Larsi said.

The young man sheathed his sword and left, while Larsi lowered the tray, displaying three plates of stew, three mugs, and a few other implements.

When Larsi had served out the contents of the tray and departed, Kelder took a good look around the room, which showed him that, except for an occasional nervous glance, the other customers had returned to their own affairs.

Thus reassured, he turned to Asha and said, "All right, now, tell us the whole story. What were you doing out there following your brother? Why was he a bandit in Angarossa, if you're from Amramion?"

Asha was shoveling stew into her mouth with a wooden spoon, and Kelder realized that she probably hadn't eaten all day. He waited until she paused before repeating his questions.

"Amramion isn't exactly the other side of the World from here," Asha retorted. "Two days ago I was still living at home."

Kelder frowned. "All right, then," he said, "why aren't you living at home *now*?"

"Because I came after Abden."

"But *why*? Aren't you a bit young to be out on your own?"

Asha hesitated. She studied Kelder's face, and then Irith's. "I ran away," she said.

"Go on," Kelder said.

"I ran away," she repeated, "and I didn't have anywhere else to go, I didn't have any family or friends to stay with, except Abden."

"And he was one of those bandits?"

She nodded. "He ran away last year," she said, "and he didn't know where else to go, so he went east, and he got stopped by bandits, and he didn't have any money, and he wasn't worth any ransom, but he was big and strong and knew how to fight, so they let him join. He sent me a message and told me about it."

"And then they all got killed today," Kelder said.

Asha nodded again and sniffled.

"But what were *you* doing?"

"I ran away the day before yesterday," she said. "I couldn't ... I mean, I wanted to see Abden and stay with him. I found him this morning, and he said that I couldn't stay there, that they didn't have any way to take care of me, but I hung around and tried to think of something, because I couldn't go back home. And then the scout came back and said a caravan was coming, so they all rode out to meet it, and I ran after them, but when I got there they were all dead, and you two were there and nobody else was, and I didn't know what to do, so I followed you."

She looked up at him. "And here we are," she said.

He looked down at her. "How old are you, Asha?" he asked.

She frowned. "Not sure," she said. "Nine, I think."

Not sure? Kelder started at that. How could she not know how old she was?

He pushed that aside and said, "Nine's too young to be out on your own."

"I *know* that," she said. "That's why I came to stay with Abden!" She sniffled. "And he's gone now."

"So shouldn't you go home, then?" Irith asked.

"No," Asha said flatly.

Kelder looked at Irith, who shrugged, tossing her hair delightfully.

"What *are* you going to do, then?" Kelder asked.

Asha looked down at the table. "I don't know," she whispered.

"What would you *like* to do?" Irith asked.

The child looked up again. "I'd like to find that caravan and kill everybody in it! They killed my brother, and he wasn't going to hurt anybody!"

"You don't know that," Kelder said. "Or at least *they* didn't know that. And he was going to rob them, wasn't he? That might well hurt them; they make their livings trading, they could starve."

Asha glared at him and said nothing.

"Being a bandit is a dangerous business," Kelder pointed out. "Your brother must have known that."

She turned away.

"Killing them wouldn't help your brother any, you know."

"Nothing can help him now," Asha said bitterly. "He won't even get a decent funeral."

"Well," Kelder said, considering that, "maybe we could do something about that, the three of us. We could go back and build a pyre for him." The prophecy was running through his head—a champion of the lost and forlorn, honored by the dead. "We don't have a theurgist or a necromancer to guide his soul, but at least we could set it free."

"No, we couldn't," Asha said.

"Why not?" Kelder asked, puzzled.

"Because," she reminded him, "they took his head."

Kelder had completely forgotten that unsavory detail. Asha was quite correct; as he had noticed, the caravan had taken all the bandits' heads, impaled on pikes as a warning to other would-be attackers. That was standard procedure for thieves, Kelder knew, but he had never before considered the religious consequences.

If someone died and nobody burned the body, the soul would be trapped for weeks, or months, or even years, unable to fly free and search for a way to the gods of the afterlife. It would be prey to ghost-catchers and nightstalkers and demonologists, who respectively enslaved souls, ate them, or used them to pay demons for their services. That wasn't just theory; there were enough ways for magicians to communicate with the dead that the exact nature of ghosts was well established.

And one established fact was that you couldn't burn a body properly unless you had at least the heart and the head. It was better to have the whole thing, but the heart and head were the absolute minimum.

Cutting off a thief's head and posting it suddenly seemed like a rather nasty custom.

It also, it seemed, offered Kelder an opportunity to do something that was a very clear and definite step toward achieving his promised destiny. If he were to champion Asha, who was undoubtedly lost and forlorn, by freeing her brother's soul, he would doubtlessly be honored by that dead soul; that was a good part of his fate right there.

It would also impress Irith, which he wouldn't mind at all. He could be a hero to this little girl and her dead brother, at any rate, and without slaying any dragons or doing anything else all that dangerous.

"Maybe," he said hesitantly, "maybe we could get his head back somehow."

"Are you *crazy*?" Irith said, even as Asha looked up at Kelder with dawning hope in her eyes.

That was not the reaction Kelder had hoped for. "I don't

think so," he replied, a bit defensively. "I mean, why couldn't we? They don't need them *all*, just for display!"

Irith frowned, opened her mouth, then closed it again.

"You *are* crazy," she said.

Kelder glowered at her—this was not at all the reaction he had expected, but he was not about to back down now in front of Asha, after getting her hopes up—and especially not with part of the prophecy at stake. "It wouldn't hurt to *ask*," he said. "What harm could it do? You know that the caravan is here in town, we both saw it . . ."

Asha suddenly became very attentive indeed, and Irith sighed.

"Listen," she said, "the whole thing is insane, but if you've just got to try it, take some time to think it over, all right? You don't want to be roaming the streets of Angarossa at night, and I'm not going to tell you how to get there from here. Let's just wait until morning, and if Asha's still here and you still want to try it, we can talk then."

"All right," Kelder agreed. The idea of dashing out into the night was not very appealing, once he stopped to consider it, and this sounded like an excellent compromise.

"But what do I do *tonight*?" Asha wailed.

Kelder looked down at her, then across at Irith.

Irith's hair was gleaming golden in the lamplight; her white tunic had somehow managed to stay clean on the road, and that and her pale skin made her look like an island of light against the dark wood paneling behind her. He and she would be taking a room at the inn, of course—it would use up almost half of his remaining funds, he estimated, but that didn't seem important. He had been looking forward to sharing a room with her again.

The shapeshifter nodded slightly. Kelder sighed. There were, he now saw, some serious drawbacks to being a champion of the lost and forlorn.

"You can stay with us tonight," he said reluctantly.

CHAPTER 8

There were times during the night when Kelder se-
riously considered trying to approach Irith, despite the little
girl curled up beside the sleeping shapeshifter, but he resisted
the temptation. He woke several times, as he was unaccus-
tomed to sleeping on a wooden floor; there was only one bed,
and Asha and Irith were sharing that. Each time he woke, he
thought over the situation and stayed where he was.

It was easier after the candle had burned out, and he could
no longer see the graceful curve of Irith's body on the bed.

When he awoke for the day, not particularly well rested, Irith
was already up and dressed and gazing out the window. Asha
was still asleep, curled into a tight little ball on the bed.

Judging by the light, it was an hour or more after dawn—
Kelder felt vaguely guilty about sleeping so late, but then he
had certainly not slept well, so perhaps it balanced out.

"Should we wake her?" Irith asked in a whisper, gesturing
toward the bed.

"No," Kelder said, "let her sleep. The poor girl must have
been exhausted. She should be safe at home, not out walking
the highway."

Irith nodded agreement. "It's awful about her brother, isn't
it?"

Kelder nodded in return. "What about breakfast?" he
asked.

"I haven't done anything about it yet," she replied.

"I'll go see what's to be had, then," Kelder suggested.

"Do that," Irith agreed.

Kelder found his way downstairs. In the dining room a

dozen people were eating—most of them, he noticed, just fin-
ishing up. Larsi spotted Kelder as he looked around. "Are you
and the Flyer ready to eat, then?" she asked. "I suppose you
worked up an appetite last night."

Kelder started to make a defensive answer mentioning
Asha's presence, but thought better of it. After all, when they
had taken the room they had said it was for two, not three,
and an extra charge was not inconceivable.

Instead, he simply said, "No, we didn't." Almost as an af-
terthought, he added, "But we'd like breakfast, anyway."

"Well, you're in luck; the chickens were laying well today,
and I've got four eggs left. There's salt ham, and pears, and
plenty more. Eggs, ham, and tea for a copper round. Do you
want a tray for your room, or will you eat down here?"

"Is there a charge for the tray?" Kelder asked.

Larsi smiled. "Well, now that you mention it, yes," she admitted. "But it's only two bits."

"We'll eat down here, then," he said. "I'll be right back."
He turned and headed back to the room.

He knocked, in case one of the girls was using the chamber
pot or otherwise in want of privacy, and then entered.

Asha was still curled up asleep; Irith was gone.

Puzzled, Kelder looked around, but she was indisputably
not to be found anywhere in the little room. He stepped back
out into the passageway, but there was no sign of her there,
either, and he could see no exit save the stairs he had taken.

He had never gotten past the foot of those stairs; she could
not have slipped past him unseen.

He stepped back in the room and looked around again, and
this time noticed the open window.

They were on the inn's upper floor, a good ten feet above
the ground, and it was a very small window, but Irith had her
magic. Kelder doubted he could squeeze through the opening
himself, but Irith was thinner than he was, and once she was
halfway out she could have grown wings easily enough.

He crossed the room and looked out.

The wall below the window was not sheer; there was a narrow ledge a foot or so down, but it was much too narrow for

a person to stand on. From there to the ground the wall was smooth dressed stone.

The alley below was muddy—apparently it had rained at some point in the night—but there were no footprints.

If Irith had left by the window, she must have flown. He leaned out, so as to see past the overhanging eaves, and studied the sky. He could see no sign of her, but that meant little, given his limited area of view.

He shrugged and ducked back inside, whacking his head loudly on the frame. He swore.

Asha was still soundly asleep. He marveled at her ability to slumber so long and so soundly.

Irith had said he should see about breakfast, so presumably she wouldn't be gone long. He sat down on the edge of the bed to wait.

Sitting and doing nothing, when one is recently awakened and hungry, is not much fun. Kelder looked around, bored, but there was nothing of any interest in the little room. At least, nothing except Asha. He studied her face as she lay sleeping.

She was a skinny little thing, and he realized suddenly that the big dark area on one cheek that he had taken for a smudge of dirt was a half-healed bruise. He leaned over and looked her over more closely.

She was wearing only a cotton shift; he lifted the sheet and investigated.

Her arms bore bruises old and new; so did her legs, and, he saw with dismay, her throat. There were old scars on her legs, as well—something had done considerably worse than mere bruises once.

Kelder frowned and pulled the sheet back in place.

"Is something wrong?" Irith asked.

Kelder started and whirled.

She was standing by the window, looking just as if she had never left.

"I didn't see you come in," he said. He hadn't heard wings, either, he realized.

"You weren't supposed to," she replied, smiling.

He smiled back a little uneasily. Marriage to Irith would probably be full of surprises. "Breakfast downstairs any time you're ready" he said.

Her smile vanished. "Thank you," she said, "but I think we might want to skip it."

"Why?" he asked, startled.

"Because the caravan has already left, and I think they're already out of sight of Castle Angarossa; at least, *I* couldn't see them anywhere, and the stablemaster at the caravanserai said they left over an hour ago."

"How far did you look?" Kelder asked.

She shrugged. "I didn't go very high," she admitted. "I didn't want to attract too much attention. But I can't see them from the roof of the inn."

Kelder frowned again. He looked down at Asha, up at Irith, past her at the window.

"Forget it," he said. "We'll catch up with them eventually. She needs her rest, and I need breakfast."

"All right," Irith said, with evident relief. "I didn't really want to argue with them about somebody's head, anyway." She made a face at the thought.

Kelder noticed that she seemed to have concluded that they would be leaving the caravan alone, which was neither what he had said nor what he had intended, but he didn't bother to correct her.

"All right," he said, "let's go eat." He saw Irith glance toward Asha, and added, "Let her sleep."

Irith nodded, and the two of them walked downstairs, hand in hand.

As they ate, Kelder considered the signs of battering on Asha's body. Had Irith noticed them? Were the bandits responsible? If not, who was? Were those marks the reason she had left home and why she would not speak of it?

"What will happen to the bodies?" he asked Irith.

She looked up from her egg. "What?" she asked.

"The bodies of the bandits—the caravan just left them all lying there by the highway. What will happen to them?"

Irith shrugged. "*I* don't know," she said. "I guess they'll just lie there."

"Until they rot?"

She shrugged again.

"That won't make that stretch of highway very pleasant," Kelder pointed out.

Reluctantly Irith answered, "There are . . . well, you know, animals and stuff."

That was even worse. "Shouldn't someone do something about them?" Kelder asked.

"Like who?" Irith asked. "I mean, if they have families somewhere and they find out, I guess they could do something, or maybe if King Caren decides it's a good idea his soldiers could bury them or something."

"What about Asha's brother?" The idea of doing a good deed, of freeing the trapped soul, still appealed to Kelder.

"What *about* Asha's brother? Are you really going to try to do something about him? Kelder, the caravan is *gone*, they aren't there, and I don't think they left her brother's head sitting on a table somewhere!"

"We can catch up with them," Kelder insisted. "They don't move very fast."

"And if we do that, what's going to be happening to the *rest* of him? I mean, *gross*, Kelder!"

"Maybe we could go back and do something . . ."

"And then the caravan will get so far ahead we'll never catch it, and it isn't any of our business *anyway*, Kelder, so just forget it, all right?"

"No," said an unsteady voice from behind.

Irith turned; Asha was standing on the stairs in her shift, listening to them.

"Oh . . ." Irith said.

"Asha, don't worry," Kelder said quickly. "Look, we can go back and build a cairn over your brother's body to keep it safe, and then we can go catch the caravan and get his head back—they're headed for Shan, same as we are, so we're bound to catch up with them somewhere. I mean, there's only the one Great Highway."

"Build a *what*?" Irith asked.

"A cairn. Like a box made of rocks, I mean. Isn't that called a cairn?"

"I don't know," Irith said, "I never heard of anything like that. Do they do that in Shulara?"

"No," Kelder said, "but I heard about it in an old story about an enchanted princess."

"What kind of story?" Irith asked suspiciously.

"Just a story my grandmother told me," Kelder said.

"It sounds weird to me," Irith replied dubiously.

"We should do it," Asha said.

Kelder nodded agreement.

Irith looked from one to the other and then announced, "You're both crazy, but all right, we'll do it."

CHAPTER 9

*I*rith *eyed the structure critically.*

"So I never built a cairn before," Kelder said defensively. "I don't see you helping much."

"I never even *heard* of a cairn before," Irith said, tossing her hair, "and I think the whole idea is stupid. I wish I still hadn't heard of one."

Asha staggered up holding another rock, one she could barely carry. Kelder quickly took it, then looked over the stone oval, trying to decide where to place it.

"Are we just going to leave all Abden's friends lying here?" Asha asked as Kelder set the stone in place.

Kelder looked around at the mutilated corpses, wrinkling his nose at the sight and the stink, and then said, "Yes."

Asha shrugged. "All right," she said. "I just thought I'd ask."

"Go find another stone," Kelder told her.

"This is stupid," Irith said, sitting down cross-legged on the grass. "And boring, too. How are you going to make it cover him without falling in and squashing him?"

"I thought I could make it arch over," Kelder said.

Irith grimaced.

Kelder frowned. "I don't think it's going to work," he admitted. He looked around, as if hoping to find inspiration.

All he saw were headless, decaying corpses and an equal number of dead horses. The horses, at any rate, mostly still had their heads attached.

Irith, too, looked around, wrinkling her nose. "Ick," she said. "I hate to say it, but what if you used some of the saddles to cover him and then covered those with rocks? They look stiff enough to work."

Kelder considered the matter, then nodded.

"That should work," he said. He headed for the nearest horse. "I'm surprised nobody's taken the saddles yet."

Irith shrugged. "Looting corpses isn't much fun," she said. "Probably most people who pass this way have better things to do. Besides, they might be worried about getting cursed or something. But even with the smell, and curses or not, I bet you won't find any purses here anymore."

Kelder looked up from the cinch strap he was tugging at. "Do you think there might really be any curses here?" he asked.

"Don't be silly," she said. "Why would anyone curse us for trying to help a little girl give her brother a proper funeral?"

Kelder had no answer for that; besides, he was discovering that pulling a thick leather strap out from under a dead horse, even a mangled one, takes a great deal of strength. Being a champion of the lost and forlorn wasn't much fun, so far. It didn't seem to impress his intended bride, either.

"Um . . ." he said, as he lost his grip and fell backward, "could you give me a hand here?"

Irith gave a loud sigh, then came to help.

Together, they freed the saddle; Kelder then carried it over and fitted it across his half-built "cairn," like a barrel-vaulted roof.

It fit just fine, and looked strong enough to serve as a frame for a stone covering. He turned to Irith. "Thank you for the help, and for the suggestion," he said.

She waved away his gratitude. "I just didn't want to be stuck here all day while you were finding out how hard it is to build arches," she said.

Three hours later the job was done; Abden's headless remains were entombed in leather and stone. It had taken three saddles to cover the cadaver.

"You're sure it's the right body?" Kelder asked, looking around at the others, still lying scattered across the grassy verge.

Asha nodded.

"Good," Kelder said, straightening up and rubbing his lower back. It was stiff and sore. "Then let's get going." He looked up at the sun. "I doubt we'll catch the caravan today, but we can at least get started."

Irith shook her head. "No, we can't," she said.

Kelder glared at her. "Why the hell not?" he demanded.

"Because it's more than four leagues from Castle Angarossa to the town of Sinodita, and there isn't a decent inn anywhere in that four leagues," Irith said. "We've taken more than half a day on this stupid job, and *I* don't want to be walking around here after dark."

Kelder looked up at the sun again, then back at Irith. "It's not much more than an hour past noon," he said. "How far is it to the Angarossan border?"

Irith thought for a minute. "About two leagues, I guess," she said.

"Are there bandits all over Sinodita, too?"

"What do you mean?" Irith asked, eyeing him warily.

"I mean, is the King of Sinodita as crazy as King Caren of Angarossa and letting bandits run wild there?"

"Queen," Irith told him. "Sinodita has a queen. And no, she's perfectly sensible and there aren't a lot of bandits."

"Well, we can reach the border well before sunset, and we should be safe enough on the highway in Sinodita; I know it will be dark by the time we reach the town, but the greater moon should be up tonight, I think, and if it's not we could stop somewhere until the lesser moon rises, or carry torches, or something. We don't have anything bandits would want, anyway. I say we go on."

"Maybe *you* don't have anything bandits would want, Kelder of Shulara," Irith said, putting her fists on her hips and glaring at him, "but *I* don't care to risk getting raped!"

Kelder glared back rather wearily. She did have a point, he supposed, and he didn't want anyone bothering his destined bride—even if she didn't yet know anything about her destiny. "Then *you*, Irith the Flyer," he said, "can fly on ahead and meet us at the gate when we get to Sinodita."

"There isn't any gate," Irith said. "It's not walled."

"Fine. Then you pick a place that a couple of fools like us can find, and we'll meet you there."

Irith continued glaring and chewed her lower lip. Then she turned and called to Asha, who was waiting for them several paces up the road to the east, "Do you want to walk another four or five leagues today?"

"No," Asha called back, "but I will if I have to, to catch the caravan."

Irith frowned, looked back at Kelder, then threw up her hands in disgust.

"Oh, I give up," she said. "I just give up. You two are hopeless. I can't let that little girl walk that far, after she's spent the whole morning hauling those rocks around! She's about ready to fall over right now!" She pointed.

Kelder looked and realized that Irith was right.

He had not considered that, but it was true. Asha was just a child, after all; she was not strong enough, really, for a journey like this. Kelder was about to surrender, to agree to stay another night in Angarossa, when Irith turned into a horse.

Kelder blinked; Asha stared, then grinned, then burst out laughing.

Irith had transformed herself instantaneously into a horse, a fine white mare, and she was just as remarkably beautiful as a horse as she had been in human form. Her mane was long and flowing, her tail came within an inch or two of the ground; she was long-legged and graceful, slim and splendid. Her white tunic had become a saddle blanket, recognizable by its blue and green embroidery; her other garments had vanished.

"I didn't know you could do that!" Kelder exclaimed. He wondered where the other garments had gone, and whether they would reappear when she changed back.

The horse snorted and gave him a withering glare. He had had no idea a horse was capable of such an expression.

"Can you talk?" he inquired.

The horse shook her head.

"This is so Asha can ride?" Kelder asked.

The equine Irith nodded.

"Should we both ride?"

Irith tried to kick him, but he dodged in time. He noticed that her hooves were not shod. That made sense; after all, she went barefoot in human form.

"I guess not, huh?"

She glared at him again.

"Asha," he called, "come here!"

The girl approached, very hesitantly. Irith lowered her head for the girl to pet, but Asha shied away.

"Come on," Kelder said, "it's just Irith."

"But she's ... is she a horse?" Asha asked, almost whispering.

"She certainly looks like one," Kelder said.

"I never rode a horse," Asha said, still standing back. "I've never even touched one."

"Well, this isn't a *real* horse," Kelder said reassuringly. "It's just Irith enchanted to look like one."

That did not seem to reassure Asha very much, but she took another step toward the magical beast.

Kelder picked her up and lifted her carefully onto Irith's back. "Lift your leg over ... higher, don't kick her ... There!"

Asha settled uneasily into place.

"Hold onto her mane," Kelder advised.

Asha did, but she was still not particularly steady.

"I'm sure Irith will walk slowly at first," Kelder said, patting Asha's hand, "and you'll get used to it. You'll see."

Irith took a step; Asha, frightened, grabbed the mane more tightly. Kelder kept a steadying hand on Asha as the threesome started walking.

"Maybe we should get a saddle," Kelder suggested, seeing how Asha swayed.

Irith turned her head and glared at him.

"No?"

She shook her head no.

"I'm all right, Kelder," Asha said, "really!"

"All right," Kelder said, and walked on. "There's at least

one good thing, Irith," he said, when they had gone a few steps farther. "At least this way you don't need to worry about being raped."

She tried to kick him again, and Kelder had to dodge, then duck quickly back to catch Asha as she lost her balance.

CHAPTER 10

*K*elder had remembered correctly; the greater moon lit their way into the town of Sinodita. Even by the moon's dull orange glow they had no trouble in following the highway—and no trouble in noticing the changing terrain.

The countryside had grown steadily and visibly flatter since they passed the Angarossa/Sinodita border, and the soil had grown drier and sandier. They no longer passed trees of any sort, and the farms on either side of the highway were far from prosperous. They seemed to raise nothing but goats and horses; the coarse, sparse grass would not feed cattle, and the sandy soil would not support crops.

Twice they passed grazing stallions that looked up and whinnied at Irith. Fortunately, there were solid fences between pasture and highway.

Irith plodded along, head down, ignoring everything, except when she turned to glare at Kelder.

Kelder did his best to ignore Irith's annoyance; his own feet were aching and swollen, and the thought of removing his boots was approaching obsession. To distract himself he concentrated on his conversation with Asha, who had pains of her own to try to forget, ones far more lasting than sore feet.

It was as the sun was setting, in a spectacular display of color, that Asha finally admitted why she had left home.

"My father makes *oushka*," she explained. "He has a still out in the barn, and he grows corn and makes *oushka* out of it. He sells some of it—maybe you've heard of him, Abden Ildrin's son? Abden the Elder? He's supposed to make the best in Amramion."

Kelder and Irith both shook their heads. Kelder resisted the temptation to comment that "the best in Amramion" wasn't saying much; one of his own neighbors, back in Shulara, had claimed to make the best *oushka* in five kingdoms.

Asha shrugged. "Well, he sells some, but he drinks an awful lot himself." She shuddered, and Irith tossed her mane in response.

Kelder just nodded.

"He's drunk most of the time," Asha said. "Ever since our mother died. She was having another baby, and something went wrong, and she and the baby died. Abden—I mean Abden the Younger, my brother; Dad's Abden, too, of course, so my brother is Abden Abden's son. I mean he was. Anyway, Abden said that when our mother was alive our dad didn't drink anywhere near so much, but I don't really remember that. I was four when she died, and I don't remember her much."

"I'm sorry," Kelder muttered.

Asha ignored him.

For a moment they continued in silence; then Kelder said, "Your father beats you?" His tone made it a question.

Asha asked, "You saw the marks?"

"Yes," Kelder admitted.

Asha nodded. "Yes, he beats me. He used to beat Abden, too, but finally Abden ran away. And that cheered me up a lot, you know? It meant I could get away eventually, too. So I did, I ran away to be with Abden, but then he got killed." She sniffled slightly, and Kelder realized for the first time that she was crying.

"Don't worry," he said as reassuringly as he could, "you don't have to go back to your father."

"I can't live by myself," she said, snuffling. "I'm too young, and I don't know how."

"We'll find you someplace," he said.

He had absolutely no idea how he could carry out such a promise, but he intended to do it somehow.

After all, wasn't he a champion of the lost and forlorn?

Maybe those yet unborn who were to honor him someday would be Asha's children.

"Thank you," Asha said.

They plodded on together.

When they reached the town of Sinodita, Kelder tugged at Irith's mane. She stopped and turned a questioning look toward him. He reached up and lifted Asha down; the little girl had been half asleep and woke up with a start.

"We're here," he said, setting her on her feet.

"Where?" she asked, looking around.

Irith transformed back into her natural form—or, Kelder corrected himself, at least her *usual* form, that of a beautiful teenage girl. All her clothes seemed to be back where they belonged, and her hair was unmussed.

It had occurred to Kelder that he had no way of knowing whether it was her natural shape or not. He had never dealt with shapeshifters before; he wondered if there were established protocols about such things.

And if her natural form wasn't human, did he want to marry her?

"Why did we stop here?" Irith said.

Kelder blinked, puzzled. "Because this is Sinodita, isn't it?"

"I thought we'd go on to the Flying Carpet," Irith replied. "It's up toward the other end of town."

"Oh," said Kelder, "that's an inn?"

Irith nodded wearily. "About the only decent one in this whole town," she said.

"Oh," Kelder said again. "I didn't know."

Maybe, he thought, looking at Irith's face in the dim moonlight, she wasn't really fifteen at all. Maybe she was an old hag who could transform herself into a girl again.

Did he want to marry an old hag?

"Well, it is," Irith said.

"Come on, then," he said.

"I'm not turning back into a horse," Irith said warningly.

"That's fine," Kelder said. "Asha can walk—can't you, Asha?"

The girl nodded, and the three of them trudged onward.

A few minutes later Kelder rapped at the door of an inn; above his head a signboard creaked in the warm breeze that blew from the east. Kelder hadn't been able to make out the picture on the sign, but Irith assured him this was the right place.

Dinner was cold and greasy, and the only room left was a garret where Kelder was unable to stand upright without hitting his head on the tie-beams.

The innkeeper was apologetic. "We weren't expecting anyone so late," he said.

"At least they weren't completely full," Asha said sleepily, before toppling onto the down pillow the innkeeper had found to serve as her mattress.

That left Irith and Kelder sitting on the two straw ticks. Irith was massaging her legs; Kelder looked at her curiously.

"Horses use their leg muscles differently," she explained, glaring at him. "I'm not used to walking so far in horse shape."

"Oh," he said.

After a moment of awkward silence, he added, "Thank you very much for carrying Asha."

Irith shrugged. "It wasn't anything much," she said, rubbing her shins.

After another moment Kelder asked, "Can you turn into *anything*?"

Irith sat up and looked at him. "What?" she asked.

"I mean, well, you turned into a horse, and I didn't know you could do that. I mean, I knew you could grow wings, and you said you were a shapeshifter—can you turn into anything you want?"

"You mean, could I turn into a dragon and burn you to a crisp?" Irith asked, smiling at him in a way he didn't like at all.

He nodded.

"No," she said, turning her attention back to her legs. "I have seven shapes, and that's all, and a dragon isn't one of them."

"Oh." That was a relief—if it was true. "So you can't disguise yourself as someone else?"

"No. Why would I want to?"

"I don't know; I was just curious." He was not about to admit that he had suspected her of being an ancient crone.

"Well, I can't."

"Seven shapes?"

She made a noise he took for agreement.

"Well, a horse is one," Kelder said.

"And this is another," she replied.

He considered, and asked, "Wings—is that three?"

She nodded.

"Uh . . . what are the other four?"

"None of your business, that's what they are," she said, straightening up and then lying back. "Go to sleep."

"But . . ." As her future husband, he felt that they certainly *were* his business, but he didn't want to tell Irith about his plans for her, her prophesied role.

"Shut up and go to sleep, Kelder. I'm too tired for this." She curled up on her bedding and closed her eyes.

There was another matter he had wanted to discuss with her, as well, and now he wished he had brought it up first. Mentioning it now seemed impolitic.

It would have to come up eventually, but he was too tired to worry about it; he would leave it until morning.

It would *need* to be discussed then, though.

The matter was money; he didn't have any more, beyond a few copper bits. He had no way of paying the bill at the inn if it was anything like the last few.

Fortunately, given the accommodations, it would probably be somewhat less.

Life was becoming very complicated, even with the prophecy to guide him. Irith was clearly the one he was destined to wed, and she was as beautiful and cheerful as he could wish, but marrying a shapeshifter with a secret past was not altogether a reassuring prospect. Asha clearly provided him with someone lost and forlorn to champion, and freeing her brother's soul was obviously the way to be honored by the dead, but catching up to the caravan and getting Abden's head from it might not be all that simple.

Well, Zindré had never said that his life would be *easy*.

And could he refuse his promised future if he wanted to? If it was all too much for him, could he just give up and go home?

Well, who was going to stop him?

And for that matter, maybe it was all coincidence after all; maybe Zindré was a fraud, in which case he was fooling himself, and going home would be the only sensible thing to do.

With a sigh, he leaned over and blew out the candle, then stretched out on his own ticking.

He thought he would be awake, thinking about money, and about Zindré's predictions, and about Irith, for hours.

He was wrong; within three minutes he was sound asleep.

CHAPTER 11

"*That's all you've got?*" the innkeeper demanded.

Kelder nodded silently. Behind him, Irith muttered, "Oh, gods, how utterly embarrassing! Kelder, I can't *believe* you're doing this—and in the Flying Carpet!"

Asha had the good grace to keep her mouth shut, for which Kelder was grateful.

The innkeeper glared at the coins as if they were a direct personal affront.

"Oh, come on," Kelder said. "It's only three bits short, and I swear, it's all we've got."

The proprietor let out a long, dramatic sigh. "Oh, all right," he said, "but I really shouldn't. Now, go on and get out of here, and don't you ever tell a soul I was so soft-hearted and stupid!"

"*Thank* you," Kelder said with a bow. "May all the gods bless and guard you, sir!" Greatly relieved, he turned and hurried for the door, before the man could change his mind.

When they were safely out of the inn and on the streets of Sinodita, Kelder turned left. Irith corrected him, grabbing his arm and turning him around.

"That's west," she said. "We're going east."

Kelder stood where he was and shook his head. "No, we aren't," he said. "Or at least, *I'm* not."

"You're not?" Asha asked, looking up at him.

"No," he said, "I'm going home, to Shulara."

Irith put her hands on her hips and snorted. A lock of hair fell across her face; she blew it out of her way and glared at Kelder.

"What about me?" Asha asked timidly. "What about Abden?"

Kelder looked down at her. "I'm sorry," he said. "But I'm tired, and I don't have any more money, and I can't see what we can do, anyway. If we caught up to the caravan, what would we do? Why would they help us? And how long will it be before we catch them, anyway? Where will we eat and sleep?"

"I don't know," Asha whispered.

"Neither do I," Kelder said, "and that's why I'm going home. I can sleep on the grass by the roadside and pick a little food from the fields, and that should last me long enough to get home to my family—if I turn back now." That probably meant giving up on Zindré's prophecy, but just now, tired even after a night's sleep and humiliated by his experience with the innkeeper, Kelder didn't care.

And maybe he could try again in a few years, become the champion of the lost and forlorn then. It was much easier to be a hero when one had money.

"What about *me*, though?" Asha asked. "I can't go back to my family!"

Kelder frowned. "Don't you have *any* relatives except your father?" he asked.

Asha shook her head; a tear ran down one cheek.

"Kelder of Shulara," Irith said, with her hands on her hips, "if you think for *one minute* that I'm going to let you break your promise to that poor child, then you're a complete blithering idiot! *We*, both of us, are going on to Shan with her, and we're going to find her brother's head and bring it back and build a proper pyre! And after that we'll find someplace for her where she'll be safe. And *then*, if you want, you can creep back home to your stupid little farm in Shulara and let your mommy and daddy take care of you—but not *until* then! Do you hear me?"

Kelder blinked. "Irith," he said tiredly, "I don't. Have. Any. More. *Money*."

"Well, so *what*?"

"So I can't go *anywhere*."

"Kelder, you're being stupid! What do you need money for? We aren't just any bunch of travelers, you know; you aren't in this alone. You're with Irith the Flyer!"

Kelder looked at her for a long moment, then asked, "So what?"

"*So*, you silly ass," Irith replied, "I'm a shapeshifter and a famous magician! Everybody on the Great Highway knows me. I can get money any time I want!"

"You can?"

"Of *course* I can! Do you think I've lived all these years off people like you?"

Kelder had not thought at all about how Irith supported herself; the question had simply never occurred to him. Now that it had been pointed out, he felt rather foolish.

"Oh," he said.

He thought for a moment.

Asha was staring up at Irith now, and the expression on her face and in her eyes looked suspiciously like adoration. Kelder felt a twinge of envy; wasn't it *he* who was supposed to be the honored champion?

"I must be just as stupid as you said," he said. "I don't see how you can get money any time you want."

Irith let out an exasperated hiss and turned away in disgust, then turned back to say "I *work* for it, silly! I can do things that nobody else can!"

"But how do you find work?" Kelder asked.

She shrugged. "I ask around. And if there isn't anything handy, I borrow money—people know I'm good for it."

"Oh," Kelder said again. He hesitated and then asked, "Do you have any money now?"

"Of *course* I do!"

"You do?" Kelder's weariness and confusion began to give way to annoyance. "You *do*?"

"Yes, of *course*!" Irith repeated.

"Then . . ." Kelder stopped, calmed himself, and tried again. "Then why . . ." Again he paused, but finally the entire thing burst out, unrestrained.

"Then why in all the depths of Hell didn't you TELL me

that before I embarrassed us all in front of the innkeeper?" he shouted.

"Because you didn't ask!" Irith shouted back. "*I* didn't know you were out of money! You didn't tell me! The first I knew of it was when you counted out your coins for Bardec!"

"Well, why didn't you say something *then*?" Kelder yelled back.

"Because I was too embarrassed, that's why!"

Kelder started to say something in reply, but no words came; his breath came out in a rush. He took another breath, but it, too, came out as wordless noise.

"Are you really going back to Shulara?" Asha asked.

Kelder looked down at her, and his anger dissipated.

"I don't know," he said.

"It's only two days from here to Shan," Irith said. "At most; we could make it in less if we pushed."

Kelder looked at her, remembering the long walk from Shulara, and then looked down at Asha again.

"No," he said, "no, I guess I'm not going back to Shulara. Not yet, anyway." He turned back to Irith. "Two days?"

"Less, really," she said. "It's three and a half leagues to the Castle of Dhwerra, which is right on the edge of the desert—after that we're out of the Small Kingdoms entirely. There's nothing but the Great Eastern Desert from there to Shan—it's about another three and a half leagues. Seven in all. Most people make it two days because of the heat."

"What heat?" Kelder asked.

"The heat of the desert, of course! But it isn't bad this time of year, really."

"Seven leagues," Kelder said, considering.

Irith nodded. "I could fly it in a couple of hours," she said.

"And we've come how far since we met?"

She shrugged. "Oh, I don't know," she said. "Maybe fifteen leagues?"

Kelder thought for a moment longer, then asked, "Do you really think we can do anything for Asha?"

Irith pursed her lips. "Well," she said, "I don't know about anything really, you know, long term, or anything, but it shouldn't be all that hard to get her brother's head back and build him a pyre."

Kelder mulled this over, and Irith added, "Besides, don't you want to see Shan on the Desert? I mean, it's a really interesting place. The market—they call it the Bazaar—is wonderful. They specialize in sorcery, or at least they used to."

That *did* sound interesting—one of the great cities he had been promised.

Really, the prophecy was still holding up just fine. His bride, the cause he was to champion, a great city to be seen—it was all coming together, wasn't it?

He couldn't just give it all up and go back to being a boring old farmer, with no special destiny.

"All right," he said, "let's get going. We'll all walk at first, and if you get too tired, Asha, we can stop, and maybe Irith can turn into a horse again . . ."

Irith glared at him.

Kelder glared back.

Asha ignored them both and started walking, and a moment later they followed.

CHAPTER 12

The Castle of Dhwerra, unlike most of the castles along the Great Highway, was not actually very near the road. Instead it was built atop a huge mass of rock that thrust up from the sandy earth, half a mile or more to the northwest of the highway's closest approach.

The highway was no longer heading east. From Amramion to Sinodita it had run east by northeast; from Sinodita it had run due east for three leagues; now, though, it curved around and ran due north.

In doing so, it described a quarter circle around the Castle of Dhwerra and around the great stone promontory upon which the fortress was built. Along that arc were located a dozen or so inns, but no real town.

And at the end of the arc the road arrived at the top of a long, steep escarpment.

Kelder had grown up among mountains—small ones, but mountains—and was not particularly bothered when land went up or down, but he had never seen anything quite like this particular feature of the landscape. The cliff seemed to extend endlessly in both directions, a dividing line across the World, as if something had long ago split the World in half and then put it back together without lining the pieces up properly. The higher portion, where he stood, was sandy, but still mostly green, and had various features of interest—the castle soaring up on his left, the inns behind him, the occasional bush.

The lower portion, at the foot of the slope, consisted of

nothing but golden sand, shining so brightly in the midday sun that he could not look at it without squinting.

It was undoubtedly a vast plain—another phrase fulfilled, at least in part.

"The Great Eastern Desert," Irith said. He turned, startled; a moment before she had been a horse, with Asha on her back. Now she stood on two feet again, instead of four, and Asha stood beside her.

"But it's north," Kelder said.

Irith glared at him. "Don't be stupid," she said. "The boundary isn't perfectly straight, silly! There's a piece of the desert that sort of sticks out to the west, and Shan's in the middle of it, and we're on the south edge of it, here."

"Oh," Kelder said, looking out over the gleaming sands again.

Far away, on the horizon, he thought he could see something glistening. He wondered if it was their destination, the fabulous city of Shan on the Desert.

Were they really going there? Was he really going to see someplace that exotic?

Vast plains, great cities, and beside him the bright and beautiful girl he intended to marry—even if the prophecy somehow didn't all come true in every word, he was already sincerely grateful to Zindré. Her words had at least given him the impetus to make this journey, and despite his sore feet and empty purse, that was something he wouldn't want to have missed.

Especially since meeting Irith had been a part of the journey.

"How big is the piece that sticks out to the west?" he asked. "It must be pretty big if we can't see across it."

Irith shrugged. "Oh, maybe ten leagues across," she said. "Not all that big."

"Ten leagues isn't big?" Kelder threw her a startled glance.

"Not compared to the whole thing," Irith replied. "I mean, they don't call it the *Great* Eastern Desert for a joke, Kelder— it's *huge*. Covers one entire side of the World."

"What's on the other side?"

"Of the *World*?" Irith stared at him as if he were quite thoroughly mad.

"No, no," Kelder explained hastily, "I mean the other side of the ten leagues!"

She shrugged again. "Empty grassland. Lots and lots of it."

He nodded. "And Shan's about three or four leagues from here?"

"About that," she agreed.

Kelder looked down the escarpment, down at the empty sands, and asked, "How do we get there?"

"Walk," Irith said, pointing.

Kelder followed her finger and discovered that the road did not vanish at the top of the cliff, as he had first thought; it turned a sharp angle to the right and wound its way slowly and torturously down the slope, to disappear into the sand at the bottom.

"The sand blows onto the highway, but there are markers every half mile or so," Irith explained. "It's paved, really, but the sand covers it."

Kelder sighed and looked up. The sun was slightly past its zenith.

"I guess we had better get going," he said.

Irith nodded. "Asha," she said, turning to the girl, "can you walk for a while? It's sort of steep along here, and it's not good for horses, and besides, I'm getting tired of being a horse."

"All right," Asha agreed. She immediately started walking on ahead, picking her way carefully down the rather abrupt drop that took the road over the edge of the escarpment and down the first five or six feet.

Kelder and Irith followed.

"Is it uncomfortable, being a horse?" Kelder asked, genuinely curious, as they made the turn and the road leveled out somewhat as it cut sideways across the face of the slope.

"No, of course not," Irith answered. She giggled at the idea. "It's sort of nice, being big and strong like that. But I get tired of not seeing any colors and not being able to talk, and my fingers that aren't there get stiff, sort of, from being hooves and being walked on."

"Not seeing colors?" Kelder asked, startled.

"That's right," Irith said with a nod. "Horses don't see colors, just grays and black and white. Sort of like in the evening, when it's mostly dark? Except that it's not dark, there just isn't any color." She hesitated, then amended that to "At least, when *I'm* a horse, *I* don't see colors. I don't know about natural horses, really."

"Oh," Kelder said.

A moment later he said, "Could you ask them?"

"Ask who?" Irith asked, startled.

"Natural horses. Can you talk to them, when you're a horse?"

"No, silly!" she said. "Horses don't talk!"

"Not even among themselves?" Kelder asked. "I mean, I know they don't speak any of our languages, but don't they have languages of their own?"

Irith giggled again.

"Well," Kelder said defensively, "they do in all the old stories."

"Oh, Kelder," Irith said, "those are just *stories*! Hardly any of them are true!"

"Well, how should I know that?" he asked.

"Because it's foolish! Horses can't talk unless they're magical, somehow. The gods taught *people* to speak, not animals!"

Kelder marched on half a dozen steps in silence, then said, "What about the other things you can turn into?"

"What other things?" Irith asked, not looking at him.

"You said you could change into seven different shapes," he said. "Can the others see color? Can they talk?"

"Well, it doesn't matter whether I have wings or not," Irith said, "I'm still *me*, and I can still see colors and still talk."

"What about the others, though?"

Irith sighed. "Which others?"

"All four of them!"

"I can't talk in any of the others. I can see colors in two of them."

"Which ones?"

"None of your business."

That effectively ended the conversation, and they trudged on down the escarpment in silence.

The silence continued for the entire descent, and well out onto the sands. Kelder simply didn't have anything to say except questions that Irith didn't want to answer, Asha was concentrating on walking, and Irith's thoughts were her own.

It was finally broken when Asha wailed, "This sand gets into everything! Irith, could you be a horse again?"

"No," Irith snapped. She marched on.

"Here," Kelder said, "You can ride on my shoulders for a little while, until you get the sand out from between your toes." He reached out his arms.

Asha looked up at him, considering, then shook her head.

"No, Kelder, but thank you all the same," she said. "I'll walk." She turned and trudged onward, slogging through the drifting sand.

Kelder dropped his arms, then shrugged. "Suit yourself," he said, a little annoyed. Was that any way for a person to treat her champion?

He marched on, frustrated and resentful. Fulfilling a prophecy wasn't turning out to be as much fun as he hoped.

He glanced over at Irith, at her flowing golden hair and the curves that showed through her garments as she walked.

On the other hand, he told himself, it did have its points.

He trudged on, thinking about the future.

CHAPTER 13

They covered the last mile or so largely by the glow that spilled out over the walls of Shan on the Desert; the sun was down, the greater moon not yet up, and the lesser moon not enough to help.

Shan, though, blazed like a fire before them, lighting the sky orange.

Asha was staggering with exhaustion, and in the end she gave up and let Kelder carry her the last hundred yards, through the city gates and into the Bazaar.

They had not caught up with the caravan; Kelder had secretly hoped they would, but they had seen no sign of it.

He hoped that they hadn't passed it, perhaps safely tucked away at Dhwerra. It *should* be waiting for them in Shan, Kelder told himself.

Once inside Asha stared about, wide-eyed, as Kelder lowered her to the ground. They were in the central square of the Bazaar, and Kelder and Asha both looked about in wonder. Irith waited impatiently for them to get over their awe.

The Bazaar at Shan was unique among all the markets Kelder had ever seen in that it was built on two levels—at least two levels, perhaps more. The ordinary open market was surrounded not by the usual taverns and inns and shops, but by a maze of galleries and arcades, alight with torches and lamps of a dozen varieties, with merchants of every description lining every side, displaying their wares to crowds of eager customers.

And atop the galleries and arcades, on their flat roofs, there

99

were still more merchants, still more customers, to be reached by innumerable staircases.

Most of the upper level was unroofed, or covered only by tents and awnings, but in a few places the upper tier, too, was partially enclosed by more substantial structures. Kelder could not see, in the tangle of firelight and shadow, whether there were still more merchants up on a third level.

Where there were no permanent stalls, there were blankets heaped with goods, or blankets covering momentarily untended goods, or wagons or carts or other vehicles. Entire caravans had set up shop under the colonnades around the market square; some of them had obviously been there for quite some time.

Nor was the Bazaar simply a single square. Oh, there was a central square, and a larger one than Kelder had ever seen before, but the galleries and arcades, colonnades and courtyards, stairways and stalls all extended for blocks, to left and right and straight ahead, inward from the city walls. Kelder could see no end to the labyrinth of buyers and sellers and goods.

It seemed to him that the Bazaar must surely occupy the entire interior of the city walls—but that was absurd.

Wasn't it?

"I don't understand," he said. "Where do they all *come* from?"

"Where do all what come from?" Irith asked, startled. That was not the question she had been expecting.

"The merchants," Kelder said, with a wave of his hand. "Look at them all! Where do they live? And where did all these people *buying* things come from? We didn't see that many on the road, certainly. And we're in the middle of the desert, and I don't see any farmers here with their crops— what do they all eat? Where do they get all those things they're selling?"

"Oh, don't you know?" Irith replied, startled. She giggled. "Really, Kelder, sometimes it seems like you don't know *anything*!"

Slightly resentful, but too awed and curious to worry about it, Kelder asked, "What do you mean?"

"I *mean*, it's all done by magic, of course! We aren't in the Small Kingdoms anymore, you know—they take their magic seriously here."

"What sort of magic?" he asked, eyeing her cautiously. Magic, after all, was something she knew far more about than he did—and while he wanted to know more, he had a fair appreciation of how dangerous it could be. In fact, the thought of unfamiliar and perhaps hostile magic made him distinctly uneasy, especially after what had happened to those bandits back in Angarossa.

"Oh, I guess wizardry, mostly, these days," Irith said, "but a lot of sorcery, too—it used to be *mostly* sorcery, but these days sorcerers aren't what they used to be . . ."

"What are you talking about?" Kelder demanded. "What do sorcerers have to do with all this?"

Irith put her hands on her hips and glared at him.

"I am *talking*," she said, "about *this place*—about Shan on the Desert!"

Kelder glared back, waiting for her to continue. Somewhere in the back of his mind he remembered that she had told him that the Bazaar specialized in sorcery, but he was in no mood to admit it.

She threw up her hands in disgust.

"Aah! Don't you know *anything* about Shan?" she shouted.

"No," Kelder answered, "I don't. Except that it's at the end of the Great Highway and is supposed to be the best place in the World to buy certain things." He glanced around at the Bazaar and added, "Which I can believe."

"All right, then," Irith said, "I'll explain." She took a deep breath and began, "Shan isn't part of the Small Kingdoms—it wasn't part of Old Ethshar. What it *is*, is the last bit of the old Eastern Command, that fought under General Terrek in the Great War. You know about that?"

"A little," Kelder said. "I mean, of course I know about the *war*, and I've heard of General Terrek, I think. He got killed by a demon, didn't he?"

Irith nodded. "A whole bunch of demons, actually. His whole command got wiped out, pretty much—all the demons of Hell got loose at once and went running all over the east, blasting everything. That's where the Great Eastern Desert came from—it wasn't desert before that."

"Oh," Kelder said, thinking about the vast, empty wasteland that surrounded Shan and trying to imagine what could have caused it. By comparison, the demons who wiped out the bandits looked pretty trivial.

That reminded him of the caravan they had come to find; he glanced around but recognized none of the wagons in sight.

A few did have heads on pikes, as it happened, but none of them were recent. Two were actually just skulls, rather than heads, and the others were approaching a similar state.

Irith continued, "Right, the demons did all that, and they were going to go on and destroy everything else, but the gods themselves came down from Heaven and fought the demons and defeated them."

Kelder nodded, partly listening and partly still looking for the caravan; that part, about the gods coming and stopping the demons, he had heard before.

"But it was too late for General Terrek, of course, and all of his people—except for Shan." She made a sweeping gesture, taking in the entire Bazaar. "See, this was Terrek's main supply depot, and he had all his magicians here at the time, and they had all their protective spells up and everything, and they were able to hold the demons off until the gods came and rescued them."

"Oh," Kelder said again, still looking around.

"Anyway," Irith continued, "after the war ended, there were all these people here, magicians and supply clerks and quartermasters and people like that, and they had all these supplies intended for General Terrek's army, but the army was gone, so they just kept all the stuff themselves and started selling it."

Kelder nodded, turning his whole attention back to Irith.

The whole thing made sense, so far, except for one little detail.

"That was more than two hundred years ago, though," he said. "They must have sold it all off long ago!"

"Well, of *course* they did, silly!" Irith agreed. "But they bought other stuff, or made it, and they're all still buying and selling. And since this was the biggest cache of magical supplies in the entire World for so long, it's still where magicians come to buy and sell, a lot of the time. Not just magicians, either. And the people here make things, too—they make glass here better than anywhere else, better even than Ethshar of the Sands. There are miners who bring in jewels from the desert to sell here, too. Let's see . . ." She paused to think.

Kelder waited.

"Well, glass," she said, "I said that. And sorcerers' stuff, and supplies for wizards except you can get most of those in Ethshar just as well now, and medicines, I think—some of them—and perfumes, they make wonderful perfumes here, and there are dyes—all kinds of stuff." She shrugged. "It used to be nicer, actually. Business has dropped off a lot since I first came here."

"They must be expensive," Kelder said. "I mean, it's a long way to come, all the way out here." He remembered another unexplained detail and asked, "So where did all the buyers come from, anyway? We didn't see anywhere near this many people on the way . . ."

"It's the off season," Irith said. "It's *much* more crowded than this sometimes!"

Kelder looked about at what must have been several hundreds, perhaps thousands, of people.

"A lot of people don't come by the highway," Irith continued. "The wizards fly, or use some other kind of magic to get here. People from all over the eastern Small Kingdoms come overland to Dhwerra and get the highway from there, and they would all have gotten here hours ago, so we wouldn't have seen them on the road. And there are other ways, magical ways, I think—I've heard stories about tunnels under the desert."

"Oh," Kelder said. "But what do they all eat? Where do they stay?"

"Oh, there are places to stay," Irith said. "Inns for the customers, tenements for the natives. And they get their food by magic, mostly."

While this discussion had been taking place, Asha had rather blearily wandered over toward a nearby merchant's stall.

"Oooh!" she exclaimed, distracting Kelder and Irith. "Look!"

The two looked.

Asha had lifted the velvet cover from a glass sculpture of a dragon; the creature sparkled vivid gold in the yellow lamplight. Its jaws were open in silent rage, crystal fangs glittering; it stood crouching on three taloned feet, the fourth raised to strike, claws outstretched. Its tail wound gracefully to a needle-sharp point, and its wings, like sheets of ice, swept up and back, ready to bear it instantly aloft.

Kelder found himself drawn to it.

Irith looked but called, "It's getting late, and I'm really hungry; can we get some dinner now? And find somewhere to sleep?"

Kelder and Asha stared at the glass dragon.

"Kelder?" Irith called. "Come on, let's get something to eat!"

Kelder reluctantly tore himself away. "Did you see this thing, Irith?" he called.

She shrugged. "Not that one," she said, "but I've seen others. I've been here before, Kelder, lots of times. You can make lots of nice things out of glass."

"Nice things" seemed a rather inadequate description, to Kelder—he thought the dragon was quite spectacular. He didn't argue, though.

He did hesitate.

"It will still be there after we eat," Irith pointed out, and Kelder tore himself away.

"Come on, Asha," he called. "Let's get dinner."

The little girl hesitated, as Kelder had. He reached out and took her hand and led her away.

Following Irith's lead, they headed out of the square to the northwest, pushing their way through the wall of traders under the first ring of columns.

Once they had pierced that veil, Kelder suddenly saw what Irith had meant about the off season and a decline in business.

The arcades and merchants' stalls still continued as far as Kelder could make out, but now he could see that many of them were empty. Some of the merchants who were there were sitting alone and ignored, without a patron in sight.

And many of them did not look at all prosperous; Kelder could see men and women who were dirty and unkempt and tired. Some were slouched against pillars, or curled up on the ground asleep, not even pretending to look for customers anymore. All this had been hidden by the crowd in the central square.

It struck him as odd that so many people should be clustered there, rather than spread more evenly throughout the market; he said as much to Irith.

She shrugged. "Well, the galleries around the square are where those new caravans are—probably a lot of the people doing the buying are really the merchants from these other places." She waved a hand at the largely vacant inner arcades.

"I didn't see the . . ." Kelder began, and then he stopped.

He had been about to say that the caravan they had followed should be there somewhere, if new caravans were what attracted customers, but before he could finish the sentence he spotted something.

Far off to the right, to the northeast of the market, he could see a face impossibly high up, almost brushing against the stone arch overhead, torchlight from below lighting it unpleasantly. And it was *only* a face, with no body below.

He blinked, and realized that he was looking at a head on a pike—a fairly fresh head. That presumably meant that the caravan they wanted was right there; in fact, the head he was looking at might well be Abden's. Asha's brother.

He chewed on his lower lip for a second or two, considering.

His stomach growled, deciding him; he wouldn't point the caravan out just yet. Being Asha's champion could wait a little.

"You didn't see what?" Irith asked.

"Nothing," he lied. "Do you know someplace good to get something to eat?"

"Of course," she said. "This way."

She pointed ahead, down a colonnade lined with crates and barrels. A table a few paces away displayed tall green bottles—wine, Kelder assumed. At least some of the barrels were presumably full of spirits, as well—this particular arcade would seem to specialize in strong drink. He glanced down at Asha, remembering what she had said about her father.

She was staring ahead rather fixedly, not at the bottles or barrels but at a man who lay sprawled against a pillar.

Kelder grimaced and looked ahead.

That first drunk was not the last; others were sitting or lying here and there along the arcade. In fact, there were about as many drunks as there were vintners.

Annoyed, Kelder wondered why the merchants didn't shoo these sorry specimens away. He quickly reconsidered, however, when he realized that there were no sober customers in sight—why should the sellers chase away the only people who were actually buying, at the moment?

He sighed. The World was not the pleasant place he would have wished for, had he been offered the job of creating it.

"Come on," Irith said, taking his hand.

Asha had been holding the other hand, so Kelder found himself being dragged along as the central link in a three-part chain. Irith pulled vigorously—she must be very hungry indeed, he thought. Asha was too tired to move as quickly as Irith moved, and was slowed further by shying away from an old man who lay mumbling in their path. She whimpered.

Irith turned at the sound, and the drunk looked blearily upward at the trio.

"Irith!"

Kelder looked down in astonishment.

The drunk was staring at Irith's face. He dropped the empty bottle he had held clutched in one hand and reached up toward her.

"Irith," he said, "you've come back!"

CHAPTER 14

*I*rith stared down at the weathered face, the red nose, the bloodshot eyes, the dirty, ragged beard, and the matted hair. She dropped Kelder's hand and stepped back.

"Eeeew," she said.

"Irith, it's *me*," the drunk said, scrabbling against the paving stones as he tried to get his feet under him.

Asha dropped Kelder's other hand and backed away.

"Listen, old man . . ." Kelder began.

"Irith," the drunk called, ignoring him, "don't you remember me?" With one hand on the pillar, he got to his knees. His foul breath reached Kelder's nostrils.

"*Remember* you? I never saw you before in my life!" Irith replied angrily.

"Yes, you did," he insisted. "It's been years, the gods know, too many years, but you knew me, all right, don't you remember?" He made it to his feet, panting, his hand still on the pillar. "Don't you know me?"

He stared back at her blank face, no flicker of recognition showing, and suddenly shouted at her, *"Don't you know me?"*

"No!" Irith screamed back. *"I never saw you before!"*

"Listen, old man, you leave her . . ." Kelder began, trying to push between Irith and the drunk. He was uncomfortably aware that the confrontation was attracting attention; several of the wine merchants were staring, and assorted other people were turning to see what the disturbance was about.

The old man, with strength truly astonishing in one so decrepit, shoved Kelder rudely aside and took a step toward Irith.

She shrank back, and her wings appeared suddenly. She stretched them, as if to take flight, to escape this loathsome apparition, but the tips brushed against the arcade's vaulted ceiling. She glanced up, startled, at the prisoning stone, then looked around, panicky, at the people, staring at her from all sides, watching her intently. Her wings vanished.

"Get away from me!" she cried. "Everybody get away!"

Kelder, recovering from his surprise, thrust himself at the old drunk, arms outstretched, and knocked him off-balance.

"Irith!" the drunk cried. "Irith!"

Irith turned and ran, down the shadowy arcade, her white tunic flashing brightly as she passed each lamp, then fading into the next patch of darkness.

"Follow her!" Kelder barked to Asha. Tired as she was, the girl obeyed, scampering after the fleeing shapeshifter, while Kelder pushed the drunk up against the pillar.

"Irith!" the drunk called again, looking after her, paying no attention to Kelder.

"Listen," Kelder began.

The drunk burst into tears. "No," he wailed, "I can't lose you again! Irith, come back!" He tried to shove Kelder aside.

"*Damn* it!" Kelder said, as he stumbled back against a stack of crates. He grabbed at the drunk's tunic and pulled the old man down with him.

"Let me go!" the old man bellowed, trying to tear loose. "Let me go after her!"

"*No,*" Kelder shouted back, holding on tight.

Sobbing, the drunk swung a fist at his face; Kelder dodged easily.

The drunk swung again, and this time Kelder had to loose his hold in order to avoid the blow. Cursing, he dodged. The drunk stumbled to his feet and began staggering in the direction Irith had gone.

Kelder sprang up and charged after him, tackling him from behind and knocking him heavily to the stone pavement.

The drunk's words had become incoherent babbling by this point, but his actions were clear enough; he was trying to get up, get away from Kelder, and continue his pursuit of Irith.

Gritting his teeth, Kelder hauled off and punched him squarely in the nose.

The old man's head snapped back against a heavy cask, making a sound like a slammed door—a very solid door. Blood trickled from his nose, and he slid to the ground, dazed.

Kelder's knuckles stung from the impact, and he was very worried indeed lest he had killed the old man—he'd heard somewhere that drunks had brittle bones.

This particular drunk was made of sterner stuff than that, for he didn't so much as lose consciousness completely. He did lie stunned for a moment, but then shook his head, trying to gather his muddled wits.

By that time Kelder was back on his feet, and the instant he was sure that the old man had not been killed or crippled he spun on his heel and sprinted after his companions.

A moment later the drunk was out of sight, and Kelder was as good as lost in the mercantile maze of columns and courtyards. He slowed to a stop and called quietly, "Irith?"

Asha's voice answered him. "This way, Kelder!"

Following the sound, he made his way through another fifty yards or so of market and into an alley—he had finally left the Bazaar and entered the city proper. He found Asha crouched in the mouth of the alley, watching in all directions.

"Are you all right?" he asked her.

She nodded.

"Where's Irith?"

Asha jerked a thumb in the direction of the alley's gloomy depths. Hesitantly Kelder crept into the darkness.

"Irith?" he called.

A cat meowed, somewhere ahead.

Something touched Kelder on the back, and he started, then realized it was just Asha, following him.

"She said there's a tavern down the far end of this alley that she likes," Asha whispered.

Kelder nodded an acknowledgment. "Irith?" he called again.

"Here," she answered, stepping out of the darkest shadows

ahead. Kelder could still only see a dim outline, but he was sure it was Irith. "Is he gone?"

"He's back there somewhere," Kelder said. "Um ... I hit him."

"Good!"

Kelder was surprised at the heat in Irith's response. "Where are we?" he asked.

"Horsebone Alley, it used to be called," Irith said. "I haven't been here in years. There's a real nice tavern around the corner at the far end, called the Crystal Skull—that's where we're going."

"The Crystal Skull?" Kelder asked, glancing back at Asha and seeing only a small, dark shape.

Irith nodded, then realized that that was probably not visible. "Yes," she said, "the owner had this big chunk of quartz that looked sort of like a skull. He kept it on the mantel."

"Oh," Kelder replied. That sounded harmless enough. In general he didn't like the idea of patronizing businesses with morbid names, but in this case he decided to trust Irith's judgment. Holding Asha's hand, he followed the dim outline of the shapeshifter down the alley and around the corner.

"No torch," Irith remarked, startled, when they were out of Horsebone Alley and into a broader but equally unlit thoroughfare. The shadows here were not as deep or threatening; the faint glow of the lesser moon and the stars poured down, and some of the light of the marketplace slopped over the rooftops and into the street. She pointed to an unlit doorway. "Over there," she said, leading the way.

Kelder followed, an uncomfortable, uneasy feeling stirring in his belly.

The doorway was broad and deep; above it an iron bracket projected straight out from the rough stone, with empty rings where a signboard had once hung. To either side of the doorway were black iron sconces, also empty; there were no signs of torch or ash, and even the smokestains on the wall appeared to be weathered, rather than fresh. It was plain to Kelder that this place was not open for business, but Irith ignored the signs and marched straight into the gloom of the entryway.

Kelder followed and found her standing in the open archway.

At first he thought the door was open, but then he realized that there was no door. Nor, looking through the opening, was there any roof; the same faint illumination that filled the street filled the building's interior, as well. Dusty chunks of stone and wood lay strewn about, colorless in the dim light.

"It's gone," Irith said in a tone of dull surprise.

Kelder stepped up beside her and glanced about.

"It certainly is," he agreed.

"What happened to it?" Asha asked curiously.

"How should *I* know?" Irith snapped, turning angrily on her young companion.

Asha cowered back against the wall of the entry, and Kelder thrust a restraining hand between the two.

"She's just a kid," he said.

"I wasn't going to touch her!" Irith protested.

Asha burst out crying, sliding down the wall until she sat sprawled on the ground.

Kelder and Irith looked at one another.

"Now what?" Kelder asked.

"*I* don't know," Irith replied.

"We can't eat here," Kelder said, waving his arm at the dusty ruins. "It's been gone for years, by the look of it."

That statement was simple truth, but something about it bothered him.

"Well, I haven't *been* in Shan for years," Irith said. "I usually turn around at Dhwerra when I travel the highway—if I even get that far. Sometimes I turn back at the Angarossa border."

"Do you know of any other good taverns or inns here?" Kelder asked. "Ones that might still be in business?"

"No," Irith replied, "I haven't come anywhere but here in *ages*."

"Well, where did you go before you found this place?" Kelder asked in his most reasonable tone.

"One that's been gone even longer," Irith retorted.

Kelder sighed and looked around.

"Well," he said, "we'll just have to find someplace new, then. Come on."

Irith peered apprehensively at the street. "What about that old man?" she asked.

"What about him?" Kelder asked.

"What if he finds me?"

Kelder considered that.

Two things suddenly fell into place in his thoughts.

When had Irith last been there? He looked into the ruin; it had not been abandoned yesterday, or the day before.

It looked as if it had been abandoned for years—and a good many years. If Kelder had been asked to guess, he'd have said ten or fifteen; he could believe as little as five, but less than that . . .

Irith was only fifteen. More than three years ago and she wouldn't even have been wearing a skirt yet—so to speak, since she was wearing breeches, in defiance of tradition. She wouldn't have been welcome in a tavern unescorted.

How could she have come to the Crystal Skull? And the way she spoke of it, she had been in here more than once.

That was one thing.

And the other . . .

"How did that old man know who you were?" Kelder asked.

"What do you mean?" Irith asked, uneasily.

"I mean," Kelder said, "he called you by name. He said he didn't want to lose you *again*—he definitely said 'again.' When did he lose you before?"

"He didn't," Irith said uncomfortably. "He's crazy, or lying, or something."

"But how did he know your name?"

"He probably heard one of you two say it," she suggested, "and maybe he got me mixed up with some other Irith. I mean, it's not an unusual name, you know." She made a face that was almost a sneer. "It's about the *second* most common name in the World, isn't it, *Kelder*?"

Kelder did not rise to the bait; he was used to jokes about his name, and he knew perfectly well that it was the most ordinary name in the World.

And Irith was quite right, her own name was also very popular, probably the most commonly used feminine name—though nowhere near as widespread as Kelder, and maybe not up with some of the other masculine names. He'd heard plenty of jokes and stories that used Kelder and Irith as names for a boring peasant couple, and wasn't bothered by them.

"You're sure you didn't know him, when you were little?" Kelder asked.

"Of course I'm sure!" Irith snapped. "Ick, *him?*"

"I mean, he's not your father, or your old master, or an uncle or something?"

"Kelder, of *course* not! Don't be stupid. My father's dead, and I don't have any uncles anymore, and he's not my old master, he's just a creepy old man who's got me mixed up with someone else." She turned away and muttered, "I mean, he's *got* to be."

"When you came here before, were you alone? I mean, why were you in this tavern? You must have just been a little girl."

"No, Kelder, don't be silly, it wasn't *that* long ago!"

"But . . ."

"Hai," she said, "just drop it, all right? Let it go."

Reluctantly, Kelder let it go. "All right, then," he said, "let's go find somewhere to eat and to sleep. And in the morning we can see . . ."

"In the morning," Irith interrupted, "we can get *out* of here!"

"Out of where?" Kelder asked, startled.

"Out of *Shan*, of course! We can head back to somewhere *civilized*, not all these dreary *ruins* and old *drunks* and things!"

Asha stopped crying and stared up at Irith.

Kelder hesitated.

"What about my brother?" Asha asked.

"Oh, *forget* about your brother!" Irith snapped. "I want to get away from this awful place and that nasty old man!"

"Wait a minute . . ." Kelder began.

"You promised!" Asha shrieked.

"I did not!"

"You did!"

"Hai!" Kelder shouted. "Quiet down, both of you!"

The girls subsided, glaring angrily at each other. Kelder sighed. This was all getting very complicated; he hadn't expected his promised wife to have a mysterious past and troublesome moods, nor had he expected championing the lost and forlorn to be as tricky as it seemed determined to be. "Listen," he said, "we did promise her, Irith, but as soon as we get Abden's head off that pike, we can get out of here."

"Well, how long is *that* going to take?"

"Not long," Kelder insisted. "I mean, I saw the caravan back there, I think—it should be easy enough."

"How?" Irith demanded. "It's up on a pike, out of reach, and they aren't going to get it down for us."

"You can fly, can't you?" Kelder replied. "Asha and I can make a distraction of some kind, so no one will be looking, and you can fly over there and snatch the head right off the pike, and no one will even see you, in the dark."

"You mean tonight?" Irith asked. "Now?"

Kelder opened his mouth and then closed it again. His stomach growled.

"Maybe tonight," he said. "After we eat."

CHAPTER 15

"*Maybe we shouldn't try it tonight,*" Kelder said, chewing on the steak. The meat here required considerable gnawing—not, as Irith had pointed out, like the food at the Crystal Skull.

"We should have found someplace better," she had said.

"There may not *be* any place better anymore," Kelder had replied. "And I'm hungry."

And now they were in Big Bredon's Tavern, gnawing on meat that had probably come from some caravan's superannuated draft animal. Little Asha was having trouble staying awake, her head constantly on the verge of falling forward into her fried potatoes.

"Why not?" Irith asked.

Kelder pointed his fork at Asha.

"I'm all right!" Asha protested. "I'm just tired."

"We all are," Kelder agreed. "So maybe we should just rest and worry about it tomorrow night."

Asha frowned, blinking. "What if the caravan leaves again?"

"Oh, it won't do that," Kelder said, not quite as confidently as he would have liked. "I'm sure they'll be staying in Shan for several days yet. Right, Irith?"

"*I* don't know," Irith said, jabbing her fork viciously at her potatoes.

Kelder glared at her resentfully. "Well, anyway," he said, "I think we're all too tired tonight. We'd probably mess up somehow. Tomorrow night should be fine."

"*I* don't want to stay in Shan all day," Irith said resentfully.

116

"This place has really gone downhill since I was here, you know that? It's a dump now—ruins everywhere, half the arcades deserted ... "

"You're just mad about the Crystal Skull," Kelder said.

"Yes, well, so what?" Irith snapped. "What difference does it make why I don't like it here? I don't like it here; I want to go."

"We're not going anywhere until we at least *try* to get Abden's head back," Kelder told her.

"Fine, then let's just get it *over* with, shall we?" Irith dropped her fork and turned to Asha, then stopped and giggled.

Kelder turned to see why Irith was laughing, and found Asha sound asleep, her cheek resting on the oily potato slices. He smiled, then carefully lifted her head from her plate and transferred it to a folded napkin on the table.

"All right," Irith said, before Kelder could say anything, "we get some sleep. But we don't need to wait all *day*—why don't we get up really, really early, maybe two hours before dawn, and ... and do it then? And then we can still get out of town before anyone from the caravan wakes up, and they'll probably be too busy doing business to come after us right away even if they notice it's gone and figure out where we went."

Kelder considered that for a moment, wishing he wasn't quite so exhausted himself; his fatigue made thinking difficult.

"All right," he said at last. "That will give us about four hours' sleep, I guess, which is better than nothing."

Irith smiled at him, her first real smile since that morning. "Oh, good!" The smile vanished. "It's going to be really yucky, you know, pulling that head off that pike."

Kelder grimaced. "I guess so," he said. "You have to do it, though; you're the only one who can fly."

"I know." She sighed. "Let's go get some sleep."

They went and got some sleep. They had to carry Asha to the room Irith had rented, Kelder taking her under the arms, Irith taking her feet.

It was only at the very last moment, the candle already extinguished, that Kelder realized they were not going to wake up until midday without outside help. He staggered back downstairs and promised the night watchman six bits in copper if he got them up on schedule.

The watchman agreed.

Kelder did not even remember returning to his bed; the next thing he knew was that someone was shaking him, none too gently, and someone with beery breath and a strange accent was telling him, in Trader's Tongue, to wake up.

He was too tired to think in Trader's Tongue at first, and in Shularan he advised whoever it was to go immediately to Hell, and to speak Shularan on the way.

The shaker said, in Ethsharitic this time, that he spoke no Quorulian. This completely inappropriate response brought Kelder awake, as he tried to figure it out.

He sat up, blinking, and recognized the night watchman.

"It's not Quorulian," Kelder said. "It's Shularan."

"I don't speak that, either," the watchman said in Trader's Tongue, shrugging.

"Right," Kelder said. "Thank you for waking me."

"Eight bits," the watchman said, holding out a palm.

"Six," Kelder said. "When my friends are awake and we've checked the time."

The Shanese shrugged again. "Six," he agreed. "I wait."

Kelder glared at him for a moment, then reached over and shook Irith awake.

Five minutes later the three of them were making their way, rather blearily, through the streets of Shan. The watchman, richer by six bits of Irith's money, was back in his regular post at the inn.

"So I just fly up and take the head off the pike, and then we go, right?" Irith asked, stumbling over an empty bottle and narrowly avoiding whacking her head against a stone pillar.

Kelder nodded. "That's right," he said.

"And what are you two going to be doing?"

"Standing watch, I guess," Kelder replied. Then he corrected himself. "No, they've probably got guards. We'll be distracting the guards."

"Oh," Irith said. "All right."

"There!" Asha said, pointing. "There it is!"

"Shh!" Kelder and Irith both hushed her.

She looked up at them, startled, but said no more.

"Do you see any guards?" Kelder asked.

Irith shook her head. "They must be there, though." She sighed. "Tell me again why I'm doing this."

"Because," Kelder told her, "you promised Asha."

Irith looked unconvinced.

"Because I asked you to," Kelder suggested.

Irith sighed again, nodded, and spread wings that had not been there an instant before. She flapped them once.

Kelder started to shush her, then caught himself.

"Just testing," she said. "They're a little stiff; I haven't flown much these last few days."

He nodded. "Look," he said, "we'll meet you at the city gate, all right?"

"Fine." Her wings stretched gracefully upward, flapped, and she rose toward the night sky.

Below her, the youth and the child watched for a moment. Then Kelder shook himself out of his momentary daze and said, "Come on." Asha followed obediently as he crept toward the caravan, moving as silently as he could and trying to keep to the shadows as much as possible.

The wagons were in a line along one side of an arcade that was significantly higher and wider than most, and open on both sides. Torches were mounted on each vehicle, but most had burned out, and those that remained were hardly more than stubs. What little light they cast mingled with the orange glow of the greater moon, and with light spilling over from the central square, but even so, the arcade was shadowy and dim, the caravan's bright colors reduced to scarcely more than flame yellow and shadow gray.

Most of the wagons were closed, their shutters latched and doors barred, awnings and banners furled and stowed. Steps and benches were folded away, brakes set, wheels blocked. The draft animals and outriders' mounts had all been unhitched and taken elsewhere for stabling, the yokes and traces and other gear all neatly tucked out of sight. Each one of the wagons had a pike held to one corner by iron loops, and atop each pike was a bandit's head.

At first glance, Kelder saw nothing moving but the flickering shadows. Then something yawned loudly.

Kelder felt Asha tugging at the back of his tunic, but he ignored it as he looked for the source of the sound.

He found it; a big, burly man in a dark tunic and kilt was leaning against a pillar, whittling. A sword hung from his belt and a long spear stood within easy reach, propped against a stone upright. There could be no doubt whatsoever that he was standing guard.

The knife he was carving with glinted in the torchlight for a moment and a curl of wood-shaving spiraled to the pavement. He was awake, but not exactly intent on his job.

The mere fact of his presence, and wakefulness, was enough to make the whole job more worrisome, though.

"Damn," Kelder muttered to himself.

"Kelder!" Asha whispered urgently.

He turned, finger to lips, and said, "What is it?"

"Where's Abden?"

Kelder looked at her blankly for a moment.

"I mean, where's Abden's *head*?"

Annoyed, Kelder turned to point. "The head's right . . ."

He stopped.

Slowly he turned back to Asha.

"I don't know," he said. "What does . . . what did your brother look like? That one," Kelder said, pointing to the nearest pike. "Is that him?"

"No," Asha said. "That's Kelder—I mean, the other Kelder, Kelder the Lesser, they called him."

"Well, I knew it wasn't me," Kelder snarled sarcastically. "What about the others? Which one is he?"

Asha took a minute to peer up at those heads that were visible from where they stood. "I don't see Abden," she said at last.

The head was *not* right there, Kelder realized.

"Damn!" he said again.

CHAPTER 16

"*Now, how many heads are there?*" Kelder asked himself as he scanned the skies for Irith. "Nobody's about to take a severed head inside his wagon at night, not if he's sleeping there—that would be too creepy, just *asking* to be haunted." He glanced down at Asha, hoping for some useful suggestion, but all he saw was that she was on the verge if tears. He quickly turned his gaze upward again.

"No one would take one inside," he said, still addressing himself, "so they're all out here on the wagons, and it's just a matter of finding the right one, right?"

Asha made a muffled noise of agreement.

Kelder frowned. It was just a matter of finding the right one, but Asha was the only one who could do that, since she was the only one who knew her brother's face.

Irith must have realized this by now—so where was she? Why hadn't she come back for further instructions? All he could see was a small bird, silhouetted against the lesser moon as it climbed the eastern sky.

He shrugged and looked down at Asha. "We'll have to sneak up as close as we can and see if we can find the right ... uh ... the right pike. *Then* we'll tell Irith which one it is ..."

There was a sudden flapping of wings, and Irith was descending, a few feet away.

"Kelder," she said angrily, "I don't know which head!"

"We just thought of that," Kelder agreed.

"So what do we do?"

"Can you carry Asha when you fly? Then she could point it out."

Irith looked the girl over, considering, then shook her head. "No," she said. "Not a chance."

Kelder had expected that. "All right, then," he said, "We sneak Asha up as close as we can on foot, and let her look until she finds the right one,"

"Maybe Irith could get all of them?" Asha suggested. "Then we could go back and burn *all* the bodies . . ."

She realized that both Kelder and Irith were glaring at her, and her voice faded away.

"No," Irith said. "Just one."

"All right," Asha said. "I'll go look. But I can't go alone."

"Of course not," Kelder agreed.

Irith glanced over at the wagons, the patchwork of light and shadow, the big man scraping away bits of wood with his knife.

"You two go ahead," she said. "I'll wait here."

Kelder started to agree, then paused. Irith was the one who had to know just where the head was, after all. But it wasn't worth the argument. "All right," he said. "Come on, Asha."

Together the two crept closer.

There were a dozen wagons; the guard stood beside the seventh in line, by Kelder's quick count, and they had approached near the ninth. "This way," he whispered, beckoning Asha toward the front of the column.

After all, there were more wagons in that direction, even if it was farther to go.

The head on the eighth wagon was facing the opposite direction, but Asha shook her own head no; the hair was wrong.

The next faced them, but again, Asha indicated that it was not the one they wanted. They were both tiptoeing now; if the guard happened to look up from his whittling, and if he wasn't blinded by the tangle of shadows and torchlight, he would be looking right at them.

The head on the sixth wagon was facing away, and Asha was not completely sure, but didn't think it looked like Abden.

Kelder was beginning to think they should have turned the other way and checked the tail end first when Asha made a strangled noise.

"That's it," she said, pointing. "That's Abden."

The fifth wagon was green trimmed with gold, and the Ethsharitic runes on the side said something about someone named Doran of someplace—Ship-something, safe place for ships, something like that; Kelder did not bother to puzzle the whole thing out. It was obviously the name of some Ethsharitic merchant. The pike at the front corner displayed the head of a young man, and Kelder thought there might be some resemblance to Asha, but he wasn't sure he wasn't just imagining it.

"All right," he whispered. "Let's go back and tell Irith."

Asha nodded, turned, and began to scamper back.

Her bare feet slapped on the paving stones. Kelder started after her and had taken perhaps three long steps when something registered.

He turned, and saw that the guard had lowered his knife and carving and was peering out into the gloom, following the sound of Asha's footsteps.

Kelder decided that he didn't want to be seen just yet. He fell back into a nearby shadow, under the overhang of a two-story shopfront.

"Irith?" Asha called. "Where are you?"

Kelder hissed to himself with exasperation.

"Irith?" Asha called again, more loudly.

She was standing, Kelder thought, at about the spot where they had separated, plainly visible in the light of the two moons. The guard was watching her intently now.

What's more, another guard, whom they had not previously seen, had heard the sound and was peering between the wagons from the other side of the caravan. This one was tall and thin, with a black beard that needed trimming—it straggled messily down onto his chest.

There was no sign of Irith.

A cat meowed nearby, and Kelder turned for an instant,

looking for the animal, but didn't see it. He turned quickly back to Asha.

"Kelder!" a breathy voice said behind him, quietly.

He started and turned to find Irith standing there, finger to her lips.

"How did you . . ." he began.

"Which one?" Irith whispered hoarsely.

"Which what?" For a moment he thought she was asking something about the two guards, and he tried to figure out what she wanted to know.

"Which *wagon,* stupid?"

"Oh," Kelder said, collecting his wits. "The green one, right there." He pointed.

Irith nodded and spread wings that had not been there an instant before. "You go distract them," she said.

Then she launched herself fluttering upward.

Kelder blinked and looked up, watching her ascent.

"Irith?" Asha wailed. "Kelder?"

Kelder frowned; the best distraction was probably the simplest, he decided. He stepped out of the shadows. "Over here," he called. He trotted toward the little girl, who was standing alone in the street, on the verge of panic.

The first guard had stepped away from the pillar and tucked his carving under his belt. Now he slid his knife into its sheath and picked up the spear. The other guard was between two of the wagons now, facing away, scanning the little plaza on that side of the arcade.

Kelder tried hard not to be seen looking at either of them as he came up to Asha and said, a little more loudly than necessary, "Here I am, Indra."

Indra was the first girl's name he could think of, other than Asha or Irith.

"Kelder!" She spotted him and dashed toward him, arms out.

At least that was one advantage of having the most common name in the World, he thought; nobody was ever going to track him down by using it.

He met Asha halfway and picked her up in a big embrace,

then spun her around—which gave him a chance to look at the nearer guard without seeming to.

The man was standing, watching the two of them. He was not looking at the green and gold wagon. Kelder forced himself not to look at it, either. He lowered Asha to the pavement and then glanced casually at the guard.

That individual was now looking either way along the row of wagons. He might, Kelder thought, have guessed that this little scene was being played out to distract him.

At least, that was why Kelder was doing it; Asha had apparently lost track of what she was supposed to be doing and was acting on impulse. In her excitement over finding Abden's head she had completely forgotten everything else about the plan. That was fine, really; she was doing an excellent job of being a distraction and probably acting far more naturally than she would have if she had remembered.

They did not, however, want the guard to realize he was being deliberately decoyed.

The other guard, Kelder noticed with a twinge of concern, was not in sight at the moment.

Spear in one hand, his other hand on the hilt of his sword, the visible guard was peering into the darkness.

"Looking for something?" Kelder called.

Startled, the guard turned to look at him silently for a second and then shook his head. He said nothing.

"I've lost my wife," Kelder said, pressing on. "The girl's sister. She's tall, with black hair, wearing a green tunic and a brown skirt—have you seen her?" He tried very hard to ignore Asha's expression of surprise as she heard him tell such lies.

The guard shook his head again.

"You're sure?" Kelder insisted.

"Haven't seen anybody," the man said in a surprisingly high-pitched voice. "Except you two."

"Well, if you do . . ." Kelder began.

"Excuse me," the guard said, interrupting, "I've got rounds to make." He began walking along the line of wagons, stooping every so often to peer under them, occasionally poking his spear into the shadows. He called something Kelder didn't catch and was answered by a deeper voice from the other side.

Kelder was very relieved indeed to see that the near-side guard had started out toward the back of the line, rather than the front. He hoped the other one had, as well.

"Well, if you see her," Kelder shouted after them, "tell her we'll meet her at the inn." Then he turned away, taking Asha by the hand and pulling her along.

"Kelder," Asha said, starting to protest.

He jerked viciously at her wrist, and she followed without further objection.

He led her quickly around a building, into an alley, and out of the guards' sight. Then he stopped, held a finger to his lips, and peered cautiously back around the corner.

"What is it?" Asha asked.

Kelder waved a hand at her, and she fell silent.

The heavier guard had reached the last wagon; the one with the sloppy beard met him there, and the two exchanged a few words—Kelder could just barely hear their voices, and could not make out any at all of what was said.

Above the arcade, orange moonlight shone briefly on a fluttering white wing, and a shadowy shape rose toward the heavens, something vaguely round cradled in one arm.

Kelder smiled.

"All right," he told Asha, "now we go around the block and run for the gate, as fast as we can. Irith has the head."

"You're sure?" Asha looked up at him doubtfully.

"Just go," Kelder said, giving her a shove.

He was destined to be Asha's champion, but that didn't mean he had to like her, and just now, tired and frightened as he was, he did not think much of her at all.

CHAPTER 17

To Kelder the double moonlight on the desert sand looked somehow unnatural. It was brighter than moonlight had any right to be, even when both moons were full and at zenith—and in fact, that wasn't the case. The moons were both past zenith, the lesser descending quickly toward the western horizon, the greater still high overhead, and neither was full—the lesser was close, but the greater was only about three-quarters. The familiar rosy glow of the moons combined with the gold of the sands to make an odd, burnt-orange color that Kelder didn't like at all. "Are you sure we shouldn't wait for sunrise?" he asked.

"Come *on*," Irith said. "Let's get *out* of here!"

Asha said nothing, but she obviously agreed with Irith; she was tugging at Kelder's sleeve. Reluctantly he came.

"I can see why you're in a hurry, Asha," he said. "You want to set your brother's soul free. But I don't know why *you're* rushing so much, Irith."

She glanced back over her shoulder; the city wall gleamed ruddily in the moonlight, and the open gates were a tangle of torchlight and shadow. She thought she saw something moving, and wasn't sure if it was just a flickering shadow or really someone there.

"Let's just say I don't much care for Shan on the Desert anymore," the Flyer replied.

"Is it because that inn was gone?" Asha asked.

"No," Irith answered.

"It's that old drunk, isn't it?" Kelder said, "or at least that's part of it. But I don't see why he has you so upset."

"It's not him, either," Irith said with another glance behind.

Kelder looked at her, then turned his gaze to his feet and trudged onward through the cool orange sands.

She was lying, he was sure. It *was* the drunk.

They had gone no more than a league when the lesser moon set; the greater moon was working its way toward the horizon, as well. Color faded from their surroundings, and Kelder began to worry.

"Are we still on the highway?" he asked.

For several seconds, no one answered. Then Irith said, "I don't know. I can't see that well."

They stumbled on for a moment longer, and then Kelder remarked, "Well, if we're not, at least the caravaners won't find us."

"Those demons could," Irith replied.

Asha started crying quietly.

"You would have to say that," Kelder muttered, not really meaning Irith to hear.

"Oh, shut up," Irith said.

"We're going to wander around in circles until we die!" Asha wailed.

"No, we aren't," Irith snapped.

Kelder took it upon himself to expand on this. "We're all right, Asha," he said, "really. We know we're going south because the greater moon is on our right, see? And look, off to the left." He pointed. "There's light on the horizon, that's the sun coming because it's almost dawn, so that's east. So even if we lose the highway, we'll reach that big cliff eventually, and then we can find the road again."

"Oh," Asha said, struggling to stifle her tears. A moment later, when they were under control, she whined, "I'm tired."

"We all are," Kelder said.

"Then why don't we rest?"

Kelder halted in his tracks with the intention of making some biting retort, and then stopped. "You're right," he said, "why don't we? They probably aren't going to come after us. Even if they realize we've left the city, why should they go to all that trouble? They have plenty of heads. So what's the hurry?" He sat down on the cool sand. "I'm tired, too, and I'm going to sit here and rest until the sun comes up and we can see what we're doing."

Asha smiled and plopped down beside him.

Irith had proceeded a dozen paces farther, but now she stopped, as well, and turned back to look at the others. "Here?" she said. "Out in the middle of the desert?"

"Why not?" Kelder asked. "What's going to bother us?"

Irith looked back at Shan, still visible as a dark, uneven line on the horizon and a faint glow in the sky.

"Besides," Kelder said, "if anything comes after us, we'll see it in plenty of time. You can grow wings and fly away."

"It'll still get *us*," Asha said, momentarily concerned.

"It would," Kelder agreed, "if anything was going to come after us, but nothing is. And besides, if Irith got away, she'd find some way to save us, I'm sure."

Irith looked at Kelder doubtfully, suspecting—with reason—that he was being sarcastic.

"All right," she said. "We can rest here for a little while, I guess." She folded her legs and sank to the ground.

None of them really intended to sleep; the idea was merely to rest for a few minutes.

On the other hand, none of them had had much more than four hours' sleep in the past twenty-four, and they had walked a very great distance in that time, as well as going through the various excitements in Shan. Kelder had punched an old man, Irith had pried a severed head off the point of a spear, and Asha had participated in the rescue, as she saw it, of her brother's soul.

Within five minutes, long before the sun rose or the greater moon set, they were all sound asleep.

Even as he lay sleeping, something nagged at Kelder. He knew he shouldn't be asleep, and that knowledge troubled his dreams.

Still, exhaustion had a firm grip on him, and he slept on.

The sun rose, and its warmth on his face, its light on his eyelids discomfited him; he struggled to wake up.

Something threw a shadow over him briefly, and the sands

shifted slightly—the sound of footsteps reached Kelder, even asleep. He stirred slightly and tried to pry his eyes open, tried to make his arms and legs move.

A low voice spoke, something brushed—and Irith shrieked. Kelder was awake at last, scrambling to his feet.

Irith screamed, long and piercing; she was sitting up, hands out to fend off, and as Kelder's eyes focused her wings appeared and spread. She kicked off, flapping, and skittered across the sand for a moment, heels dragging, before she managed to get herself airborne.

As she did, a dark, ragged shape that Kelder could not immediately identify threw itself at her, trying to grab her, hold her down, bring her back—but unsuccessfully. She slipped away and soared upward. Kelder and Asha watched her go.

She didn't hesitate, didn't slow, didn't look back; she flapped strongly and steadily as she drove southward toward the horizon.

The ragged creature wailed and wept, calling after her; most of the words, if they were words, were unintelligible, but the name Irith was repeated frequently. It staggered along for a few paces, then collapsed, sobbing, into a miserable, huddled heap. Then it lifted its head. With a shock, Kelder realized that the creature was the old drunk who had accosted Irith back in Shan.

"Irith," the old man called, "come back! I won't hurt you, I swear it, I just want to talk! *Please!*"

The distant speck that was Irith the Flyer continued to dwindle.

"*Now* what do we do?" Asha asked.

Kelder looked about. His pack was still lying where he had left it; the bundle containing Abden's head was there, as well. He looked up. It didn't look as if Irith were coming back right away.

He considered. He knew that he would find her again—Zindré's prediction was that he would marry her and bring her home to Shulara with him, so he knew he would find her again.

He didn't know when, where, or how, though.

That would have to take care of itself; there were more immediate concerns. "We can go on and build the pyre ourselves," Kelder said. "But first, I want to know just what in the World is going *on* here!" He stepped forward and grabbed the old man by the shoulder.

The filthy cloth of his tunic felt greasy and unpleasant under Kelder's hand, but Kelder ignored that. The old man started slightly at the youth's touch, but didn't resist; he didn't even turn to look, but instead kept staring after Irith.

"Old man," Kelder said, "who *are* you?"

The drunk simply stared at the departing Flyer.

"*Talk* to me, damn it!" Kelder shouted. "Who are you? Why is she scared of you?"

That penetrated.

"Scared of me?" The old man turned and looked up at Kelder, astonishment plain on his face. "Why would she be scared of me?"

"That's what *I* want to know!" Kelder snapped. "Who are you?"

The man blinked, as if considering a new and surprising idea.

"What's your name?" Asha asked, stepping up beside Kelder.

"Ezdral," he replied. "My name is Ezdral."

"Just Ezdral?" Kelder asked.

The old man shrugged. "Mostly," he said. "Back in Shan they call me Ezdral the Sot, mostly." He blinked. "That'll do. I'm not drunk right now, haven't touched a drop since I saw Irith in the arcade last night, but I've been pretty sodden for a long time, there's no sense in denying it."

"All right, Ezdral," Kelder said, withdrawing his hand and resisting the temptation to wipe it on his own tunic. "How do you know Irith?"

The old man looked down, coughed, spat something out, and wiped his mouth on a grubby sleeve. He turned, squatted, then sat down, crossing his legs slowly and carefully.

Kelder waited.

Ezdral looked up at him and then gestured at the ground.

Asha took the hint and dropped down, sitting facing Ezdral. Kelder took a moment longer, but joined them.

"When I was eighteen," Ezdral began, "I met . . ."

"When was that?" Asha interrupted.

Ezdral frowned. "What year is it now?"

"It's 5222," Kelder told him.

"Then I'm . . . let me see . . . sixty-two, is it? Born on the first of Thaw, 5159 . . ."

"Sixty-three . . . no, sixty-two," Kelder agreed.

"So it would have been forty-four years ago." Ezdral looked at them for agreement.

Asha nodded. Kelder said, "Go on."

Ezdral took a deep breath and let it out slowly.

"When I was eighteen," he said again, "I met a girl, a beautiful girl with golden hair, like I'd never seen before. I was working in a stable in Mezgalon, and she was passing through, and I thought she was the most beautiful thing I'd ever seen. We got to talking, and she said her name was Irith the Flyer, and when I asked how she got a name like that she showed me how she could grow wings and fly."

Kelder and Asha looked at one another.

"Forty-four years ago?" Kelder asked.

Ezdral nodded.

"It can't be the same one," Kelder said. "She's only fifteen. She said so."

Ezdral shook his head wearily and peered at Kelder from beneath heavy lids. "She was fifteen then, too," he said.

Kelder's lips tightened. "Go on with your story," he said.

"We talked, and I fell in love with her," Ezdral said. "I mean, wildly and madly in love. She was *so* beautiful, so sweet. And we left Mezgalon together, and we traveled the Small Kingdoms from Shan to Lamum, Fileia to Lurethon." He smiled. "Oh, we had some good times, we did. Filched a jeweler's best stones once in Hlimora just so Irith could play with them. Danced naked in the Forest of Amramion. Got roaring drunk with the crown prince of Tuyoa, and Irith challenged his court wizard to a duel of magic and almost got herself killed. She could do other magic, not just shapeshifting, you know—had maybe half a dozen spells. Wasn't any match for a real wizard, though." He sighed.

The recitation paused for a moment, but Kelder and Asha waited without protest this time.

"We were together a little over a year, I think," Ezdral said, resuming his tale. "I was nineteen, maybe twenty, by then. I started to think about maybe settling down somewhere, maybe having children someday. And one day I woke up and Irith wasn't there. We'd been at her favorite inn in Shan on the Desert, a place called the Crystal Skull, and I still was, but she wasn't."

Kelder glanced down at Asha; she was sitting rapt, taking this all in. "Why did she leave?" the child asked.

Ezdral turned up an empty palm. "Who knows?" he said. "Maybe she just got bored with me."

"So what did you do?"

"Well, I waited, at first—I waited a month, to see if she would come back. When she didn't, I went out looking for her, going up and down the Great Highway and around to all the places we'd gone together, but I didn't find her. I'd hear about her now and then—how she had flown over Castle Angarossa shouting insults, or been seen playing with the Queen of Ophera's cats—but I never caught up to her, never saw her myself. And after a time I sort of drifted back to Shan, doing odd jobs or begging, and I stayed there and waited for her."

"Why didn't you just forget about her?" Kelder asked. "Find yourself another girl?"

"Because I *couldn't*, damn it!" Ezdral shouted, in the first display of temper Kelder had seen from him. "I *couldn't*! Don't you think I *tried*? But I couldn't go to sleep at night without thinking about her, couldn't look at another woman without thinking that Irith was prettier . . . I was in *love* with her, so damnably in love—and I still *am*, damn it all to the Nether Void!" He pounded a fist on the sand and then went on more calmly, "I started drinking to try to forget her, I just drank all the time, whenever I could get money, and it was even starting to work, a little, after twenty years or so—and then last night I looked up and there she was, I saw her walking past me, as big as life, looking just as she always had. And at first I thought I was dreaming, or that the wine was giving me visions, though I hadn't drunk that much, and then I thought I was dead and had died and this was her ghost, and I could see her because I was a ghost, and then I finally realized it was real, she'd come back, and I called to her."

He fell silent for a moment, and Kelder remembered the previous night's events, not with satisfaction but with a growing dismay, like a weight in his belly.

"I called to her," Ezdral repeated, "and she said she didn't know me, she ran away screaming, and then you hit me, and I fell down."

"I'm sorry," Kelder whispered.

"You didn't know," Ezdral said, waving it aside. "*I* knew, though. I knew she had been deliberately avoiding me all these years, that that was why she hadn't come back to Shan, and I knew she'd leave again now that she knew I was there, but I had to talk to her, I had to tell her that I loved her, so I went to the gate and waited, and I hoped she wouldn't just fly over the wall. And she didn't, but you were with her, and I didn't want a fight, so I followed, trying to think of what I could say, what I could do that would make her talk to me, make her stay with me." He let his breath out in a long, shuddering sigh.

Asha didn't know what to say. Kelder couldn't say anything at all, and Ezdral had finished. For a time they all sat silently on the sand, thinking their own thoughts.

CHAPTER 18

"*M*aybe it was her mother," Asha suggested. "Or her grandmother."

Ezdral shook his head.

"But Irith is only fifteen," Kelder pointed out. The thought that his intended bride was not just a Tintallionese runaway who had visited Shan as a child was deeply disturbing; the idea of his own Irith roaming the Small Kingdoms with another man, before Kelder had even been born, was intolerable, and he was groping for a way to deny it.

"Oh, yes," Ezdral agreed, "she's always been fifteen."

Kelder sat back and considered that, and considered Ezdral, as well.

He looked every day of his claimed sixty-two years, and then some—his hair and beard were long, white, thinning, and uncombed; his face was rough and lined, his eyes sunken and bloodshot. His lips were a pale, unhealthy color, his skin yellowish. He wore a tunic that hung loose on his sunken chest; the garment had once been brown but was now blotched, stained, and faded, so that it was black here, gray there, and a washed-out tan elsewhere. His breeches were tanned leather, with large shiny patches on the knees—and probably, Kelder guessed, on the backside as well. They ended in tatters just below the knee, and from there down, his legs and feet were bare.

His hands were thin and bony and stayed curled and clawlike at all times, apparently involuntarily; the nails were cracked and blackened, the hairs on the back white and wire-like. When he lifted a hand to gesture, it shook. His wrists were bone and tendon and loose skin, with no fat at all, no muscle tone. He wore no ornaments of any kind, and his garments had no trim or embroidery and were of the plainest possible cut—not only were they decrepit, they hadn't been much to start with. His belt was a twisted strip of rawhide, with a single pouch hung on it, a drawstring bag about the size of Asha's head.

It was very hard to imagine him as a strong young man, adventuring with Irith.

On the other hand, why would he have made up such a tale? And he spoke with an unquestionable sincerity.

But it *couldn't* be the same Irith as the one Kelder meant to wed. "Her grandmother, it must have been," he said.

Ezdral shook his head. "I don't think so. She's *magic*, remember?"

"She's only fifteen," Kelder repeated.

Even as he said it, though, he was remembering all the puzzles and peculiarities about Irith—how she claimed to have done so much since leaving her apprenticeship, even though that couldn't be more than a year or two; how she remembered an inn in Shan that had obviously been abandoned for years; all the other references to times and places and doings that she could scarcely have fit into fifteen years. The Tintallionese theory didn't explain it all; in fact, it hardly explained *any* of it, really.

If she was actually sixty or seventy years old, her youth and beauty magically preserved, *that* would explain it.

But it wouldn't explain *her*, Kelder thought. It wouldn't explain the person that Irith was.

Kelder liked to think of himself as grown up, not a kid anymore; compared to a few years ago, he *was* grown up. Realistically, though, he knew he was hardly a mature adult. It wasn't a matter of size or strength, of gray hair or wrinkles—adults acted differently, presumably because they had learned better, had been changed by experience.

But Irith didn't.

Irith acted like a girl of fifteen. And it wasn't just acting, like players in the annual pageant taking the roles of ancient heroes—she *was* a girl of fifteen.

But how could she be?

It didn't make sense. There was all this evidence that she was far older than she looked—her own stories about what she'd done, and everything Ezdral said, and the fact that she was known to people all along the Great Highway—and then there was an equal amount of evidence, in her appearance and behavior, that she was just what she claimed to be, a girl of fifteen.

Kelder couldn't make the two possibilities resolve themselves.

Irith would be able to settle the matter, of course—if she ever came back, or when he found her again. He looked up at the southern sky but could see no trace of her.

He knew he would marry her anyway, but this—this changed things, somehow.

"I guess I believe you," Kelder said. "Maybe it *is* the same girl. But it doesn't really matter, since she's gone now." He knew *he* would find her again, but there was no reason to think Ezdral or Asha would.

Ezdral looked up and said hopefully, "She might come back, though—she likes you, I saw that she likes you."

Kelder shook his head. "I don't think so," he said. "At least, not while *you're* here. She's scared of you."

"But I'm nothing to be afraid of!" Ezdral wailed.

Kelder shrugged.

"You do look scary," Asha said. "Your beard goes all over, and your hands look nasty, and you're all dirty, and you smell of wine, or *oushka*, or something."

Ezdral looked down at himself.

"I suppose you're right," he admitted. He looked up again, first at Kelder, then at Asha. "Are you two going to wait here for her to come back? Maybe I could get cleaned up and then come back here and meet you? . . ."

"No, no," Kelder said quickly. "We can't stay. We've got a very important errand to run, back in Angarossa—we need to hold a funeral for Asha's brother."

"Oh," Ezdral said.

"We should get going," Asha suggested, with a meaningful glance at Kelder.

Kelder knew what she meant—that they should get away from this crazy old man as quickly as possible. He felt something of the same urge himself.

For one thing, he wanted Irith back, and as he had just told Ezdral, she wouldn't be coming back while the old man was there.

"You're right," he said, getting to his feet and picking up his pack. "Come on." He turned to Ezdral and said, "Have a safe journey back to Shan, and I hope you find your Irith someday."

As long, he thought, as Ezdral's Irith was not Kelder's Irith.

Ezdral leaned forward on his hands, struggling to rise. "I'm not going back to Shan," he said. "She's not going to go to Shan again for years, after this. I'll have to go looking for her elsewhere."

"Oh," Kelder said, a bit disconcerted. "Well, good luck, then." He took Asha by the hand and started walking, southward across the trackless sands, toward the cliffs that he knew lay just below the horizon.

A moment later he realized that Ezdral was following them. He started to turn and protest, and then stopped.

What could he say? After all, the man had a right to walk on the same sand as everybody else. As long as he stayed out of reach, what harm could he do? And what could Kelder do to stop him?

"You know," Ezdral called out, "I'd love to talk to you two about Irith. What have you done together with her? Where have you been? Do you have any idea where she might be?"

At first Kelder ignored this, but as they walked on Ezdral kept up an intermittent barrage of questions, shouted across the intervening five-yard distance.

"Come on," Kelder told Asha, "hurry up; if we move fast enough he won't be able to keep up, he's a sick old man."

Asha nodded and hurried, but it did no good. Kelder by

himself could easily have outdistanced Ezdral, but Asha was only nine, and small for her age—she didn't have the long legs or the stamina to keep up with Kelder's pace when he hurried.

And Ezdral, decrepit as he was, *could* keep up with Asha's best pace.

If Kelder left Asha behind, he could easily get away from Ezdral—but what sort of champion of the lost and forlorn would he be then? Reluctantly he gave in and slowed down again, and the three of them proceeded, two in front, and the old man a few paces behind.

By the time they reached the escarpment that marked the end of the Great Eastern Desert and the beginning of the Small Kingdoms, Kelder had yielded to the inevitable—the three were walking side by side, chatting companionably.

Ezdral was sadly unaware of recent events—he hadn't heard about the Angarossan king's support of banditry, or the use of demonologists as caravan guards, or the rumors about someone named Vond the Warlock building an empire in the south. He didn't even know what a warlock *was*, though he did remember all the disturbances on the Night of Madness, twenty years ago.

"That was when the Crystal Skull got wrecked," he said.

Kelder was not pleased to hear that. It might be that the old drunk was running two different memories together, or simply fantasizing, but it did seem to make sense, and if it was true it would completely destroy any possibility that Irith was really only fifteen.

Unless she had somehow acquired the memories of someone older? She seemed too certain of things to have simply been told about the Crystal Skull, but what if those memories had been magically transferred to her, somehow? Kelder had heard of witches doing that sort of thing, so maybe wizards could, too.

Or what if she had been simply *gone* somewhere for forty-odd years? Suppose that wizard she'd dueled with had turned her to stone, and then she had finally been turned back just recently—wouldn't *that* account for everything?

Kelder thought it would; he rather liked the theory, in fact. It still meant that his Irith had once wandered the Small Kingdoms with someone else, with the young Ezdral who had deteriorated into this drunken wreck in the intervening years, but at least she really would have only lived fifteen years or so, not sixty or more. Somehow, the thought of her being an unchanging fifteen for all that time was far more discomfiting than any knowledge of a previous boyfriend.

He didn't mention the theory to Asha or Ezdral, though. He told himself that he wanted to work out the details a little more first, but the truth was he was afraid they would find enough flaws in the idea to unravel it completely.

Of course, if that *was* what had happened, then Irith might not have deserted Ezdral at all, she might have been kidnapped from his side—and while knowing that might comfort the old man, Kelder decided that he didn't want to discuss that possibility.

What if he was wrong, he asked himself, why get the old man's hopes up?

Even as he thought that, though, he knew he wasn't really as concerned with Ezdral's feelings as his own.

When they reached the escarpment they had missed the road completely; studying the sky and the landscape, Kelder finally decided they had arrived somewhere to the east of their intended destination, so with a shrug he turned right and led the party along the foot of the cliff.

It was midafternoon when they finally found the road again, and by the time they reached the top and were back on the relatively level ground of Dhwerra the sun was almost on the western horizon.

Ezdral looked about at the patchy grass and weeds and remarked, "Been a long time since I was up here and saw things growing out of the ground like that."

Asha gazed around and then up at Ezdral wonderingly. The idea of going for years without seeing greenery was very strange to her, indeed.

Kelder remarked, "Maybe you should go on to Amramion, then, and see the forests."

"Maybe I will," Ezdral agreed, "if my feet hold out. I'm getting tired, though. Isn't it about time we found an inn, or at least something to eat?"

Kelder grimaced. "If you want anything to eat," he said, "I'm afraid you'll have to beg for it. That's what we'll be doing. And I guess we'll just have to sleep by the roadside. We don't have any money."

"You don't?"

"No," Kelder snarled, "we don't. I spent all mine, and Asha never had any, and Irith was paying our way back in Shan, before you frightened her off. I'm just glad we had full canteens when we left!" A thought struck him. "Do *you* have any money?"

"A little," Ezdral admitted, "a few bits. Not enough for an inn, but I can get us all some bread."

"You can?" Asha looked up at him, surprised and grateful.

He nodded. He looked at the road ahead, curving gracefully around the Castle of Dhwerra, and at the scattered buildings along its length. "Which inn is best?"

Asha looked at Kelder, and Kelder looked at Asha.

"I don't know," he said. "Just pick one."

With a shrug, Ezdral picked one.

CHAPTER 19

*T*he bread was rough and a bit stale, but it was filling, and the innkeeper had had leftover cabbage that she had thrown in free; the three had hardly dined well, but at least their bellies were relatively full when they settled onto a hillock at the roadside for the night.

Kelder had two blankets, one for himself and one for Asha; Ezdral claimed he was fine without one.

"I've got this to keep me warm," he said, pulling a squat black bottle out of his belt pouch. "Been saving it."

"What is it?" Asha asked.

"*Oushka*," Ezdral replied, grinning. "The very best *oushka*, Adréan's Pure Barley Liquor, from Sardiron of the Waters. It fell off a caravan wagon last month, and I picked it out of the mud." He displayed the label.

Asha turned away; Kelder nodded politely, but showed no further interest.

"Been saving it," Ezdral repeated to himself as he pried the cork out.

As he huddled under his blanket, Kelder wondered whether he should have asked for a drink. Something warming might be nice, and he had no philosophical objection to *oushka*. He had tasted it on occasion, back home in Shulara, for various special events.

Asha, though, with her drunken, malevolent father, wanted nothing to do with any sort of alcohol, and Ezdral, even after he had cleaned himself up a little for dinner, was scarcely an advertisement in favor of strong drink.

143

"Are you sure you don't want some, Kelder?" Ezdral said, his voice already starting to slur. "It's good stuff, and one hates to drink alone."

Kelder curled himself up more tightly, pretending to be asleep, and decided that he would never drink *oushka* again.

"It's your loss, if you don't," Ezdral said, shrugging. He gulped noisily, pouring the liquor down his throat, and Kelder shuddered.

A moment later the bottle clinked against a stone as Ezdral dropped it; a heavy thud followed as the old man fell back against the ground. Kelder lay still, huddled and waiting, finding now that he was not really all that sleepy yet.

A snore sounded, and Kelder uncurled enough to peer over his shoulder.

Darkness was descending, the sun down and the lesser moon still low in the east, the greater moon not due up for an hour or more; the little party had not bothered to build a fire. All Kelder could see of Ezdral was a shadowy lump.

He could hear him plainly enough, though; the old drunkard was snoring steadily and loudly.

"He's asleep," Asha said in a conversational tone.

"Hush!" Kelder called in a hoarse whisper. "You'll wake him!"

"No, I won't," Asha said, speaking normally. "He's too drunk. Nothing's going to wake him up for hours. He got that whole bottle of *oushka* down in about five minutes; even my father couldn't do that!"

Kelder watched Ezdral uneasily. "Are you sure?" he asked.

"I'm positive," Asha replied. She sat up, a vague shape in the gloom. Kelder watched as she crept over and prodded Ezdral with a finger; the drunkard snored on without stirring. "See?"

Kelder nodded. "I see," he said.

"So are we going to stay here with him, or are we going to get away and lose him?"

Kelder considered. "I'm not sure," he said. "He's not so bad, really."

"He stinks, and he's dirty."

"That's true," Kelder admitted. "But if he was cleaned up . . . He knows a lot, he's done a lot of traveling. He might be useful. Having an adult along could be helpful." Having someone along who had money could be helpful, for one thing, he thought, but he didn't say that aloud. Nor did he mention that he wondered what else the old drunk might know about Irith.

"*You're* an adult."

Kelder shook his head. "Not really," he said. "I'm only sixteen; if I was an apprentice—well, in most trades I'd still be an apprentice. It'll be another two years before I really count as an adult."

"Oh," Asha said, "I didn't know."

"There's no reason you should have," Kelder said.

The two of them sat for a moment, on opposite sides of the sleeping Ezdral, not saying anything.

"Is he asleep?" a voice called from somewhere overhead.

Kelder looked up, startled, and found Irith hovering above them, wings gleaming rose in the light of the lesser moon.

"Yes!" Asha shouted up to her. "Come on down!"

The winged girl descended slowly and cautiously and settled to the ground a few yards away. Asha jumped and ran to her and gave her a long, enthusiastic hug.

Kelder was a little more controlled about it, but he, too, went over and embraced her.

When they had exchanged greetings, Irith said, "Come on then, let's get away from him while we can!" She gestured for the others to follow and started down the slope toward the highway.

Kelder noticed that her wings did not vanish, as they usually did when she walked anywhere; she was keeping them ready, in case Ezdral woke and she had to flee again.

Of course, that would mean leaving Asha and himself behind again . . .

"Wait a minute," he said.

"What?" Irith asked, startled. She turned back to face him.

"I'm not sure this is right," he said. He glanced down at Ezdral. Drunk and snoring, the old man looked lost and forlorn, and Kelder was the prophesied champion of the lost and forlorn, wasn't he?

And it was time to settle a few things. If he was going to marry Irith—well, marriage was a partnership, and he intended to be an equal partner, at the very least, not giving in to Irith on everything. Her magic gave her an advantage; he had to make up for that by stubbornness.

"What do you mean?" Irith asked. "Of course it is! Why would we want to be anywhere near a dirty old drunk? Come on, let's get away while we can! He'll be fine where he is, he doesn't need us."

"How do you know that?" Kelder countered.

"Well, he got along just fine all those years in Shan by himself, didn't he?" the Flyer demanded, hands on her hips.

"It's not the same, and you know it," Kelder told her. "Besides, there are things we need to settle."

"Such as what?" Irith demanded. "Has he been telling you lies?"

"I don't know," Kelder said. "Maybe they were lies, maybe they weren't. Did you hear any of what he told us?"

"Only a little."

Asha was standing at Irith's side; now she looked up, startled. "You did hear a little?"

"Maybe," Irith admitted. "I'm not sure."

Asha asked, "How could you have heard?"

"She has ways of not being seen if she doesn't want to be, Asha," Kelder said. "I don't know just what they are—but I'd like to."

Irith glared at him; even in the darkness he could see that.

"You want to talk about all this, Kelder?" she asked.

"Yes, I think I do," Kelder replied.

"Do we have to do it out *here*, in the cold and the dark, with that old drunk snoring like a pig?"

"No," Kelder said, "but I'm not going any farther than the nearest inn without him, until you've explained a few things."

Irith stamped her foot in annoyance. She looked down at Asha, then back at Kelder.

"Well, all *right*, then," she said. "We probably couldn't get very far tonight anyway, in the dark. We'll talk at the inn over there, all right?"

"All right," Kelder agreed.

CHAPTER 20

By the time they reached the inn Irith's wings were
gone and some of her annoyance, as well. She didn't so much
as grimace when she realized that she would be paying for
everything.

"At least we'll be comfortable in here," she said.

The inn was arranged with tables along the walls and high
backs to the benches that accompanied them, forming booths
and providing an unusual degree of privacy. The three of
them took one of these booths and ordered two ales and a
lemonade from a young man with an apron and a tray.

As soon as the young man had departed, Asha asked Irith,
"How could you watch us without us seeing you?"

Irith sighed. "Do I really have to tell you?"

"I think so," Kelder said. "At least, if you want us to travel
with you."

"All right, then," she said. "Mostly I was either a cat or a
bird; sometimes I was invisible, but I have trouble with that."

"What's 'invisible'?" Asha asked.

"It means I'm still there, but nobody can see me. Except
it's not comfortable and I can't see very well when I do it,
and it only lasts a few minutes, so mostly I didn't get very
close or anything, I just stayed a bird and flew overhead, or
a cat and watched you from a distance. Except cats and birds
... well, cats can't hear low noises very well, so I couldn't
hear what anyone was saying when I was a cat. Birds can
hear low noises, but they don't hear very *well* sometimes. So
when you were coming up the cliff I sneaked up close as a cat
and then turned invisible and listened, and you were talking to

148

that old man and he was talking about going to Shan with me years ago, but he *didn't*, I never went there with him!"

"You're sure of that?" Kelder asked.

"Of *course* I'm sure! I never traveled with that scruffy old drunk!"

"Well, he wasn't a scruffy old drunk, back then," Kelder pointed out.

"When?" Irith demanded.

"Forty years ago—forty-three, I think it was, actually." Kelder watched her reaction closely. Would she be surprised, declare the whole idea of her doing *anything* forty years ago to be ridiculous?

"Forty years ago?" Irith stopped and stared.

That was ambiguous, Kelder thought; she hadn't dismissed it as ridiculous, but she hadn't accepted it, either. "Were you around forty-three years ago?" he asked.

"Well, of course I was, but I wasn't associating with dirty old men!"

There it was. She had been around back then; it wasn't her mother or grandmother. Asha stared. Kelder swallowed and said, "He was nineteen, maybe twenty."

"Oh," Irith said, taken aback. "Oh, I guess he would have been, wouldn't he?"

Kelder nodded.

"I hadn't thought of that," she said.

"Did you know him?"

She frowned. "I don't know," she said. "What's his name?"

"Ezdral."

Irith stared. Her eyes grew wider than Kelder would have thought possible.

"*Ezdral?*" she said. "*That's* Ezdral of Mezgalon? It *really* is?"

"That's what he says," Kelder told her.

"I was sort of afraid it might be somebody I knew once, you know," Irith said, the words spilling out in a rush. "And I really hated to think about anyone I know getting old and icky like that and drinking so much and lying around, so I didn't like it when he said he knew me and I wanted to get away from him—but I *never* thought it might be Ezdral!" She blinked. "That's *awful!*"

"He says you traveled with him when he was young, then one day he woke up and you weren't there."

"Well, that's sort of true," Irith admitted. "I mean, I was there, at first, but he didn't see me. And I'll bet he didn't mention that we'd had a fight the night before, did he? Or that he'd been being a real pest, talking about all this stupid stuff about settling down and raising kids."

"What's stupid about it?" Asha asked, before Kelder could react.

"I'm too *young*, that's what!" Irith said quickly.

Asha and Kelder looked at each other. Kelder's visions of a life of domestic bliss with Irith suddenly seemed much less attainable.

"Oh, it was all a long time ago, anyway," Irith said.

"Irith," Kelder said, "it *was* a long time ago, more than forty years ago, but you keep saying you're only fifteen."

"I *am* only fifteen!" she retorted angrily.

"*How* are you only fifteen?" Kelder asked. "Where were you between then and now? Were you under a spell or something?"

"A spell?" Irith stared at him.

"Turned to stone, maybe?"

"Silly," she said, almost laughing, "of course not! I've been traveling, enjoying the World."

"For forty years?"

"Longer, really."

"How long?"

"Oh, well . . ."

"*How* long?" Kelder demanded.

"*I* don't know," she said defensively. "I haven't kept track."

Kelder found himself momentarily baffled by this response. How could anyone *not know* something like that?

Irith stared at him in mild irritation. "Why are you asking so many questions? What difference does it make?"

"When were you born?" Kelder asked. "What year?"

"Oh, well, if you put it like that," Irith said, "I was born in 4978."

"That's more than two hundred years ago!" Kelder said, shocked.

"Yes, I guess it is," Irith admitted.

"So you're more than two hundred years old?" Asha asked, fascinated.

"No," Irith insisted, "I'm fifteen! I've been fifteen for two hundred years, and I'll *always* be fifteen!"

"Always?" Kelder asked.

Irith nodded. "It's part of the spell," she said.

Asha and Kelder exchanged glances. "So you *are* under a spell?" Asha asked.

"No, not like that," Irith said.

Kelder asked, "Then like what? What spell are you talking about?"

"Well, the one that made me what I am, of course," Irith said. "The one that made me a shapeshifter and everything."

Just then the young man in the apron returned with their drinks; they accepted them and waited until the young man had departed again.

Kelder sipped his ale, then turned back to Irith. "I think," he said, "that you're going to have to tell us all about it."

Irith looked at him, at the unsmiling expression on his face, and then down at Asha, sitting beside him, her own little mouth set firmly.

Irith sighed.

"Oh, all right," she said, "I'll tell you the whole story." She shifted on the bench and then remarked by way of preamble, "You know, you two aren't being any fun at *all*!"

The others just sat, and Irith began. "It's called Javan's Second Augmentation of Magical Memory," she said. "The spell, I mean."

"Tell us about it," Kelder said.

"How did you learn it?" Asha asked. "Were you a magician?"

Irith frowned. "I guess I'd better start all the way back at the beginning," she said.

She took a deep breath and began, "I was born in the Third Military District of Old Ethshar, which was already being called Dria—it was run by someone we called a colonel, but he declared himself king when I was five. It was a lot bigger then than Dria is now—the colonel ruled everything as far east as Thuth."

She saw the rather blank expressions on both Kelder's and Asha's faces and explained, "That's all on the eastern plains, between the mountains and the desert—south of here."

"But that's not Ethshar," Asha protested. "Ethshar's way off to the west."

"That's the *new* Ethshar," Irith said. "The Hegemony of Ethshar, it's called. That was originally all conquered territory, and Old Ethshar was where the Small Kingdoms are now. It sort of fell apart, though."

"Go on," Kelder said.

"Well, anyway," Irith said, "I grew up in Dria, and it was still part of Old Ethshar, sort of, but only because of the Great War. You know about that, right? How we were all fighting against the Northern Empire? And they had demons and sorcerers fighting for them?"

Kelder said, "We know about the War."

"Well, because we were all scared of the Northerners, none of the Small Kingdoms fought each other much, and a lot of people just kept breaking off little pieces and setting up their own kingdoms, and nobody could do anything about it because we couldn't afford to fight among ourselves, you see? But it made it harder and harder for the four generals to raise armies and protect us. So the war had been going on for hundreds of years, maybe a thousand years, but it was beginning to look as if we might lose, or at least that's what my parents thought. The news from the generals was good, mostly— General Gor was doing well in the west, and General Anaran was raiding the Empire's borders, and everything—but Old Ethshar was coming apart."

"What does this have to do with your spells?" Kelder asked.

"I'm getting to that!" Irith glared at him.

"Get to it, then!"

She glowered for a moment longer, then continued, "So everybody was very worried when I was growing up, and I heard a lot of stories about how terrible the Northerners were, and my parents were always talking about how everybody had to do everything they could for the war effort, and the king was always issuing proclamations about how Dria would fight to the last inch of ground and the last drop of blood, and all this stuff, and it was all exciting, and really scary, and I think it was a pretty bad way to grow up, but I didn't have any choice, you know? So I was scared all the time, but I wanted to do my part, so I went and got tested at Dria Castle when I turned twelve, and they said I would make a good wizard, and the war effort always needed good wizards—we had much better wizards and theurgists than the Northerners did, which is why they didn't win, even though they had much better sorcerers and demonologists."

Kelder, seeing that this might actually lead somewhere, nodded encouragingly.

"So they signed me up as apprentice to a wizard who had retired from combat duty to train new wizards," Irith went on. "Not in Dria Castle, up in the hills to the west. And he was a nice enough master, I guess, but he was older than anything, hundreds of years old, and he'd never married or had any kids or anything, so even though he knew just about all the wizardry there was, he wasn't very easy to get along with, and he didn't understand anything about what it was like for me, being a girl growing up like that."

Kelder made a vaguely sympathetic noise.

"And I never really wanted to be a wizard anyway, and old Kalirin wanted to send me out to General Terrek on combat duty when I'd finished my apprenticeship, and he talked about my maybe doing research, but I knew that research wizards all get killed—I mean, they're lucky if they last a month! And I hated it, all that fussing around with weird, icky stuff like lizard brains and spider guts and teardrops from unborn babies, and I mean, yuck! Who wants to be a wizard?"

Asha started to say something, and Irith cut her off. "Oh,

all right, so it's really great when a spell works the way it's supposed to and everything, but there's all that preparation and setup and ritual first, and everything has to be just perfect—it isn't *all* fun, you know. And they wanted me to learn all these awful spells for fighting with, that weren't going to be any use for anything else, like blowing people into bits, and they didn't care about any of the *good* stuff, like flying or shapechanging or anything. So I hated it. And by the time I was fifteen and was getting the hang of it all, the war was going badly in the east, and General Terrek was falling back, and how was *I* supposed to know he was luring the northern army into a trap? I thought we were going to lose the war, and the Northerners were going to come in and rape everybody and then kill us all, or torture us forever, or something. So one day when he was out somewhere I borrowed Kalirin's book of spells and looked through it for some way to get myself out of it all, and I found Javan's Second Augmentation."

"Kalirin was your master?" Kelder asked.

"That's right," Irith agreed, "Kalirin the Clever. He'd been training wizards forever, practically—I must have been about his two hundredth apprentice."

Kelder nodded. "So what *is* Javan's Second Augmentation of whatever it is?"

"Well," Irith said, "do you know anything about wizardry?"

Kelder considered for a second or two, then admitted, "Not really."

"All right, it's like this," she explained. "Wizardry, as near as anybody can figure out, works by tapping into the chaos that reality is made out of—and if you don't understand that that's fine, because I don't, either, that's just what Kalirin told me. It does this by taking magically-charged symbols—stuff like dragon's blood or mashed spider legs—and ritually combining them in patterns that break through into that chaos. Or at least, that's what the wizards *think* they're doing, but nobody really knows for sure, they just know that if you do this and this and this, then that'll happen. If you put a pinch of brimstone on the point of your . . . um, on your dagger and fling it in the air while you say the right magic word, it'll start a fire—but nobody really knows *why* it does that, and why it doesn't work if you try it with, say, phosphorus—I mean, phosphorus burns better than brimstone, so it ought to work, right? But it doesn't. And it has to be a dagger that's enchanted a particular way, too."

Kelder nodded.

"And some of the spells take *hours* to do, or even *days*," Irith said, "and some of the ingredients are a real nuisance to get hold of, you know? So it's just not very *convenient*, being a wizard. It's not like theurgy, where you can just call on a god and ask for a favor, or warlockry, where I don't know *what* they do but it seems to work right away without any spells or equipment or anything."

"So . . ." Kelder prompted.

"So," Irith said, "this wizard Javan, who was some kind of genius or something, started looking for ways to get rid of all the rituals and magic words and rare ingredients and things. He wanted to find some way to get right at that chaos or whatever it is without all the in-between stuff. And he figured that if the ingredients are just symbols for something in the underlying chaos, then why can't we use *symbols* of symbols? The way we use words as symbols, maybe. And he found a way he could sort of do this, sort of. He found a way to put spells right into a wizard's brain, or his soul, or somewhere. He still had to do the whole ritual and everything, but he didn't have to do it all just when he wanted the spell to work, he could do it in advance and sort of store the spell in his head, ready to go. I mean, he could take some petrifaction spell or something that would take two days to perform, and he would run through the whole two-day ritual, and then his own little spell with it, and that would put the whole thing in his head, and then he could carry it there as long as he wanted, and then when he saw the person he wanted to pet-rify, he could just point and say a word, and that whole big fancy two-day spell would come pouring out of his head and down his arm, and *bang!* The person would be turned to

stone." Irith paused. "I think witchcraft works sort of like that, too," she said, "but I'm not sure."

Kelder nodded; Asha looked slightly confused. "But then, if wizards can carry spells around like that, why . . ." she began.

Kelder hushed her. "Irith will explain."

"Right," Irith agreed, "I will. So, Javan came up with this, and he called it Javan's Augmentation of Magical Memory, Javan's *First* Augmentation of Magical Memory—because you carry the spells in your head like memories, you see? Anyway, it's a pretty good spell, it's hard to do but it's useful, and it's still around, but not all that many wizards know it, because it *is* hard to do, and besides, there are some problems with it."

"Like what?" Asha asked.

"Like, you can only do maybe three spells with it, four if they're simple ones, maybe only two if they're big, complicated ones. You can store them away in your head—but while any of them are still in there, you can't do any *other* magic. And sometimes they go bad while they're stored, and they don't work right when you try them. And each one is good only once—use it and it's gone. So if you did a petrifaction spell, and the person you want to use it on has a couple of friends with him with swords, you could be in big trouble, because it'll work only once. Oh, and there's no way to get the spells out *without* using them, so if you store up a curse, and then your victim dies before you use it, you need to find someone *else* to put the curse on, or it'll stay in your head forever and you won't be able to do any other magic at all until you get it out. So it's not all *that* useful a spell."

Asha nodded.

"So that's the First Augmentation," Kelder said. "What's the second one?"

"I'm getting to that," Irith said. "So Javan had this spell, but it wasn't everything he wanted, right? I mean, you could carry only three spells and they didn't always work right, and it was a hard spell to perform in the first place. So he tried to come up with an improvement on it."

"The Second Augmentation," Kelder suggested.

"That's right," Irith agreed. "except it wasn't exactly an improvement after all, it's just different. It lets you carry about a dozen spells, if you do it right, and you can use each one over and over, as many times as you like—but they *never* come out. And you can't learn any more magic, ever."

Kelder blinked. He thought that over.

"And there isn't any counterspell, at least not that anyone's ever found. Which is why there wasn't any Third Augmentation—because Javan tried out the spell, and loaded a dozen spells into his head, or maybe a dozen anyway, and from then on he could use them all as easily as snapping his fingers, but he could *never get them out*, and he couldn't do *any* other magic, *ever*, and no other wizardry would even *work* on him, he was so charged full of magic, and since he hadn't used any youth spells or immortality spells or anything in his experiment, that was the end of him—he lived about another thirty years, I guess, and he could do those ten or twelve spells all he wanted, but he wasn't any use for anything else." She grimaced. "Anyway, he'd written the whole thing down, so anyone who wanted—I mean, any wizard who could work high-order magic, because it's not an easy spell—anyway, anyone who wanted to could see how the spell was done, but nobody ever tried it again." She took a deep breath.

"Except me," she said.

CHAPTER 21

Irith had paused in her story, but Kelder and Asha just waited, and after a moment she began where she had left off.

"It was ... well, I'd heard the story from Kalirin, about how the great Javan went and ruined himself, and I was worried about the war, and I didn't want to be a wizard, and I was really sick and tired of being an apprentice—I mean, for three years I had worked the skin right off my fingers, doing all this weird stuff," Irith said. "And it seemed like a good idea, to go ahead and do the spell, and then I'd know some magic, but I couldn't go into combat because I wouldn't know the *right kind* of magic, and I'd *never* be able to do research—I wouldn't be able to do any other magic, ever. So I started picking out the spells and practicing up. The book said that Javan's Second Augmentation was a seventh-order spell, but it looked a *lot* easier than that, and I was doing fourth-order spells without much trouble, and I figured that if it didn't work I wasn't any *worse* off. I mean, usually, when a spell doesn't work right, nothing happens at all. Sometimes it goes wrong, and all kinds of horrible things can happen when that happens, but usually it doesn't, you see?"

Kelder nodded.

"So I started picking out the spells I wanted and collecting all the ingredients for everything. I can still remember what I needed for the Augmentation—maybe one reason I liked the idea was that there wasn't anything really yucky in it. I needed three left toes from a black rooster and a plume from a peacock's tail and seven round white stones, six of them exactly the same weight and the seventh three times as much, and a block of this special incense that had been prepared in the morning mist of an open field, and then I needed my wizard's dagger." Irith smiled dreamily, leaning on one elbow. "You know, I haven't thought about this stuff in *ages*! All that stuff, to work magic!"

"You don't have a wizard's dagger now, do you?" Asha asked.

"Of course not," Irith said, sitting up again. "I had to break it as part of the spell. I cut my knee doing it, too."

"Go on," Kelder said.

"Well, it took a couple of months to get ready," Irith said. "And then an entire sixnight to work all the spells together. They didn't all work—I'd picked some that were too hard for me. And some that sort of worked didn't work right, like the invisibility spell. It was supposed to be Ennerl's Total Invisibility, but it doesn't act the way Kalirin's book said it would; it's a fifth-order spell, and I didn't really know how to do stuff above fourth-order, but I figured I could give it a try." She shrugged. "It's better than nothing."

"So what other spells did you try?" Asha asked.

"Oh, I picked all the best ones I could find," Irith said, "but not stuff that the army would want. And I didn't make Javan's silly mistake; the very first one I did was a spell of eternal youth, and if that hadn't worked I wouldn't even have done the rest, I don't think. I'm not really sure, because the magic messed up my memory a little bit—but anyway, the spell worked, so I was fifteen then, and I'll always be fifteen—I can't get any older unless something breaks the spell, and there *isn't* anything that can break the spell!" She smiled brightly.

"What else?" Kelder asked.

"Well, there's a Spell of Sustenance that they used to use on soldiers so they didn't have to feed them—see this?" She lifted her head and displayed her throat, pulling away the velvet ribbon, and for the first time Kelder realized that the bloodstone she wore there was not on a choker, but set directly into her flesh. "As long as that stone is there, I don't need to eat or drink or even breathe—but I usually do any-way, because it's fun, and besides, if I go without too long it feels really weird and I don't think it's good for me. And I don't get tired if I use it, I mean, not the usual way, but it . . . I don't like to use it too much." That explained how she could dance along the road for hours, Kelder realized—and also why she didn't always, why she had gotten tired when carry-ing Asha on horseback.

"And I can change shape, of course," Irith continued. "I have seven shapes. That's Haldane's Instantaneous Transformation, and it was the hardest part—I had to make bracelets from the skin of each animal and soak them in my own blood stirred with butterfly wings."

Kelder remembered the bands around her ankle and, once again, a mystery evaporated.

"Seven shapes?" Asha asked. "What are they?"

Irith hesitated. "Oh, I guess it won't hurt to tell you," she said finally. "I can be a horse, or a bird, or a fish, or a cat, or me, or me with wings, or a horse with wings. And before you ask, I can't carry much when I fly, even as a horse—I couldn't have just flown us all to Shan. Flying with anything more than my own weight is *hard*."

"How did you get skin from a flying horse?" Kelder asked. He had never heard of flying horses, and certainly had never seen any.

"Well, I didn't, really," Irith admitted. "I used strips of or-dinary horsehide braided together, with dove feathers woven in. And for just growing wings, I used dove feathers wound in my own hair."

Kelder nodded. "Anything else?" he asked. "Shape-changing, invisibility, eternal youth, the Spell of Sustenance—that's four, and you said there were a dozen."

"I said you could *maybe* do twelve," she corrected him. "I only tried ten, and half of them didn't work." She shrugged. "I was only an apprentice, after all."

"Half—so is there one more?"

Irith bit her lip, and Kelder thought she blushed slightly; he couldn't be sure in the dimness of the tavern.

"There is, isn't there?" he said. "At *least* one more."

"Just ... just one, I think," she admitted. "And I wish it didn't work, and I'd gotten one of the protective spells instead, or the one that would let me walk on air, or the one to light fires. I *still* can't believe I messed *that* one up—the fire-lighting spell. I mean, it's about the simplest spell there is, one of the first things every wizard's apprentice learns. I think I must have left it until last, and I guess by then I was really tired ..."

"Irith," Kelder said, cutting her off, "what's the other spell?" He was not going to let his wife keep any important secrets from him, and while Irith wasn't his wife yet and didn't know she would ever be, *he* knew.

"... I mean," she said, "here I was doing seventh-order wizardry, and I couldn't get Thrindle's Combustion! ..."

"Irith."

"Or maybe," she went on desperately, "I never even tried it after all—maybe I forgot, or decided it would be too useful for the army. After all, if you use it on something that's already burning, it explodes, so that would be almost like a weapon, wouldn't it? So I must have decided not to use it, and my memory's been playing tricks on me ..."

Kelder leaned across the table and grabbed her by both wrists.

"Irith," he said, in what he hoped was a low and deadly tone, *"what was the other spell?"*

She stared at him for a moment, then surrendered.

"It was a love spell," she said. "Fendel's Infatuous Love Spell."

Kelder sat back, puzzled; why had she been so reluctant to name it? What was so terrible about a love spell? The local farmers back home had told some stories about love potions, and they hadn't sounded particularly horrible.

"There might have been another one, maybe," Irith said, speaking quickly, "I don't know. It's really, really hard for me to think about magic sometimes now, and everything I remember from when I was getting the spell ready is all sort of blurry. But if there were any others, they were one-time things, like the youth spell, not anything I can use over and over . . ."

She was trying to distract him again. A dreadful thought struck him.

"Irith," he said, "did you try that love spell on *me*?"

She stopped in midbreath and stared at him, shocked. Then she burst into giggles.

"*No*, silly!" she said, "of *course* not! You don't love me that much, or you wouldn't be arguing with me all the time and asking me all these questions! Don't you know how love spells . . . well, no," she said, calming, "no, I guess you don't know."

"No, I don't," he said coldly.

Even as he spoke, he was thinking. The possibility still remained that she might use the love spell on him in the future; maybe that was why he would marry her. No, he told himself, that was silly. He already wanted to marry her, without any spell—didn't he?

"It isn't *all* love spells work that way, anyway," she explained, "but there's a reason this one is called Fendel's *Infatuous* Love Spell."

"You've used it?" Kelder asked.

"Well," she said, "I was worried about the Northerners, you see. So I picked the transformation so I could grow wings and fly away, or turn into a fish and swim away, and I picked the invisibility spell so I could hide from them, and the sustenance spell so I wouldn't need any food while I was hiding—and the youth spell didn't have anything to do with the Northerners, I just didn't want to grow old and mean like Kalirin. But the love spell was so that if the Northerners *did* catch me, somehow, I could make them love me, so they wouldn't want to hurt me, you see? That's all."

"But the Northerners never came," Kelder pointed out.

"No, they didn't," Irith agreed. "After I made the spell, and it worked, mostly, I ran away and hid, and then when I didn't see any fighting or anything I sneaked into a tavern and listened, and I found out that General Terrek had just won a big battle, his retreat had just been a trick, and the Northerners weren't coming. But I didn't dare go back then—I'd deserted in time of war, and that meant a death sentence. So I hid out in the mountains for three years, working my way north toward the Great Highway and sneaking down to get news sometimes, and in 4996 the Northerners turned a whole army of demons loose and blasted General Terrek and the eastern territories into the Great Eastern Desert, and I thought we were all going to die after all, except it would be demons instead of Northerners, and they could probably find me no matter how well I hid and the love spell probably wouldn't work on them. But then the gods themselves came and fought the demons off and wiped out the Northerners, and the war was over, and I stopped worrying, and after a while I stopped hiding. And I ran into Kalirin one day, and I thought he was going to kill me, but he didn't care anymore, he said that with the war over it didn't matter, and there wasn't any point in punishing me anyway, because of the spell. So I stopped hiding, but I didn't have anywhere to go back to, so I just started traveling around the Small Kingdoms, mostly along the Great Highway." She took a deep breath and concluded, "And I've been here ever since."

"And you used that love spell on someone anyway, even though there weren't any more Northerners," Kelder said, certain that Irith would have been unable to resist testing it out. He still didn't see why she was so embarrassed and secretive about it, though.

"On Ezdral, I bet," Asha said.

Kelder started. That idea, obvious as it now seemed, had not yet occurred to him; he threw Asha an astonished glance in response to her unexpected perspicacity, then looked back to Irith.

The shapeshifter nodded. "That's right," she said, "I enchanted Ezdral."

"So that's why he's in love with you?" Kelder asked. "That's why he's been looking for you all these years?" The embarrassment and reticence suddenly made sense.

Irith nodded unhappily.

"Well, why didn't you take the spell *off* when you left him, then?" Kelder asked.

Irith stared at him in surprise.

"Because I *can't*, stupid!" she shouted. "I don't know how! All I can do is put it *on*, not take it off!"

This revelation left Kelder speechless.

Irith filled the silence by babbling on, trying to explain. "I didn't know how it worked, don't you see? I mean, I'm only fifteen, and I'd been cooped up in Kalirin's stupid house in the hills near Degmor ever since menarche, and the only people I ever saw were wizards and army officers and a few servants with the brains of a turnip among them, so I didn't know *anything* about love or sex or infatuation or any of that stuff, and there wasn't anyone I could try the spell out on, to see how it worked, and there's a counterspell, yes, but it isn't part of the spell itself, and I didn't include it, maybe I tried, I don't remember, I *can't* remember, and *I can't do any other magic*! I couldn't even *touch* Kalirin's book of spells anymore!"

"But that spell . . . From what Ezdral said, it ruined his whole life!" Kelder said.

"Well, *I* didn't know it would do that!" Irith said defensively. "I didn't know how it worked! I'd used it a couple of times, but those were different, and they're all dead now, and Ezdral was so *cute*, when I saw him there—he was big and handsome and he was so good with those horses, they calmed right down when he petted them, I mean, I almost wanted to turn into a horse so he'd pet *me* that way, and he wouldn't even look at me hardly, and before I knew it I'd done it. And he came and talked to me, and he was so sweet, and it was just *wonderful*, and we had a great time, we went all over the place together and did all sorts of stuff, and he was the best-looking man everywhere we went, and he was gentle and playful . . ."

"Then why did you leave him?" Kelder asked.

She shrugged. "Well, it got boring," she said, "and he was talking about us staying together forever, and I knew we weren't going to do that, because I'm only fifteen, I'm not ready to settle down, and he was getting older, and everything, and besides, I knew he didn't *really* love *me*, he was enchanted, and I was young and pretty and everything, and even *that* was magic, so it wasn't *real*, you know? So it didn't count. So I didn't want to stay with him forever, and I knew I'd have to leave sooner or later, and when we had that fight about my dancing I decided it might as well be sooner, and *I thought it would wear off*! I thought that if I wasn't there, the spell would wear off, and he'd forget all about me."

"Really?" Asha asked.

Irith blushed again and looked down at the table.

"I thought it *might*," she muttered, "I didn't *know*. I thought it might wear off. But I guess it didn't, at least not right away."

"Not *ever*," Asha said. "He's still in love with you."

Irith shuddered. "Well, I'm certainly not in love with *him*," she said. "Can't we just forget about him and go on without him?"

Kelder knew at once what the answer to this was—no, they couldn't. Maybe Irith was capable of that sort of selfishness, maybe even Asha was, but *he* wasn't. Not when he was who he was, and not when he was fated as he was.

He did not say so immediately, however; he paused to think it over, to consider not just what to say, but the entire situation.

He expected to marry Irith—Zindré's prophecy said he would, and he had liked the idea very much. Irith was bright and cheerful, incredibly beautiful, and her magical abilities gave her all the appeal of the mysterious and exotic.

He still liked the idea, but it was obvious that Javan's Second Augmentation had changed her into something that wasn't quite the girl she appeared to be, and the thought of loving and marrying a creature that might not be quite human anymore was a bit frightening.

And he knew that Irith was far from perfect; she could be selfish and thoughtless. In particular, it was obvious that she would leave him when he started to show any sign of age—or maybe even just signs of maturity.

He did not want a wife who would leave him when he aged; the Shularan custom, and his family's tradition, was to marry for life. He had assumed that that was what Zindré had prophesied for him, that he would have Irith with him for the rest of his life, but now that he knew Irith, knew who and what she was, that looked very unlikely.

But then, was that really all that bad? He would survive if she left him, just as he would if he were widowed, and while the marriage lasted, she could certainly be an agreeable companion when she chose to be.

Still, he had doubts. This whole adventure was turning out different from what he had expected, and he was not sure yet if it was better or worse. The Great Highway was a dirt road, most of it ugly. He had seen the great city of Shan, but only very briefly and without pleasure; he had seen the vast plain of the Great Eastern Desert, and it had frightened and depressed him more than it had awed or exhilarated him. The wife he had been promised appeared to be a flighty and unpredictable creature, an immortal shapeshifter rather than an ordinary woman. Championing the lost and forlorn he had expected to be a matter of facing down thieves or slaying a dragon or some such traditional act of heroism, not stealing a dead bandit's severed head on behalf of an abused child, or defending the rights of an ensorcelled drunkard.

If this was the destiny he had been promised—and really, how could he doubt that it was?—then he had to consider whether he *wanted* it.

And if he decided he did not, could he refuse it, or was he foredoomed?

He really couldn't say; he had hardly been thinking of such things when he spoke to Zindré as a boy of twelve. He might be doomed to carry out his destiny, or he might not, he simply didn't know.

If he wasn't trapped, did he *want* to go on?

Well, discharging his promise to Asha was easy enough now; he would certainly go on and hold Abden's funeral, as he had said he would.

But did he still want to marry Irith?

She was as lovely as ever, and he thought he would enjoy her company for as long as they were together, but there was the little matter of what she had done to poor Ezdral. That was not something he wanted hanging over his married life, that some dismal old sot was madly in love with his wife, that she had been completely responsible for it, and that she didn't seem to care.

And that spell of hers—that wasn't anything he wanted hanging over him, either. What if Kelder tired of her before she tired of him, or even if he just refused her now and turned away—what if he decided not to marry her after all, and she decided otherwise? Would she use her spell on *him*?

Would he know it if she had? Would he even *care*? Ezdral knew that Irith had deserted him, had avoided him, but he was still in love with her, still looking for her.

Kelder had no desire at all to live out his life under such a curse.

Of course, spells could be broken—Kelder knew that, at least in theory. Irith had said there was a counterspell for the love charm—or at least, that she thought there was; by her own admission, she was unreliable on any question having to do with magic.

Could the love spell be broken?

Could *Irith's* spell be broken—Javan's Second Augmentation of Magical Memory? Irith hadn't been able to do any magic for two hundred years, so anything she might say would be out of date; maybe a counterspell had been found long ago. If she was restored to an ordinary, nonmagical existence, that would certainly simplify any marriage plans.

Of course, he didn't know if Irith *wanted* all her spells broken, but there was certainly one she would like to be rid of—Fendel's Infatuous Love Spell.

There was supposed to be a counterspell for that. The prophecy hadn't mentioned anything about it specifically, but Kelder knew where all the great wizards were supposed to be, and Zindré had said he would see cities, plural. Shan was one; there had to be another.

The three of them had been sitting in silence for several

seconds, thinking their several thoughts; now Kelder broke the silence.

"Listen," he said, "suppose that after we're done in Angarossa, after Abden's funeral is all done and his soul set free, we all go on along the highway, all the way to Ethshar, all four of us—you, Irith, and you, Asha, and me, and Ezdral—and see if we can't find a wizard who can break the love spell."

"All four of us?" Irith asked, startled.

"That's right," Kelder said, gathering enthusiasm, "all four of us! It would give poor old Ezdral a chance to be with you one last time, just as far as Ethshar—I'm sure we could find a wizard there who could cure him of his infatuation."

"But why bother?" Irith asked.

"So Ezdral can live out the rest of his life in peace, of course," Kelder said, annoyed. "And so you can either get rid of the love spell permanently, so you won't accidentally use it again, or so at least you can learn to dispell it if you *do* use it."

As he finished saying this he suddenly realized that he might be making a mistake—if she could turn the love spell on and off, Irith might well use it more often. That was scarcely a good thing.

She would be able to use it on *him*, whenever they argued.

Well, he told himself, the words were out now, and it was too late to take them back.

"You're probably right," Irith agreed thoughtfully. "If one of them *could* break the spell, I guess that would be nice for poor old Ezdral, wouldn't it? I mean, it wouldn't give him his forty years back or anything, he'd still be a horrible old man, but maybe he wouldn't be so bad." She brightened. "And then he wouldn't have any reason to follow me around anymore, or bother me at all—not even sit and wait for me, or anything!"

Kelder nodded, pleased that she seemed to have missed his accidental suggestion.

"That would be great!" Irith said. "I don't like the idea of that awful old man thinking about me all the time." She paused. "Do we *all* need to go?"

"Well," Kelder said, "we probably need to have you there so the wizard can see how your spell works, and we need Ezdral so we can use the counterspell on him, and Asha doesn't have anywhere else to go except with us, and *I* want to see that everything works out all right."

Irith nodded. "I don't like the idea of being around him," she said, "but I guess I can stand it as far as Ethshar."

"Why do we have to go all the way to Ethshar?" Asha asked plaintively.

"Because that's where all the best wizards are, of course," Irith told her.

"There are wizards in other places besides Ethshar, aren't there?" Asha asked.

"Of course there are," Kelder agreed, "and we'll look them up along the way—we'll ask in every village and castle along the Great Highway. I've always heard, though, that for real, serious wizardry, the best place to look is Ethshar of the Spices." Besides, Zindré's predictions clearly implied that he would see Ethshar before returning home; what other great city was there? The Great Highway ran between Shan and Ethshar, it didn't go to Sardiron of the Waters or Tintallion of the Coast or any other important cities.

"You can find good magicians in any of the three Ethshars, really," Irith said, "but Ethshar of the Spices is supposed to be the biggest and best, and it's certainly the closest. I've never been to the other two." She sipped her ale and added, "And I haven't been to Ethshar of the Spices in *ages*!"

"There are three Ethshars?" Asha asked in a pitiful little voice.

"Four, actually," Irith said, counting them off on her fingers. "There are the three in the Hegemony of the Three Ethshars, of course—Ethshar of the Spices, Ethshar of the Rocks, and Ethshar of the Sands—and then there's a place that calls itself Ethshar of the Plains that's one of the Small Kingdoms, one of the smallest, over to the southeast of here, just south of Thuth. It split off from Dria right after the Great War ended, I think. Or maybe even before the war ended."

"I didn't know that," Kelder remarked. "I thought there were just the three big ones."

Irith shrugged. "Well, nobody knows all the Small Kingdoms," she said, "or at least I don't think so. There are more than a hundred in all, and who could remember that many? But I know a lot; I've traveled all over the northern half of them, not just along the Great Highway."

"Well," Kelder said, lifting his ale in salute, "you've certainly had time for it."

Irith eyed him, trying to decide whether he meant anything insulting, and decided that he did not. She smiled at him and sipped her ale.

Kelder watched her, wondering whether her enchantments could all be broken, whether she would be any different if they were, and whether, if both of those were the case, the changes would all be for the better.

CHAPTER 22

The first sign that Ezdral was finally waking up was when he let out his breath in a long, loud *whoosh* and stopped snoring.

Kelder and Asha turned to watch him; Irith, sitting by the window brushing her hair, paid no attention.

The old man had not stirred, his eyelids had not so much as flickered, when the three of them had carried him inside, hauled him up the stairs, and dumped him unceremoniously on the little rag rug in their rented room. He had slept the night through without complaint.

Fortunately, his snoring had not been constant, so that the others were able to sleep, as well.

Now he smacked his lips noisily, wheezed slightly, and then blinked.

His eyes opened, widened, and then closed again. His hoarse breath stopped for a moment. He made a guttural noise and brought one clawed hand up to wipe at his gummy eyes. Then he slowly, carefully, lifted his lids.

He was looking at a tidy little rug, a well-swept plank floor, and one corner of the featherbed Kelder and Irith had innocently shared. Kelder had wished that they hadn't been quite so innocent, but with Asha in the cot nearby and Ezdral on the floor, he hadn't pressed his point.

The old man turned his head and spotted first Asha, and then Kelder. He blinked, and slowly, cautiously pushed himself up into a sitting position. He made a noise that might have been construed as "Good morning" by someone who

171

spoke archaic Mezgalonese, then cleared his throat and said the same thing, more clearly, in Trader's Tongue.

Then he turned and looked around the room—or at least, he started to.

When his gaze fell upon Irith, sitting by the window humming to herself, it was as if he had been struck. His mouth fell open, his eyes widened; his shoulders tensed, jerking his hands up off the floor, and he swayed unsteadily.

"Irith," he said hoarsely.

"Good morning, Ezdral," Irith said, not looking at him.

"Irith," he said again, his voice stronger now. He started to rise.

Irith turned to face him and announced, "If you touch me, Ezdral, I'll be out this window and flying away before your fingers can close, and I swear by all the gods that if that happens, you'll never see me again."

Ezdral froze as he was, crouched on one knee, staring at her.

"And don't stare at me," Irith said pettishly. "It's rude."

Ezdral quickly averted his gaze, looking at the rug instead.

"Irith," he said, "it's been so long . . ."

"Yes, I know," she said. "I guess it must have been pretty awful."

"I love you," Ezdral said.

"I know," Irith replied. "You can't help it."

"I'll *always* love you," the old man insisted.

"Well, maybe not," Irith said. "We're hoping to fix that."

Ezdral blinked and risked a quick look at Irith.

The window faced southeast, and the sun was pouring in behind Irith, turning her freshly brushed hair into a halo of golden fire, outlining her in light. Ezdral gasped in awe.

"Kelder," Irith said beseechingly, "*you* tell him." She looked away, out the window.

"Tell me what?" Ezdral asked, still staring at Irith. Kelder could see him trembling at the sight of her.

"Ezdral," Kelder said gently, "do you know *why* you love Irith so much, even after she deserted you and you haven't seen her in so long?"

"Because she's the most perfect, beautiful creature in the World . . ." the old man replied, before his voice trailed off uncertainly.

"No," Kelder told him uneasily, "it's because she enchanted you."

Ezdral frowned and glanced quickly at Kelder before turning back to his object of worship.

"She *enchanted* you, Ezdral," Kelder insisted. "She used a love spell on you, a charm called Fendel's Infatuous Love Spell, and it's permanent, and she didn't know how to take it off! It's all magic! It's just a spell, a trick!" His voice rose until he was shouting as he concluded, "*That's* why you love her!"

Ezdral frowned again.

"No," he said, "that can't be it. I mean, maybe she did, but I'd love her anyway, I know I would. By all the gods, just *look* at her! Have you ever seen anything so radiantly lovely?"

Involuntarily, Kelder looked and had to admit to himself that in fact no, he had never seen anything else so radiantly lovely—but he didn't say it aloud. That didn't matter. Ezdral was enchanted, and besides, looks weren't *everything*.

She certainly was beautiful, though; Kelder had to swallow hard before he could continue.

"It's a spell, Ezdral, really. Maybe you would have loved her anyway, but it probably wouldn't have been such an obsession. Anyway, we talked last night, and we all agreed that it wasn't right for you to be enchanted like this, and we're all going to take you to Ethshar of the Spices and find a wizard who can break the spell. Or maybe we'll find one on the way."

"You don't need to do that," Ezdral said, his gaze still fixed entirely on the object of his adoration. "I'm perfectly happy like this."

"But you *wouldn't* be," Kelder said desperately, "if Irith wasn't here."

Ezdral's head snapped around. "She's not leaving, is she?" he asked. It snapped back. "Irith, you aren't leaving?"

Irith put down the hairbrush and let out a sigh. She stared helplessly at Kelder.

"No, she's not leaving," Kelder said, "as long as you agree to come with us to Ethshar and get the spell removed."

"All right," Ezdral said. "Whatever you want, Irith, I'll be glad to do it. If you want the spell off, that's fine."

"I want the spell off," she said, "and don't *stare* at me like that!"

Ezdral's gaze instantly dropped to the floor again.

"Whatever you want," he mumbled. "Anything, Irith, anything at all—just don't leave me again."

Kelder watched this display of utter devotion with growing dismay. Ezdral was so abject, so docile, so completely at Irith's disposal.

No one, Kelder thought, should ever be so much in someone else's power.

If this was what a love spell did, he told himself, they shouldn't be allowed.

CHAPTER 23

*B*efore they left the inn, Irith decreed that Ezdral must be cleaned up; Irith refused to go anywhere with him in his filthy, bedraggled state. Ezdral yielded to this without protest, and while the girls ate their breakfast, Kelder and two members of the inn's staff set about the task.

Hair and beard were trimmed; a comb was brought and promptly lost in tangles. Hair and beard were trimmed again, and the comb recovered and put to use.

One assistant cook tackled that, while the other took away the tunic and breeches to see what could be done with them.

Kelder drew a bath and vigorously applied washrags and sponges to the old man's back while Ezdral addressed the front himself.

Once dried, Kelder thought, he might be almost presentable.

Then the old man's clothes were returned.

The breeches had come apart; the thread holding the seams was rotten and had given way under the stress of cleaning.

The tunic was still in one piece, but looked worse than ever—some of the stains had come out, but others had darkened, and yet others had bleached, giving the garment a much wider range of colors than it had had before. Threadbare patches were more obvious with the protective layer of grease removed.

Kelder looked at the fabric in despair.

"*Now* what do we do?" he said. "You can't go marching down the highway naked!"

The assistant cooks conferred quietly, the female one casting occasional smirking glances at Ezdral's nudity.

"Do you have any more money?" the male asked.

Kelder looked up at the young man, then at Ezdral, who shrugged. "I don't know," Kelder said, "Irith might."

"Well, I've got some old clothes I'd sell," the cook said. "They ought to fit."

"I don't have any better idea," Ezdral said.

Irith did have money, and the clothes did fit.

"This is getting expensive," she complained as the four of them trudged away from the inn.

Kelder glanced at Ezdral, who was now neatly clad in a light-green tunic trimmed with yellow and a dark-green kilt with black embroidery at the hem. The old man was barely recognizable as the drunk who had accosted them in Shan.

"Isn't it worth it, though?" Kelder said. "And I think you owed him something."

Irith didn't reply.

Due to their late start they didn't reach the village of Sinodita until midafternoon, and by then both Asha and Ezdral were too tired to continue. They settled in at the Flying Carpet and rested.

Kelder apologized to Bardec the Innkeeper, but even so, that gentleman insisted that Irith pay for the room and meals in advance.

Irith grumbled but paid, and Kelder spent the remainder of the afternoon looking around the town for odd jobs whereby he could earn a few coins. By sunset he had accumulated seven bits in copper and a pouch of dried figs by chopping wood, stacking it, and helping capture an escaped goat. He had also heard scandalous gossip about the company Queen Kiramé kept in her bedchamber, gripes about the idiocy and malevolence of King Caren of Angarossa, theories that Irith the Flyer was actually a minor goddess in disguise and her presence an omen of good fortune, and considerable discussion of the prospects for the coming harvest in the richer farmlands to the south, and what the effects would be on markets and the local livestock-based economy.

It was rather pleasant, really, to hear the everyday chatter of ordinary people, to listen to voices other than Irith's velvet soprano, Asha's high-pitched whine, and Ezdral's *oushka*-scarred muttering. When he joined the others for supper he was tired but in high spirits.

Kelder was too tired even to mind particularly when he discovered the sleeping arrangements—the larger bed was too narrow to hold two adults, so Irith and Asha shared that, while he took the other bed and Ezdral got a pallet on the floor.

They made better time the following day, passing Castle Angarossa at midday and coming upon the battlefield early in the afternoon. Abden's cairn was undisturbed, but the other corpses were gone—none of the travelers could do any more than guess at what had become of them. Kelder's own guess was that some of the local inhabitants had been sufficiently public-spirited to remove such an obvious health hazard.

The hard part of their self-imposed task proved to be finding enough combustibles to build a proper pyre; with the highway tidied up there was very little to be found, and in the end Kelder resorted to knocking at the door of a nearby farmhouse and paying far too much of Irith's money, as well as all his own seven bits, for a wagonload of stovewood and some flammable trash. Pleas that it was needed for the humanitarian gesture of a proper funeral were countered with remarks about the expense and effort involved in obtaining the wood in the first place and the discomforts of eating undercooked food or sleeping in a cold house.

Several wagons and a full-blown caravan passed during the period between their initial arrival at the cairn and the eventual lighting of the pyre, and none of them stopped or provided any assistance at all. In the end, though, Kelder struck a spark, fanned it into a flame, and stepped back as it gradually spread through the pile on which Abden's mutilated remains lay.

"I wonder if we'll see the ghost," Asha said, staring.

"You probably won't," Irith said. "People usually don't,

especially after so long." She paused, then added, "Sometimes *I* do, though, because of the magic."

"Tell us if you see him," Asha said. "Tell me if he's smiling."

Irith nodded agreement, then leaned over and whispered to Kelder, "He's probably gone mad by now, being trapped in two places for so long."

Kelder frowned and whispered back, "If he has, will he recover?"

Irith shrugged. "Who knows? I'm no necromancer."

It took the better part of an hour before the corpse was consumed, and Irith did not have the stamina to watch constantly; finally, though, she glanced up and started.

"There!" she said.

The others looked, but saw nothing more than rising smoke and crackling flame.

"Was he smiling?" Asha asked eagerly.

"I didn't see," Irith said. "He was facing the wrong way, and I just caught a glimpse." She hesitated. "I'm not really sure I saw anything." She noticed the expression on Kelder's face and added, *"Really!"*

"He's gone, then?" Ezdral asked.

"I guess so," Irith said.

Kelder noticed that Asha was crying silently, tears running down her cheeks, her chest heaving.

"I guess we can go, then," Ezdral said, with a look at the descending sun. "Which way? Back to Castle Angarossa?"

Asha looked up at him. "Why would we go back there?" she asked through her tears.

"For someplace to sleep," Ezdral said. "It's the closest place."

"But it's the wrong direction," Kelder pointed out.

"It's pretty far to Yondra Keep," Irith responded. "We couldn't get there before dark."

"We can sleep outdoors, then," Kelder said.

Irith considered that as Kelder turned away from the pyre and set out westward. She ran after him and said, "Listen,

Kelder, maybe we could find a wizard in Castle Angarossa who could break Ezdral's enchantment . . ."

"Are there any good wizards there?" Kelder asked, cutting her off.

"Well, not that I know of," she admitted. "But I mean, I don't really *know* . . ."

Kelder didn't answer; he simply walked on, away from Castle Angarossa.

"Look, you like to do good things for people, right?" Irith persisted. "And all this trouble with Asha's brother was King Caren's fault, right? So maybe you could do something about it . . ."

"Like what?" Kelder demanded. "I'm an unarmed traveler without so much as a bent copper bit in my pocket, and he's a king, with a castle and guards." Championing the lost and forlorn had to have limits; a child and a drunk were quite enough. The people of Angarossa and the traders who used the highway did not strike Kelder as being sufficiently lost and forlorn to merit his attention; he couldn't tackle *everybody's* problems.

"Well, but I have my magic . . ."

"So *you* can do something about King Caren?"

Irith didn't like that idea at all.

"Oh, all right," she grumbled. "I suppose one night outdoors won't kill me."

CHAPTER 24

*The rain trailed off to nothing a little after mid-*night, and half an hour later Irith finally stopped complaining and telling the others that they should have gone back to Castle Angarossa.

When they arose and Kelder saw Asha shivering in her sopping blanket, he felt mildly guilty about his insistence on continuing westward, but he set his mouth grimly and said nothing.

Damp and miserable, they set a slow pace at first, but the clouds burned off quickly, their clothing dried, and they gradually picked up speed, reaching Yondra Keep shortly after midday. As they ate a late lunch in a little café in the village, Asha asked, "How far is the next town?"

"Only a league," Irith said, before Kelder could remember.

Asha nodded. "What about the one after that?"

Irith had to stop and think about that. "From the town of Amramion to Hlimora Castle must be, oh . . . three leagues? Four?"

"Amramion?" Asha asked. "Are we near Amramion?"

"Of course," Irith said, startled. "I think it's less than two to the border."

"Maybe I should go home," the little girl said uncertainly, peering down the highway.

"What about your father?" Kelder asked quietly.

Asha looked down at the table and began to pick carefully at a protruding splinter. She gave no answer, and the subject was dropped.

They ate in silence for a moment and then Asha said, "At least it's all over for Abden. He's out of it all."

No one said anything in response to that.

"I think we'll stop at Amramion for the night," Kelder said, breaking the silence.

That was what they did.

They were questioned briefly by the guards at the border post, but they knew Irith and could see no harm in an old man and a child. Kelder they had reservations about, but eventually they took Irith's word that he was harmless and let him pass.

The party reached the village of Amramion a little past midafternoon, where they stopped at the Weary Wanderer and took a room; Irith admitted after they left the building that her funds were now running low, and they would need to find some way to obtain more, or else would need to start relying on charity or theft.

With that in mind, the party split up; Kelder went to look for work in the village, while the other three climbed the little hill to the castle and knocked at the postern gate, seeking a consultation with the king's wizard, Pirra the Mage. Irith was recognized immediately, and the three of them were ushered in.

Kelder heard about it that night at supper, as he massaged sore muscles and wondered why the only work he seemed to get was chopping wood. It wasn't work he enjoyed at all.

Of course, he knew that was why he was able to get it—nobody else liked it, either. And it was simple—anyone with strong arms could do it, and you didn't need to worry about coaxing hostile animals or tying knots wrong or anything like that. It was something you could trust to a stranger who might be clumsy or halfwitted.

Of course, since it meant giving him an ax, you didn't want to ask a stranger who looked *dangerous* to chop your wood.

Thinking that through, he only half listened to the tale of how everybody at the castle had recognized Irith, and how Pirra had been eager to talk to her, and then had been really disappointed when she discovered that Irith didn't remember how to prepare all the spells she used.

". . . and she'd *heard* of Fendel's Whatever-it-is Love Spell," Asha said, "and she was pretty sure there's a simple countercharm, but she doesn't know what it is. She knows a *different* one of Fendel the Great's love spells, Fendel's Aphrodisiac Philtre, and she knows one that's a lot *like* Irith's, but it's Cauthen's Remarkable Love Spell, and it's different, it uses mare's sweat and stallion hairs, and she says that there are two countercharms for *that* that she knows, but she doesn't know any for Irith's spell."

That caught Kelder's attention.

"Did she say what the two countercharms are?" he asked. "Maybe we could try them—if the spells are alike, they might work."

"I don't think so," Irith said.

"Well, would it do any harm to try?" Kelder persisted. "Did she say what the charms are?"

Irith and Asha exchanged glances; Irith let out a sigh.

"Yes, she said," the shapeshifter admitted. "But, Kelder, I don't think we want to try them. Not until we know they're the right ones."

"Why *not*?"

"Well, because they're difficult," Irith said.

"What are they?"

"The easy one," Irith said, "is for the victim to drink a cup of virgin's blood each night at midnight, for four nights. A *full* cup. Without spilling a drop, or choking, or throwing up. And he has to go to sleep immediately afterward; if he speaks a word or sets foot on the ground, it won't work." She grimaced. "Have you ever drunk blood? The hardest part has to be not throwing up. And all the blood has to come from a single fertile virgin human female who has never been enchanted—no mixing blood from different people, or anything."

Kelder looked at Asha, who shook her head and said, "I'm too young."

"No," Kelder said hurriedly, "I know that, I didn't ... I just ... I mean, is that really what Pirra said? I know Irith has trouble remembering magic ..." He trailed off, flustered.

"It's right," Asha said. "And that's the *easy* one."

"What's the other?" Kelder asked, though he didn't really expect it to be any better.

"It's just one drop of blood on the back of the tongue," Irith said. "Dragon's blood."

"Well, what's so difficult about that?" Kelder asked, puzzled. "I thought wizards used dragon's blood all the time."

"They do," Irith agreed, "but there's another requirement. The blood has to come from a *gelded* dragon."

Kelder thought about that.

"Oh," he said. He sighed. "Maybe we could find someone ..." he said.

"Kelder," Irith said, "that's a *quart* of virgin's blood—if she's as small as I am or smaller, I think that taking that much could kill her, and we don't even know if it would *work*. It probably wouldn't; it really is a different spell, and I already told you that magic doesn't make sense. You can't use phosphorus for brimstone and still work Thrindle's Combustion, and I don't think you can break Fendel's Infatuous Love Spell with virgin's blood."

"Well, maybe if you got a young enough dragon ..."

The others just stared at him.

"You're right," Kelder admitted, "it's not the same spell. So it's on to Ethshar, then."

"On to Ethshar," Irith agreed.

And that, Kelder thought as he took a bite of pear, wasn't really anything all that terrible. It would be exciting to see Ethshar—the largest city in the World! Another city, and another prophetic phrase would be satisfied.

But it would have been nice, he thought as he watched Ezdral down a large mug of wine, if they'd been able to break the love spell that much sooner.

The meal continued in silence, for the most part. Asha seemed to be thinking about something; Ezdral was drinking heavily and alternately staring at Irith and forcing himself not to look at her. Irith grew increasingly uneasy under his gaze, quickly becoming too nervous to talk—not that she had anyone to speak to anyway, as Kelder was too tired.

When they had all eaten their fill, and a drudge had cleared away the plates—but left the wine bottle, which Ezdral guarded—Asha leaned over and asked Irith quietly, "Could you do something for me?"

Relieved to be able to talk to someone who wasn't Ezdral, Irith asked, "What is it?"

"Could you fly home . . . I mean, to my father's house and tell him about Abden? And that I'm all right?"

Irith's relief vanished; she bit her lower lip and looked at Kelder worriedly.

"Go ahead," Kelder told her. "He won't hurt you; he doesn't even have to see you."

"I'm really sort of tired . . ." the Flyer began.

"Oh, do it!" Kelder snapped. "I've been out chopping wood to earn a lousy copper, which your old boyfriend there just drank up—I think you should earn *your* keep!"

"Don't you speak to me like that!"

Kelder started to say something else, but then a shadow fell over him. He turned to see Ezdral standing over him, fists clenched, the neck of the wine bottle in one of them.

"You don't talk to Irith like that," he said hoarsely.

For a moment the four of them were frozen into position, Kelder and Irith sitting on one bench, Asha on the other, the three of them gaping at Ezdral standing at the end of the table brandishing the bottle.

"No, it's all right," Irith said, breaking the impasse. "He's right, I'm not really tired. I think it's really sweet that Asha's worried about her father, and I'd be *glad* to go tell him."

Ezdral wavered.

"Thank you, Irith," Asha murmured.

"Sit down, Ezdral," Irith said.

Kelder, tired and fed up with the whole situation, said, "Yes, sit down." Angry that the man he was trying to help was turning against him, he added the cruelest thing he could think of. Then, remembering the nature of the spell Ezdral was under, he immediately regretted it.

"Have a drink," he said.

CHAPTER 25

*F*or much of the next morning the Forest of Amramion was visible off to their left, and Ezdral, once he had sobered up sufficiently to focus, marveled at it. He hadn't seen a forest in over a decade.

The guards at the border post between Amramion and Hlimora waved a greeting to Irith but made no attempt to hinder the party.

Irith had been quiet ever since returning from Abden the Elder's house and didn't return the guard's greeting. She had given no details of her encounter with Asha's father, but had merely said that the message was delivered.

Shortly after crossing the border into Hlimora, though, she burst out, "Asha, how could you *live* there?"

Asha looked up, startled but silent.

"She couldn't," Kelder said quietly. "That's why she's here."

"It *stank*," Irith said. "The whole place, and it was *filthy*, and the house was practically falling down, and one shed *had* fallen down. And your . . . that man was drunk and singing to himself, and when he saw me he . . . When I gave him the message and told him his son was dead he started crying, and that wasn't so bad, I expected that, but then he started complaining about how there was no one to help him, and you'd run off, and when I told him you were all right he got angry and started swearing and saying all kinds of horrible things, and he tried to grab me, but I turned into a bird and flew away, and I heard him crying again as I left." She shuddered. "*My* father was never like that."

Asha didn't say anything.

Irith looked at Ezdral and said angrily, "He was even worse than *you* were, when we found you!"

Kelder expected for Ezdral to make some cutting reply, or to stand silently on his dignity, but instead the old man muttered, "I'm sorry, Irith; please don't be mad at me."

Kelder shuddered.

Ezdral's subservience was appalling—but on the other hand, Irith seemed to be showing more compassion than was her wont. Kelder wondered if she might be learning something from Asha and Ezdral.

He certainly hoped so.

And his own presence might not hurt, either.

They were two and a half hours from the border when Kelder stopped and looked closely at the hillside to their left.

"What is it?" Asha asked.

"This is where I first saw the Great Highway," Kelder explained. "I slept on the slope there. And it's where I met Irith."

The Flyer nodded. "That's right," she said, "I remember. At first I thought you were going to just turn around and go back to your farm in Shulara."

"I thought so, too," Kelder admitted.

It occurred to him that he could do that now—he could simply head south, up that hill and down the other side, and go back home to his family and not worry about where his next meal was coming from, or Ezdral's love spell, or Asha's homelessness.

He started to think about it. He turned to look at the others.

He saw Irith's face and forgot the whole notion. She was obviously not yet ready to go with him and settle down to the life of a Shularan peasant, and he wasn't yet ready to give up on Zindré's predictions and go home without her.

"Come on," he said, "we've still got a long way to go."

They had scarcely covered another hundred yards when the turrets of Hlimora Castle came in sight. Kelder remembered how hungry he had been that morning—when was that, a sixnight ago? If he had known how close the castle was, he would never have turned east.

And in that case, he might never have met Asha or Ezdral—but he might have met other people instead. There was simply no knowing what might have happened—not without magic, anyway.

Zindré would have known, he supposed. She must have known that he would go east, as he had—or perhaps she hadn't known any details at all, just the generalities. Perhaps he had been fated to meet someone lost and forlorn, but exactly who had not been predetermined.

The whole question of prophecy was an interesting one; despite his obsession with Zindré's predictions, he had never really thought about the mechanics before. Were *all* his actions predetermined? Some, but not others? If so, why?

If *everything* he was to do was predetermined, then he didn't really have any control over his own life at all, and nothing he did or thought mattered. That was an unsettling notion.

But if he did have control over some of it, then how could *any* of it be so certain that Zindré could predict it? That was certainly something to think about, and think about it he did, as the little party trudged onward.

They reached Hlimora Castle perhaps two hours after noon, and the question then arose of whether to stay the night or press on.

"The next village is Urduron Town," Irith said.

"Well, how far is it?" Kelder asked.

Irith pursed her lips, thinking. "I don't remember," she admitted. "Three leagues, maybe?"

Kelder considered this. "They say a man's normal walk will cover a league in an hour," he said. "The sun won't be down for about four hours yet."

"Come on, then," Irith said.

Naturally, Ezdral agreed with her, and that made the vote three to one. Asha protested in vain.

"Maybe you could be a horse for a little while, Irith?" she asked.

Kelder expected her to hesitate, or refuse, but Irith simply said, "All right." She vanished, to be instantaneously replaced by the white mare.

Ezdral stared as Kelder helped Asha up onto Irith's back; he crept nearer and reached out to touch the horse's flank.

She shied away and whinnied unhappily; Asha grabbed at the mane to keep her balance.

"Don't touch," Kelder advised the old man.

Ezdral didn't touch Irith again, but he stared intently.

It was plain to Kelder that Ezdral's interest was more than just an appreciation of equine grace. At first he was puzzled by the old man's attitude; certainly Irith was a good-looking horse, but she was scarcely as attractive in this form as in human shape. For his own part, his physical interest in Irith vanished when she was in any shape but human.

Then he remembered the love spell and realized that it didn't distinguish on the basis of appearance—or, it seemed, even on the basis of species. Ezdral was still just as infatuated with Irith as ever, regardless of her shape. To him, in his enchanted state, the important change had not been that Irith was now a horse, but that she was now virtually naked.

That added a whole new level of repulsiveness to the spell, in Kelder's opinion; he watched the old man lusting after the mare and felt nothing but revulsion. Even the pity he had felt for Ezdral was overwhelmed by distaste.

He was more determined than ever to see the spell broken, though—not for Ezdral's sake, or Irith's, or because of his prophesied role, but just because it was disgusting and unnatural.

They had gone too far to be worth turning back by the time Kelder and Irith realized that just because a man can walk a league in an hour, that doesn't mean a sick old man, a child, and a horse can walk three leagues in three hours. They had not allowed for rest breaks, or even the occasional call of nature; they had not allowed for Ezdral's unsteady shuffle, or the fact that the terrain here was hilly, the road carrying them up and down one slope after another.

With Asha on Irith's back, the real holdup was Ezdral's

pace; he was simply not interested in moving quickly. Kelder
and Asha could urge him on, but with little result; he would
speed up for perhaps three or four steps, then slow again.

He might have listened to Irith, but she was unable to
speak while in equine form.

Kelder tried to find a solution. The obvious one would be
to put Ezdral on horseback, but that was out of the question.
Irith, he was sure, wouldn't stand for two riders at once, especially not if one of them was the old man. Asha would be
no faster on foot than was Ezdral—and besides, Kelder didn't
want Ezdral any closer to Irith than absolutely necessary,
under the circumstances; putting him astride her back was
asking for trouble.

Finally, though, he hit upon a much simpler and more sat-
isfactory method of accelerating the pace; he simply whispered in Irith's ear to go a little faster and not worry about
Ezdral keeping up.

Ezdral gradually dropped back as the other three marched
on unheeding, until finally he called out, "*Hai!* You're going
too fast! Wait for me!"

Kelder called back, "No; sorry, Ezdral, but we need to get
to Urduron. If you can't keep up, you can find us there."

"Wait," he puffed, "Irith!"

Irith neighed but did not slow down.

Kelder glanced back every so often, and somehow, though
Ezdral puffed and panted and struggled, he never fell back far
enough to let Irith out of his sight.

Kelder felt slightly guilty about exploiting the love spell in
such a way—but only slightly. After all, they were taking
Ezdral along to cure him, for his own good—why let him
slow them up?

The distance to Urduron turned out to be somewhat more
than three leagues; Kelder judged it at at least ten miles, possibly eleven, but unquestionably between three and four
leagues. They finally arrived as the sun sank before them.

Here, Irith had sufficient credit and goodwill to obtain ac-
ceptable room and board at an inn inexplicably called the
Stone from the Sky—but only a small room, so small that

Ezdral and Asha took the two tiny beds, Kelder slept on the floor, and Irith took the form of a cat and spent the entire night curled up on Asha's feet. A fourth human being would have been too much, but they didn't have the money for another room, and Irith's credit wasn't *that* good.

The next day's travel was the four-league distance from Urduron to Ophera; they got an early start and made no attempt to go any farther, but instead set about earning a little money in Ophera, to help defray expenses.

Irith made a few aerial deliveries—primarily flying a packet of wizard's supplies back to Urduron, for which she was paid three bits in silver. She tried to demand more, but gave in when the Opheran wizard threatened to simply conjure up a sylph for the job instead.

Kelder had to settle for coppers, but at least this time he avoided chopping wood, and instead spent a solid three hours weeding the gardens behind the inn Irith had chosen. That covered their room and board in full.

Asha was too young to do any real work, but picked up two bits by watching babies while the mothers went about business.

Ezdral insisted that he had looked for work and failed to find any; he contributed nothing to the common purse.

Both wizards connected with Irith's errand, the sender in Ophera and the recipient in Urduron, knew love spells and countercharms; neither of them, however, admitted knowing a counter for Fendel's Infatuous Love Spell.

"I don't care for Fendel's spells," the Opheran remarked. "They're tricky and usually much more powerful than they need to be. Oh, they're easy to work, but they don't always work the way you *want*. The man was trouble; I can spot one of his spells from the style, and they're all trouble."

Somehow this did not surprise Kelder at all.

He found himself thinking rather dismally about the ease with which Irith had flown, twice, the distance they had taken most of the day to cover on foot. It made walking seem vaguely futile.

On the other hand, he realized suddenly, it was a sign of

Irith's attachment to himself—and, he supposed, her attachment to Asha, and perhaps guilt about Ezdral's enchantment, as well—that she was willing to walk all this way when she could fly.

That was cheering. He had begun to wonder if he would ever be sufficiently sure of her affection to propose marriage, and this provided some encouragement.

That night, despite halfhearted attempts by the others to prevent him from doing so, Ezdral downed three bottles of wine and had to be carried to the room. The only good aspect of his early retirement was that it meant that he got the floor, and Kelder got a bed; there were three cots this time, all narrow.

The leg from Ophera to Krithimion was another relatively short one, and at breakfast Kelder suggested pressing on through Krithimion to Bugoa.

"What's the hurry?" Irith protested. "Ethshar isn't going anywhere. It'll still be there if we take a few days longer to get to it."

Kelder pointed to the semiconscious Ezdral, who was leaning against the dining-room wall, mouth hanging open, bits of fried egg in his beard. "The sooner we get him there," Kelder said, "the better."

"The way we're rushing isn't helping him any," Irith replied. "His feet are all blistered—you shouldn't have done that, making him keep up with me the day before yesterday, when we were trying to reach Urduron."

"I'm sorry," Kelder said, shamefaced.

"Besides," Irith persisted, "we haven't been checking all the wizards all that carefully, the way we just rush from one kingdom to the next—we might miss someone who knows the cure because of your rushing!"

"I doubt it," Kelder said, recovering some of his composure. "If you want good wizards, you need to go to Ethshar—that's what my grandmother always said." He wondered for a moment whether the time might be ripe to mention prophecies, with the mention of great cities, plural, but he decided against it.

"Well, I'm not turning into a horse again, Kelder," Irith said, lifting her chin.

"Listen," he suggested, "let's just get to Krithimion, and we'll see how we're doing, and maybe we'll go on, or maybe we'll stay a night there. All right?"

Irith gave that a moment's thought and then agreed. "All right," she said.

CHAPTER 26

*T*he town surrounding Krithimion Keep actually had a name of its own, to distinguish it from the kingdom it dominated; it was the town of Krithim, with no ending.

Krithimionese, Irith explained as they neared the town, was a patois of Ethsharitic and Trader's Tongue; if there had ever been a distinct native tongue, which she doubted, it was now extinct, or perhaps spoken by a few stubborn farmers somewhere.

"When I was a little girl," Irith added, "people didn't have all these silly languages. There weren't *half* so many, and everybody knew Ethsharitic even if they didn't speak it at home."

"That must have been convenient," Kelder acknowledged.

Krithim was the largest community he had seen since leaving Shan on the Desert and a closer match to his original expectations for the Great Highway than anywhere else he had yet visited. The king's castle stood almost half a mile to the south of the highway, and the entire distance from castle to highway appeared to be a network of streets and gardens and houses and shops. A few of the major avenues were even paved.

The Great Highway itself was not paved, but it *was* lined with plank sidewalks, inns, taverns, brothels, and shops, and three broad flagstone boulevards connected it to a generous market square that lay one block to the south.

An elaborate fountain occupied the center of the square, with a basin of red marble surrounding a white marble column topped by a statue of a woman pouring water from a jug, water that flowed endlessly. Smaller carvings of various sorts adorned the rim. Kelder was not accustomed to this sort of civic display.

For a moment he wondered if Krithim constituted a "great city," but despite the urban niceties he decided it was just a large town—or perhaps a small city, but not a great one.

Children were running about the market in a vigorous game of tag, ducking out of each other's reach, dodging back and forth. One of them took a shortcut through the marble basin, splashing wildly, and Kelder shouted a protest, but no one else seemed to mind, and the boy ignored him, so he let it drop.

Asha was watching the carefree game enviously; Ezdral was eyeing the wineshops. Kelder's own feet were sore; they were out of the hills now, but the road from Ophera had been rocky in places.

"Oh, Hell," he said, "I guess we'll stay here today and go on tomorrow."

Irith smiled radiantly at him.

"Where's a good inn?" he asked.

"There are a couple of good ones," Irith said thoughtfully.

"A cheap one," Kelder suggested. "We still don't have much money."

"The Leaping Fish," Irith declared.

"The Leaping Fish?" Kelder asked dubiously. "Why would they name it that?"

Irith shrugged. "I don't know," she said, "but they did."

"Are we near the sea?"

Irith giggled. "No, of *course* not!" she said. "It must be fifty miles to the sea from here!"

"A lake, then, or a stream?"

Irith shook her head. "They just call it that," she said. "It's over that way, on the Street of Coopers." She pointed to the west.

Kelder nodded and looked at the others.

It seemed to him that they had all seen quite enough of each other for a while. "Asha," he said, "you go on and play, if you like, but be at the inn for supper. The Leaping Fish, it's called, over that way—if you can't find it ask someone for directions."

"All right, Kelder!" She ran off, and a moment later she was shouting and playing with the others.

Kelder looked at Irith and Ezdral.

Ezdral was eyeing the wineshops—but he was also watching Irith. The love spell had as strong a hold as ever, and he wasn't going to leave her side, not even to get liquor. Kelder sighed, trying to think what he should do.

Irith, however, had also seen the situation and had her own solution. She vanished.

"Irith!" Ezdral screamed. "Irith, come back!"

People turned to stare at the green-clad old man, standing in the middle of the square, whirling about as if trying to look in every direction at once, groping madly with his arms outstretched, as if he were blind and searching for something.

"Ezdral," Kelder shouted, grabbing one flailing arm, "Ezdral, it's all right! She'll be back! She'll meet us tonight at supper, at the Leaping Fish!"

It took him several minutes to calm the old man; during that time, from the corner of his eye, he glimpsed a small, graceful black cat hurrying away, dashing between legs and scampering around boots. He saw the cat turn and deliberately wink at him before disappearing into an alley.

Ezdral did not notice the cat; he was too distraught to remember Irith's other shapes. Kelder supposed that if he *had* seen the cat, he would have been in love with it—with her—but that had not happened.

Which was all for the best.

Eventually Ezdral did calm down, and stood, drooping and silent, by Kelder's side. "She'll meet us tonight," Kelder assured him.

Ezdral nodded dismally and without a word headed for the nearest wineshop.

Kelder watched him go and then looked around, realizing that he was alone in this pleasant and interesting place. He would have preferred Irith's company, but he saw no sign that she was returning, and could not see any way to be with her out in the open without having Ezdral along—and he did *not* want Ezdral along, fawning over Irith, following her everywhere as closely as he dared, constantly lusting after her. The old man was terrible company.

Alone, then, in Krithimion—that wasn't so terrible. He smiled, threw Asha a glance and a wave, and set out toward the castle with the intention of exploring the town a little before finding work.

An hour or so later, after he had had his fill of windowshopping, Kelder arrived at the castle gate, which seemed as likely a place as any to ask for employment. The gate was open, and two guardsmen were chatting idly in the archway.

"*Hai,*" Kelder called. "Excuse me!"

The guards turned to consider him. They did not speak, giving him no clue as to whether or not they knew the language in its unadulterated form. Here on the Great Highway, though, they really *ought* to know it, Kelder told himself. He forged onward.

"Hello," he said, approaching to a polite distance and still speaking Trader's Tongue. "I'm passing through and a little short of cash; would you happen to know of any way I might earn a little money around here?"

"There must be a dozen merchants in town . . ." one soldier began, in the same language, but his companion's hand on his arm startled him into silence.

"You're looking for a way to earn money?" the other asked, grinning.

Not pleased by the grin, Kelder nodded. "That's right," he said.

"Well, it just so happens," the grinning soldier said, "that I know of a wizard who said he'd pay well for some help."

Kelder did not like the guard's attitude at all, but on the other hand he remembered that Irith had been paid in silver for her errand in Ophera. Wizards did have money, generally, and were free enough with it.

He suspected that he had been badly underpaid for the work he had done in the last few towns, but as a beggar, to all intents and purposes, what could he do about it?

Here, though, he had a chance to do better—maybe.

"What sort of help?" he asked suspiciously.

"Oh, just help," the guard said, exchanging a smirk with his comrade.

It couldn't hurt to check it out, Kelder thought. "Where?"

"Senesson of Yolder, on Carter Street," the guard said, pointing. "Down the hill here, turn left at the little blue shrine, turn right on the second cross-street, and look for the shop with the green tile over the door."

"Green . . ." Kelder said, "green what?" He had never encountered the word for "tile" in Trader's Tongue before.

"Green roof," the guard said.

That Kelder understood. "Thank you," he said, with a polite half-bow.

Down the hill he went, strolling slowly until he spotted the blue shrine—it was a fountain, built into the outside corner of a bakery, with a bright blue ceramic glaze lining it and a small golden statuette of a goddess, no more than a foot tall, set into the wall behind it. The gold leaf on the idol had flaked a little, and the water that sprayed from beneath the goddess' feet was slightly discolored. He turned left, between the bakery and an iron-fenced garden.

The first cross-street was a muddy alleyway, but he counted it anyway, and turned right onto a narrow, deserted byway. He had gone almost three blocks and was just deciding that he should not have counted the alley, when he spotted a shop with a rather complex façade. A five-sided bay window, its innumerable small panes hexagonal in shape, took up most of the ground-level front, while the upstairs displayed turrets and shutters with elaborate carvings. The front door, just beyond the bay window, was of oiled wood bound in brass, with designs etched in the metal and monstrous faces carved in bas relief on the wood.

And above this door was a small decorative overhang, and on top of the overhang were three rows of curved green tile.

There was no signboard, and the window display was an incomprehensible array of arrangements of silver wire, but it looked like the right place, and when he stepped up to the door he found that the design etched into the brass bar at eye level included a line of Ethsharitic runes reading SENESSON OF YOLDER, WIZARD EXTRAORDINARY.

Kelder was about to knock when the door swung open; before he could react even enough to lower his fist, a girl charged directly into him, knocking him back a step.

"Get out of the way, stupid," she snarled in Ethsharitic.

"Excuse me," Kelder said in the same language, "but I wanted to work . . ."

"So did I, but I won't do it here!" She tried to push past him, and Kelder stepped back, but then he reached out and caught her arm.

She whirled, aiming a punch at his belly, but he sidestepped in time to miss most of it, keeping hold of her other wrist. She was short and thin, her strength unremarkable, so maintaining his grip was not particularly difficult.

"Wait a minute," he said, inadvertently slipping into the Trader's Tongue he had been using almost exclusively for more than a sixnight, "I need to talk to you."

She yanked her arm free, and he let it go. "I don't speak that," she said, still in Ethsharitic, "whatever it is."

"Sorry," he said, switching back to Ethsharitic. "I need to talk to you."

"No, you don't," she said, turning away.

"Wait!" he called. "What's wrong with working here?"

She took one step, then stopped and turned back. "You don't know?" she asked.

He shook his head.

"Are you from around here?" she asked.

"No," he said, "I'm from Shulara."

"I never heard of it," she said.

There was definitely, he noticed, something a little different about the way she spoke Ethsharitic; she spoke slightly faster than he had heard it before and slurred the consonants a bit. It was not at all like the Krithimionese he had heard spoken around town. "It's southeast," he said. "Where are you from?"

"None of your business," she said.

He raised his hands, conceding the point. "All right," he said, "but what's wrong with the work?"

She glowered at him, standing with her hands on her hips, considering, and then snapped, "You don't know?"

"No," he said. "The guards at the castle told me I could earn money here. That's all I know."

She snorted. "They were joking," she said. "Either that, or they were trying to insult you."

"Why?"

"Because," she said, her tone turning sarcastic, "you *probably* don't qualify for the job."

"Why not?"

"Senesson isn't looking for workers," she explained, "he's buying materials."

"What materials?" Kelder asked, still puzzled.

"Virgin's blood," the girl said angrily.

Kelder blinked and looked the girl over.

She was roughly his own age, he guessed, despite her diminutive stature; she had long black hair that flowed down across her shoulders in flamboyant masses of darkly shining curls, a heart-shaped face and a long straight nose, a full bosom, narrow waist, and lush hips.

"It's none of my business," he said, "but . . ." He stopped.

He had intended to ask if she qualified any more than he did, but that hardly seemed like an appropriate question to ask a stranger.

If she *did*, he thought, he'd be surprised. She was no incredible beauty, certainly not in Irith's class, but she was attractive enough.

"You're right," she said, "it's none of your business."

He smiled. "You're right," he said, "I'm sorry." He turned away from the brass-trimmed door.

"Aren't you going to knock?" the girl asked.

"No," Kelder said, "I don't think so, not if that's what he wants."

She stared at him for a moment. "I could be lying," she said. "You don't have to take my word."

"No, I believe you," Kelder said. "Do you know of anywhere else I might find work?"

She shook her head.

"Where are you going, then?" he asked.

"Back to the market square," she answered.

"Me, too," he said.

"All right," she said, and together they strolled up the street, away from the shop with the green tile overhang.

CHAPTER 27

It was half an hour before he got around to asking her name.

"Azraya," she said, throwing another pebble at the dove by the fountain, "Azraya of Ethshar."

The bird fluttered up into the air, then landed and turned to peck at the pebble, seeing if it was edible.

"You're from Ethshar?" Kelder asked, leaning back on the bench.

"I just said so, didn't I?" Azraya snapped.

"No," Kelder replied mildly, "you said that was your cognomen, not that you came from there."

"Same thing," Azraya said, only slightly mollified.

"I suppose it is," Kelder agreed. "Sorry."

They were still speaking Ethsharitic, having discovered that Azraya spoke no Shularan, Trader's Tongue, Aryomoric, Uramoric, or Elankoran, and that Kelder spoke no Tintallionese or Sardironese. Neither of them spoke Krithimionese, but Azraya could sometimes follow it, and Kelder, knowing both its constituent tongues, understood it pretty well. Still, Ethsharitic was the only language they had in common.

"So what's your name?" Azraya asked.

"Kelder," Kelder said. "Kelder of Shulara."

She looked at him doubtfully for a moment, not an unusual reaction to Kelder's name, and eventually decided that he was telling the truth. Either that, or that the truth didn't matter.

"Kelder," she said, watching the dove. "All right."

"You're heading east, on the Great Highway?" he asked.

"No," she said.

"West, then? Back to Ethshar?"

"Probably. Which way are you going, back to Shulara?"

"No, to Ethshar."

She nodded. "So this is where you hit the highway, coming from Shulara?"

"No, I reached the highway in Hlimora at first and went east to Shan on the Desert. Now I'm heading west."

She looked up, interested. "You've been to Shan?"

Kelder nodded.

"What's it like?"

He shrugged. "We didn't stay long," he said. "I think it's seen better days." He was becoming more comfortable speaking Ethsharitic, now that he'd had a little practice.

"Oh," Azraya said, disappointed. "What about the other towns along the way?"

"Well," Kelder said, "this place, Krithim, is the nicest I've seen yet."

"Oh," Azraya said again. She tossed another pebble and the dove flapped wildly for a moment, then wheeled into the air and flew away. "I guess I'll be going back to Ethshar, then."

"Why were you traveling in the first place?" Kelder asked.

"None of your—oh, damn it, it doesn't matter." She slumped forward, chin on her hands, elbows on her knees.

At first, Kelder took this to mean that she was going to answer his question, but after a moment it became clear that she wasn't going to say anything without further urging.

"Maybe it doesn't matter," he said, "but I'm curious."

She turned her head to glare at him around an errant ringlet of hair. "Why?" she demanded.

"Oh, I just like to know things," Kelder said rather feebly.

She turned back to staring at the cobbles.

"When I was eight," she said, "my parents died of a fever."

Kelder, realizing he was about to get the whole story, nodded encouragingly.

"We couldn't afford a theurgist to pray over them," Azraya continued, "or a witch to hex them, or a wizard to cast spells on them, so they died. Two of my brothers died, too, and my older sister—the neighbors were all so afraid of catching it that they wouldn't come near us, they shut up our house with us inside. That left me, and my younger sister Amari, and our baby brother Regran. I was the oldest, so I tried to take care of them, and I would sneak out of the house and steal food and things for them. And when the fever was gone, I took the boards off the doors, and then the tax collectors came and took the house away because we couldn't pay, we didn't know where our parents had hidden their money—if they had any."

Kelder made a sympathetic noise.

"So we all went to the Hundred-Foot Field and lived there, with the beggars and thieves." Azraya went on. "In the block between Panderer Street and Superstition Street, in the Camptown district. Our house was in Eastwark, but our old neighbors . . . well, we thought we'd do better in Camptown, and the Hundred-Foot Field goes all the way around the city."

Kelder had no idea what this meant—he had never heard of the Hundred-Foot Field or anything else she mentioned. Interrupting to ask for an explanation did not seem like a very good idea, however, so he let her go on.

"I didn't steal," she said, "not after we lost the house. I think Amari did, but I didn't. I begged when I had to and ran errands for people when I could—one good thing about Camptown, the soldiers usually had errands we could run, taking messages to their women, or fetching things from the Wizards' Quarter for them, or even just standing lookout when they were supposed to be on duty and wanted a nap, or a little time in bed with someone, or a game of dice." She took a deep breath. "Regran died when he was two, just before my tenth birthday," she said. "I'm not sure what he died of, he just got sick and died. Somebody had kicked him, maybe that did something, I don't know. We'd done everything we could for him, even found a wetnurse and paid her half what we earned for a few months, but sometimes babies just die. After that, Amari and I didn't stay together much anymore, and I lost track of her after a while. I haven't seen her in a couple of years now. She might be dead, too." She paused, remembering.

Kelder wanted to say something comforting, but before he could think of anything and phrase it in Ethsharitic, Azraya resumed her story.

"I told you we lived near Panderer Street," she said. "Well, the panderers noticed me, after a while, and I started avoiding them. And by the time I was thirteen I didn't run any more errands on Pimp Street or Whore Street, either."

Kelder did not recognize the Ethsharitic words for panderer, pimp, or whore, but he could make a guess what she was saying.

"And after a while, I decided that I was tired of it. I was tired of the Hundred-Foot Field, the mud and the flies and the lunatics talking to themselves and the thieves going through your bedding every time you were out of sight, and I was tired of being harassed by the pimps, and I was tired of the soldiers and their errands—they were propositioning me, too, by this time. So I went to the markets to find work, but I didn't find anything at first, just more pimps, and slavers, and farmers who wouldn't take me as a field hand because I'm not big enough. I was too old to apprentice—I should have found something when I was twelve, but I didn't, I missed my chance."

Kelder nodded in sympathy. Maybe he should have found an apprenticeship on his own, regardless of what his parents wanted—but he hadn't.

"Anyway, eventually I got to Shiphaven Market, and I thought I would sign up to be a sailor, but there was someone there looking for volunteers to join a dragon hunt in the Small Kingdoms, and I thought that would be wonderful. It was a way out of the city, and I may be small, but I'm not stupid, and I'm stronger than I look—I thought I might help in a dragon hunt. So I signed up."

"A dragon?" Kelder looked at her with renewed respect. She was brave, anyway—either that, or crazy.

She nodded. "The reward was a thousand pieces of gold,

he said. I knew I couldn't kill a dragon myself, but I thought maybe I could help out and get a share."

"Where was this dragon?" Kelder asked. "How big was it?"

"It's in a place called Dwomor," Azraya said, "south of here. I don't really know how big the dragon is—as far as I know, it's still there."

Kelder had heard of Dwomor; it was one of the larger Small Kingdoms, up in the high mountains in the central region. If one was looking for a dragon, that was a likely place to start, he had to admit. "You didn't kill it?" he asked.

"I didn't try," Azraya said.

"Why not?"

She sighed.

"They signed up a whole boatload of us," she said, "and we all sailed off across the Gulf of the East, and up a river to Ekeroa, and then they loaded us in wagons and took us to Dwomor, and we all got introduced to the king, and it all looked good, nobody bothered me, nobody tried to touch me, all they cared about was the dragon, I thought. Dwomor wasn't exactly beautiful, but it was different, anyway. The whole castle was full of dragon-hunters, and they were forming into teams, and I thought I'd be able to join a team and get a share—and then the Lord Chamberlain took me aside and explained a few things."

"Like what?"

"Like what the reward was," Azraya said bitterly. "The recruiter lied. Oh, there were a thousand pieces of gold, and a position in the king's service, but those weren't the reward; those were his daughters' dowry. The *reward* was that whoever killed the dragon got to marry one of his daughters. He had five of them, not counting the married one, so he was sending the hunters out in five-man teams. Five *men*."

"Oh," Kelder said, understanding the situation immediately. Surplus princesses were a well-known phenomenon in the Small Kingdoms, a common subject of lewd jokes—there were never enough princes to go around, and custom decreed that princesses could marry commoners only under exceptional circumstances. Slaying a dragon qualified a commoner as exceptional.

"I don't know if they'd have sent me back to Ethshar," Azraya said. "I didn't wait to find out. I just set out, to see where I went. I've been wandering for months, through Ekeroa and Pethmor and Ressamor, doing what odd jobs I could, stealing when I couldn't eat any other way, and last night I arrived here in Krithim, and now I need to decide whether to give up and go back to Ethshar, or to keep looking."

"Looking for what?" Kelder asked.

"I don't know," she said. "Just someplace to live, I guess, where I won't have to beg or whore or sleep in the mud."

She paused. Kelder thought she had finished, and was about to say something, when she added, "Or sell my blood to some slimy old wizard."

CHAPTER 28

"We're staying at the Leaping Fish," Kelder told Azraya as they parted. "If you'd like to meet us there for supper . . ."

"Don't count on it," Azraya said.

Kelder watched her go, then turned and headed back for the castle. The guards might have misdirected him before, but it still seemed to be the best place to look for work. Azraya disagreed and was going her own way.

He rather regretted that; he liked her.

Maybe, he told himself wryly, he was just a sucker for sad stories and losers. Maybe Zindré had guessed that, and had suggested he would champion the lost and forlorn not from magical foreknowledge but just from his character. Asha, with her abusive drunkard of a father; Ezdral, with his love spell and alcoholism; even Irith, with her unbreakable enchantments—they were all among the unfortunates of the World.

And poor orphaned Azraya was another.

Azraya wasn't looking for a champion, though; she could obviously take care of herself.

The four of them made a boring life on a farm in Shulara look pretty good by comparison.

This time, when Kelder asked, the soldiers at the castle gate made no jokes and grinned no grins; the one who had directed him to Senesson was apologetic, the other sullen.

"Sorry," the first one said, "if Senesson can't use you, I don't have any suggestions. There must be merchants who could use some help loading their wagons, I suppose."

Kelder was about to say something more when a cat meowed by his feet. He turned, and Irith was standing beside him.

"Gods and demons!" one of the soldiers exclaimed.

"What's the matter?" Kelder asked him.

"She just *appeared*, out of nowhere!" the guard said. "It startled me—I thought my heart would burst!"

"That's Irith the Flyer," the other one said. "She can do that."

"I know who she *is*," the first guard said, "but I never saw her *do* that before, and it startled me, all right?"

"Hello," Irith said. "I'm here to see the king's wizard—he does still have one, doesn't he?"

The guards looked at one another.

"He had one the last time I was here," she said. "Her name was Perina something."

"Perina the Wise," one guard said. "She's still here. There are also two witches and a sorcerer."

"I'm only looking for wizards, thanks," Irith said. "May we go in?"

"We?"

"He's with me," Irith said, taking Kelder's hand.

The guards exchanged glances again, and then one of them shrugged.

"What the hell," he said. "Let them in."

"I think we better send an escort," the other replied.

The first considered, and agreed.

"Wait here," he said. Then he turned and hurried inside.

While they were waiting, Kelder remarked, "There's a wizard a few blocks over that way by the name of Senesson of Yolder—do you think he might have a counterspell?"

"Who knows?" Irith said. "I know who you mean; he's a nasty old man, but we can ask him when we're done here."

Kelder nodded. He was about to say something about meeting Azraya there when the soldier returned, accompanied by yet another soldier. "I'll escort you to the wizard's workshop," the new arrival said, without preamble.

"Thank you," Kelder said. "Lead on."

The wizard's workshop proved to be at the top of a distressingly long staircase; as they finally neared the top, Kelder panting and Irith making a great effort not to, the Flyer turned to her companion and muttered, "You can do what you like, Kelder, but I'm *flying* down." She touched the bloodstone at her throat and then stood up straight, her fatigue seemingly vanished, as she took the last few steps.

"I don't blame you," he wheezed back. "I would, too, if I could."

The guardsman seemed untroubled by the climb. He paused for a few seconds at the top of the stair to allow them to catch their breath—not enough seconds, in Kelder's opinion, but a few—and then rapped on the blackened wood door.

A complex and unfamiliar rune glowed white against the black, and a hollow voice asked, "Who goes there?" It spoke in Trader's Tongue, Kelder noticed.

"Two visitors to see Perina the Wise," the soldier said in what Kelder took at first for awkward Ethsharitic, then recognized as Krithimionese. "I know one to be Irith the Flyer; the other I do not recognize."

"Kelder of Shulara," Kelder volunteered, wondering why the man was answering one language with another.

For a moment, nothing happened; then the door swung open and a woman's voice called out, in the Krithimionese dialect, "Come in, Irith, and bring your friend! Thank you, Kelder, you may go."

As Kelder hesitated, the soldier bowed quickly, turned, and headed back down the staircase.

"Wait," Kelder called after him, "she said Kelder . . ."

"That's me," the soldier called back. "Kelder the Tall. No jokes, please." Then he was gone, around a bend in the stair.

Kelder muttered, "I'd hardly be the one to joke about the name, would I?" Then he followed Irith through the door.

The workshop was a large room, with windows on three sides, tables and bookcases here and there, fur rugs on the floor, and a spiral stair in the center. Standing on the stair was a handsome middle-aged woman, a streak of white in her black hair.

"Irith," she said, descending to the floor, "how good to see you!" She spoke Krithimionese, but Kelder could follow it well enough.

"Hello, Perina," Irith said in the same tongue as she stepped into the room far enough to close the door. "This is Kelder of Shulara; he's been very helpful lately."

That was not exactly Kelder's idea of a great introduction, but he smiled and said, "Hello."

"I haven't seen you for more than a year," Perina said to Irith, ignoring Kelder as she crossed the room. "What brings you here now?"

"Well, I need a spell," Irith said. "Or a counterspell, really."

Perina came and took the girl by the hand. "Come and sit down and tell me all about it," she said as she led the way to a small settee, upholstered in gold-embroidered burgundy velvet.

Kelder, feeling out of place, followed.

"Well, it seems I enchanted someone," Irith said, as she sank onto the cushions. "I didn't really *mean* to, exactly."

Perina nodded encouragingly and sat down, as well; Kelder, seeing no space remaining, stayed standing and began to wander toward a nearby shelf as if that was what he had intended all along.

"I put this spell on him, and I sort of thought it would wear off, but it *didn't*, and now he's an old man and he still has this spell on him, and it's pretty awful, so I'd really like to know how to break it," Irith said. Kelder looked over the tidy row of skulls atop the bookcase, trying to identify them all; the human was easy, of course, and he was pretty sure of the cat and the horse, but some of the others puzzled him.

"It sounds terrible," Perina said, patting Irith on the knee. "Which spell was it, my dear?"

"Fendel's Infatuous Love Spell," Irith said. Then she added, "I think."

Kelder glanced at her, forgetting about the odd skull with the horns. This was the first time he had heard her say that she wasn't entirely certain about which spell it was.

"Oh, that's a bad one," Perina said, clicking her tongue in rebuke. "It's tricky, you know; it can go wrong in ever so many ways."

Kelder looked at her hopefully, then quickly turned back to the shelves. Directly below the skulls was an impressive array of strangely shaped bottles, none of them labeled, and he wondered not just what might be in them but how Perina could tell.

"Do you know it?" Irith asked.

"No, not really," Perina admitted. "I've *heard* about it, but the Infallible Love Philtre is so much more convenient that I never bothered with it—all those stories about people falling in love with the wrong person, or even with animals!" She shook her head in dismay. "Fendel was a brilliant man, but even the best of us isn't perfect, and that spell is just nothing but trouble. Whyever did you use it?"

"It's the only love spell I have," Irith said. "I didn't see any others in Kalirin's book, when I was an apprentice."

"Well, I don't suppose old—Kalirin, was it? Your master?" Perina asked.

Irith nodded.

"Well, I don't suppose he had much call for love spells, after all," Perina said. "It's too bad."

Kelder wondered why anyone would make a bottle with two necks, both of them twisted into complete loops. And was there a reason to use blue glass for it?

"So you don't know the counter?" Irith asked.

"I'm afraid not, my dear," Perina admitted, patting Irith's knee again. "I'm *so* sorry."

The third shelf held even more bottles, but these were more ordinary—that is, if Kelder ignored the fact that something was moving in that big one second from the left and that the one fourth from the right was watching him with green glass eyes.

"I do believe it has blood in it somewhere," Perina said thoughtfully. "I've *heard* that."

"Virgin's blood?" Irith asked.

Perina shook her head. "No, I don't *think* so," she said, "but I'm really not sure. Oh, dear."

Something thin and black from the bottom shelf was reaching out for his leg, Kelder realized; he stepped back suddenly and almost trod on Irith's foot. The tendril, or whatever it was, retreated.

"Listen," Perina said, "if you *do* find a counterspell, you tell me about it, won't you? Please? It could be useful, you know."

"Sure," Irith said. "And if you hear anything, you'll tell me?"

"Oh, assuredly!"

The bottom shelf held jars; most of them had no lids, and they all appeared to contain plants, none of which Kelder recognized. The tendril came from something resembling a malevolent cabbage.

Did that qualify as a strange beast, in the terms of Zindré's predictions? Did those peculiar bottled things? Certainly there was much magic here, though he didn't know how mighty it was.

"Is there anyone you think might know the countercharm?" Irith asked. "We're heading west—we thought someone in Ethshar might know."

Perina considered that carefully, as Kelder moved on to another bookcase. This one actually held books on most of its shelves, which seemed less dangerous.

"I'm *sure* there are people in Ethshar who would know," Perina said. "That nice Thorum the Mage, on Wizard Street—if he doesn't know himself, I'm *sure* he can find someone who does, he's just the sweetest man."

Irith nodded. Kelder tried to read the titles on a few bindings and found most were in unfamiliar languages.

"Iridith of Ethshar, if you can find her," Perina went on. "She seems to know just about *everything*, I think. But I don't have any idea at *all* where she lives—she won't say." She smiled oddly and said, "And of course there's always Fendel the Great himself—the rumor is that he's still alive, living like a hermit somewhere in Tintallion or some such place."

Kelder looked up at that, then back, and blinked. Hadn't that title been different before?

"For that matter," Perina mused, "is your old master, what was the name?"

"Kalirin the Clever," Irith supplied.

"Yes, Kalirin—is he dead?"

"Oh, I think so," Irith said. "I heard that he was, and I haven't seen him since, oh, 5025, I think it was."

"That's almost two hundred years ago," Perina said, "so I suppose he *must* be dead." She sighed.

Kelder decided that maybe he would do better to just look out a window and strolled over to one.

"So you don't have any more ideas?" Irith asked.

"No, I'm afraid I don't," Perina admitted.

Kelder looked out the window and decided maybe that was a mistake after all, because it wasn't Krithimion on the other side of the glass at all, it was someplace where waves were smashing against black rocks at the foot of a high, curving cliff and ancient, crooked buildings of rough stone stood atop it; the window seemed to be somewhere on the clifftop, looking along the rim, with the sea to the left and the buildings to the right.

That was mighty magic, he was fairly certain.

"As long as we're here," Irith said, rising, "Kelder and I are a little short of money just now. Were there any little errands that you'd like done?"

Kelder stepped to the next window and was relieved to find a perfectly normal view of Krithim, laid out below them like a collection of toys; the only unsettling thing about it was how very high up they were. The wizard's workshop was clearly atop the tallest tower in the castle.

"Oh, I can't think of any just now," Perina said, as she, too, got to her feet, "but I can loan you a few pieces of silver if you like, and when you find that countercharm that will cover it. It would be worth, oh, I'd say ten pieces to me, and I could give you half of that now."

"What if we don't find it?" Kelder asked, breaking his silence.

"Oh, Kelder, don't be such a bore," Irith said.

"Then you'll find some other way to pay me back," Perina said, dismissing the problem with a wave.

Kelder hesitated, but he was tired of doing stupid little jobs and constantly worrying about where the next meal was coming from. Five pieces of silver—that was fifty in copper, four hundred bits. Added to the handful they had, that would make life a good bit easier all around.

Irith threw him a questioning look, and he nodded.

"Thank you, Perina," the shapeshifter said, "that would be wonderful."

"Wait right here, then," she said, "I'll get my purse." She hurried to the spiral stair.

That left Irith and Kelder standing a few feet apart, with no one else in the room. Kelder said quietly, "She seems to know a lot."

"Hmm?" Irith looked at him questioningly.

"Well, I mean, all this magical stuff here, and all those powerful wizards she was talking about—if *she* doesn't know the countercharm it must be pretty obscure."

Irith shook her head. "Silly," she said, "don't let Peri fool you; she's not part of any inner circle or anything. She *inherited* all this stuff from her mother—*she* was a great wizard. And she collected stuff, weird stuff—a lot of it is accidental one-of-a-kind things that nobody knows what they do, things that happened when a spell went wrong. It's not Peri's magic. Peri's just a name-dropper; she met all those people when she was little and they visited her mother, or her mother took her along visiting them, or maybe she just heard her mother talking about them. She probably hasn't seen Thorum in fifteen years, and she probably never met Fendel at all. She probably hasn't read half these books. In fact, she probably hasn't read *any* of them."

"Oh," Kelder said.

"The countercharm could be in one of them," Irith said, "but we'd never find it. We'd probably get killed by some silly warding spell if we tried to look for it."

"Oh," Kelder said again.

Then Perina reappeared, descending the stair, a velvet purse in her hand.

"Here we go," she said, pulling out a handful of coins.

When the money was safely tucked away—three pieces in silver in Kelder's purse, two in Irith's, and the rest back where it came from—Irith kissed Perina good-bye and stepped to the window.

"Must you go?" Perina asked, as Irith opened the casement.

"I'm afraid so," Irith said, as wings sprouted from her shoulder blades.

"Well, take care." She and Kelder watched as Irith stepped up on the sill and then flew away.

Feeling suddenly awkward, Kelder said, "Well, I guess I'll be going, too."

Perina smiled at him. "Oh, I'm sure," she said. "Tell me, though, lad, how did you meet Irith?"

Kelder shrugged. "Just bumped into her on the highway," he said.

"You've taken a fancy to her, haven't you? I can always tell these things." She smiled a smile that Kelder supposed was meant to be conspiratorial; it came off as condescending, instead.

"I suppose," Kelder mumbled.

"It shows," Perina said. "At least, to someone as experienced as I am it does."

"I'm sure it does," he muttered, embarrassed.

"I might be able to do something for you, you know," she said.

Kelder blinked.

"I really don't know Fendel's Infatuous Love Spell," she said, "but I do ... Oh, it isn't *you* she used it on, is it?"

"No, of course not!" Kelder said uneasily.

He didn't *think* Irith had used any spells on him, but how could he be sure she didn't have others, less powerful than the one she had used on Ezdral? *That* was an unpleasant notion.

"Oh, good, I didn't think so," Perina continued, smiling—smirking, almost. "Well, then. I don't know that one, but I *do* know some others. There's the Infallible Love Philtre, and, well . . ." She paused and cleared her throat. "There's the Spell of Aroused Lust, which isn't *exactly* a love spell—and others, too. And I was wondering whether you might be interested."

"To use on Irith?" Kelder asked.

Perina nodded, her smile coy.

For a moment, Kelder seriously considered the idea. He wanted Irith, wanted to marry her, and if she were enchanted, the way Ezdral was, he could have her, for as long as he wanted. She wouldn't argue with him anymore. She wouldn't get bored and fly away. She would be very much in his power.

It was tempting, no doubt about it.

But it would also be cruel, and unfair, and disgusting. And it might well cause just as much trouble in the long run as the spell on Ezdral. It would be far better to let Irith make up her *own* mind. She liked him, he knew she did. She would marry him, eventually, without any spells. She would come back to Shulara. Zindré's prophecy said as much.

Of course, this might have been part of the prophecy, this offer of a love spell; by turning it down he might be voiding Zindré's promises. All the same, he was resolved to do so. Magically-induced love was not what he wanted.

And then, after he had decided that he wanted Irith to love him naturally if she was going to love him at all, he remembered something.

Spells didn't work on Irith anymore. Wizardry could not affect her. She had challenged wizards to magical duels and then laughed at them as their spells left her untouched. Any love philtre, potion, or aphrodisiac would be utterly useless on her.

Did Perina know that? Was she trying to trick him?

Or did she have some other purpose in mind?

"I don't have much money . . ." he began.

She waved that away. "No, no," she said. "For you, it's free."

"Um . . . Why?"

"Because I just want to see you youngsters *happy*, that's all!"

"Well," said Kelder, "thank you, I appreciate it, and I'll think it over."

"You do that," she said as he made his escape, out the door to the stairway.

The question of just why she had made the offer gave him something to think about all the way to the bottom.

CHAPTER 29

The question of Perina's motives stayed at the back of Kelder's mind for the rest of the afternoon, nibbling away at his attention as he met Irith at the gate and led her to Senesson's shop. This time he knocked, and the two of them were admitted to the wizard's presence.

Senesson was a bent, gray old man; Kelder wondered if he might have found some way to live past his time, but without ever learning any youth spells, because he could easily have been a century old—Ezdral would have seemed to be in the very flower of youthful vigor by comparison. The wizard had no teeth, making his speech hard to understand, and a strand of spittle hung swaying from one corner of his mouth. He cackled when anything amused him, which was often. He leered at Irith in a truly offensive manner, and Kelder could understand why Azraya had stamped out in a rage.

Senesson, who was only recently arrived in Krithimion, claimed to have met Irith before, long ago in another kingdom, but she didn't recall any such encounter. The wizard invited Kelder to take a seat in the shop while Senesson and Irith talked business in the workroom.

Kelder sat and mulled over Perina's offer, while in the next room Irith fended off the drooling old fool's lecherous advances and determined, at least to her own satisfaction, that he knew no countercharm for Fendel's Infatuous Love Spell. Kelder did pay attention to the conversation, however, and intervened when Senesson's lust threatened to get out of hand.

Irith was not as angry upon departing as Azraya had been, but she came close.

219

By the time Kelder and Irith sat down for supper at the Leaping Fish, he had come to the conclusion that Perina had either hoped to dupe him into giving Irith some other potion completely, not a love spell at all, or that she had some idea that if he used a love spell to control Irith, she could then control him, and thereby have the services of a remarkable and talented creature at her beck and call.

Kelder was not sure just what Perina would want with a tame shapeshifter, but he supposed there would be uses for one. With that out of the way, he began wondering whether Azraya would show up.

Asha and Ezdral arrived more or less on schedule; Asha was smiling and happy, Ezdral drunk and morose. The old man all but flung himself at Irith when he spotted her, and Kelder saw Irith flicker, as she started to turn herself invisible and then changed her mind.

Kelder pried Ezdral away from her, got the entire party seated around the table, and saw to the distribution of the meal the inn had supplied.

Azraya did not come, and even as he admired the way the lanterns lit Irith's hair, Kelder found himself a little disappointed.

Beautiful women, plural, Zindré had said—Kelder had not immediately thought of Azraya as beautiful, but now he realized that she qualified. Another phrase had been fulfilled, then. If the contents of Perina's tower counted for strange beasts and mighty magic, then the whole prophecy was coming along nicely. Another great city, another vast plain, then a triumphant return home with Irith as his bride, and he would have made the entire prediction come true.

That was just as well; he was beginning to tire of traveling, of eating and sleeping in inns like the Leaping Fish.

The food was good, if unexciting, and the meal uneventful, save that Ezdral's hands were so unsteady that he kept dropping things; every so often the clatter of a fork or mutton bone dropped on his plate would interrupt conversation.

After supper, the drunkard passed out on the floor of their L-shaped room before anyone could suggest he sleep elsewhere; Asha took the little featherbed that had been crammed onto the window seat in the dormer at the narrow end.

That left Irith and Kelder to share the big bed at the other end, out of sight of Asha even should she wake. Ezdral was obviously not going to awaken. The two made good use of this unexpected privacy, their first in days.

"It's only seven miles to Bugoa Castle," Irith said as they gathered up their belongings the next morning, "and maybe another eleven or twelve to Syndisha, so we should get at least that far today, shouldn't we?"

Ezdral groaned, but when Irith looked at him he immediately muttered, "Whatever you want, Irith."

Asha grimaced but agreed. "We can do that."

"Tuyoa is next beyond Syndisha," Irith went on. "About ten miles, I think. That might be too much."

"Probably," Kelder said, glancing at Ezdral.

"From Tuyoa it's about eight miles to Shesta, and then about that far again to Lamum," Irith said. "And Lamum Keep stands on the border between the Small Kingdoms and the Hegemony of Ethshar."

Kelder nodded, interested.

"Now, traditionally," Irith said, "they say it's two days from Lamum to Ethshar—one day to the Inn at the Bridge and one day from there to the gate."

"We're getting close, then," Kelder said.

Irith shook her head. "Not *that* close, though, because those days were figured by what an army could march, back during the Great War. It must be ten leagues from Valder's inn to Westgate."

Asha groaned at that, and even Kelder hesitated.

"It's not so bad, from Lamum to the inn," Irith said. "Maybe eight leagues."

"Well," Kelder said, hoisting his pack onto his shoulder, "we'll see how it goes."

"Maybe we'll find a wizard along the way who knows the charm," Asha said.

Irith replied thoughtfully, "You know, we just might."

"Oh?" Kelder asked.

"You remember Perina mentioned Iridith of Ethshar might know? Well, we might see her along the way."

That was a little vague for Kelder's liking. "Oh," he said again.

They made their way out of the town and onto the highway and had gone no more than half a mile when a familiar voice called, "*Hai*, Kelder!"

He turned and found Azraya of Ethshar striding up behind them.

"Azraya!" he called.

Irith gave Kelder a startled look, then eyed Azraya suspiciously. Asha looked mildly interested; Ezdral trudged on, a few feet behind Irith, paying no attention at all.

When the entire party stopped for introductions, Ezdral stopped, but he simply stood, hands at his sides, staring at Irith. One of his hands was twitching, Kelder noticed.

"This is Azraya of Ethshar," Kelder said in Trader's Tongue. "We met yesterday."

Azraya, recognizing her name, bowed politely.

"These are my traveling companions," he went on in Ethsharitic, uncomfortably aware that Asha didn't know the language. "This is Irith the Flyer, and Asha of Amramion, and Ezdral . . ." He paused, then looked at Ezdral's current condition and said, "Ezdral the Sot."

Irith made a polite acknowledgment, and Asha followed her lead; Ezdral managed only a ghastly imitation of a smile.

"We're bound for Ethshar," Kelder added. "Would you care to travel with us?"

"I suppose," Azraya said, "it would be safer."

Irith opened her mouth to say something, then thought better of it.

They reached Bugoa well before noon, to Kelder's pleased surprise. Asha was putting out a better effort in order to keep up with Azraya, who had a tendency to drift ahead of the others; Irith stayed even with Azraya, and Ezdral hurried to stay close to Irith. As a result, the whole party made better time than usual.

Bugoa Castle was large and rambling, with a village straggling off from its walls in all directions—but mostly, of course, between the castle and the highway, as the road came no closer than five hundred yards.

Kelder's little group, with a minimum of debate, decided to not even stop.

From Bugoa the road veered southward, rather than continuing west. Kelder suggested that the highway could have taken a straighter path, and Irith told him, "It used to, or at least there used to be an alternate route between Krithimion and Syndisha, by way of Mezgalon instead of Bugoa." She glanced back at Ezdral, who paid no attention to the conversation but whose haggard features brightened when he noticed Irith looking at him. "I'm not sure why they abandoned it," she said.

She had spoken in Trader's Tongue; Azraya asked Kelder what they were talking about, and he translated Irith's remarks, to the shapeshifter's obvious annoyance.

Whether roundabout or not, this stretch of the Great Highway was smooth and level, and again, they made excellent progress. At times, it seemed to Kelder that they were almost racing—Azraya and Irith seemed to be hurrying more than necessary. As a result, there was little or no conversation.

They were about a league from Bugoa when Asha tripped and fell, and Ezdral stumbled over her and toppled headlong. The girl burst out crying, and the drunkard simply lay facedown in the dirt.

Kelder and the two young women turned back to help. Irith lifted Asha back to her feet, but the child simply sat down again, sobbing.

Ezdral was heavier and even less cooperative, and when Azraya and Kelder between them were unable to get him upright, they settled for rolling him over on his back.

"What's wrong, Asha?" Irith asked, stroking the child's hair. "What's wrong?"

Asha shook her head.

Irith persisted, and at last Asha said, "I'm just *tired*."

"Maybe we've been hurrying too much," Kelder suggested. "Asha, would it help if you could ride?"

Irith glared at him for a second, then turned back to Asha and asked, "Do you want me to be a horse for a while?"

"No!" Asha exclaimed, so loudly that she startled everybody, including herself; even Ezdral twitched at the sound. "No," she repeated more quietly. "That's all right, Irith. Don't be a horse."

"What are they saying?" Azraya asked Kelder.

"Irith was asking Asha if she wanted to ride," Kelder replied.

Azraya looked at Kelder, puzzled. "Ride what?" she asked.

Kelder realized that the Ethsharite was unaware of Irith's magical abilities. "I'll explain later," he said.

"Can you walk again?" Irith asked Asha.

"Not yet," Asha said. "Let's just rest a little while."

Kelder relayed the suggestion to Azraya, who made a noise of displeasure. "I was hoping we could cross three kingdoms today," she said.

"I don't think so," Kelder told her.

"That's stupid," Azraya said. "Why do you travel with these people, anyway, Kelder?"

Irith glared at her.

"Asha doesn't have any family," he explained. "We happened to be there when her older brother got killed, so we're sort of taking care of her for now. And Irith accidentally enchanted Ezdral, so we're trying to find someone to break the spell."

"He's enchanted?"

"A love spell," Kelder said. "That's why he follows Irith."

"Oh," Azraya said. "So why is that your problem?"

"It's not," Kelder said. "I'm just trying to help out." Saying openly that he wanted to be a champion of the lost and forlorn seemed somehow ridiculous. Fortunately, Azraya did not press for further explanation.

Upon investigation the question of whether to press on turned out to be academic; Ezdral was unconscious.

"Now what?" Azraya asked.

Kelder sighed. "Now we wait here, eat some lunch—I have

cheese in my pack—and when we can bring him around we go on."

This did not sit well with either Azraya or Irith, but they both gave in, with ill-concealed annoyance. No one was about to try carrying Ezdral. Kelder suggested that even unconscious, he could be draped over Irith's back while she was in equine form, but she rejected the idea.

"He'll slip off," she said in Ethsharitic, "and besides, I don't want him on top of me. I don't care what form I'm in, or whether he's conscious, I don't want him on top of me."

This reference to changing forms led to Azraya asking questions about Irith's magic, which Kelder tried to answer as he shared out the cheese and wafers he had bought in Krithimion. Irith was clearly annoyed by this discussion of her past, but did nothing to stop it; she was settled crosslegged on the grass by the roadside, with Asha curled up on her lap, and any attempt to shout back or stomp off would have disturbed the child.

While they ate, they chatted idly—or tried to. Asha's ignorance of Ethsharitic, and Azraya's ignorance of Trader's Tongue, made conversation difficult. Irith grew steadily more aggravated by the constant demands either that she translate for someone or that she wait while Kelder did so.

Later on, after the last crumb was gone, the three teenagers made a concerted effort to rouse Ezdral, but without success.

"May demons eat his guts out!" Irith said, following this up with comments in several languages Kelder did not understand.

Azraya just laughed.

That was the last straw for Irith.

"I'll meet you in Syndisha," she said, spreading wings, "if you ever get there!" She flapped and took off.

Azraya stared in open-mouthed astonishment as Irith flew away to the south. "She really *does* fly!" she said.

"Yes, of course," Kelder said. "I told you she did."

Azraya looked at him with an unreadable expression, then back at Irith.

When the Flyer was out of sight, Azraya said, "Let me try

the Sot again." She began not merely shaking Ezdral, but slapping him, hard, first on one cheek, then the other.

"I wish Irith wouldn't fly off like that," Asha said, looking away uncomfortably.

"Me, too," Kelder agreed, putting an arm around the girl's shoulders.

Azraya gave up her attempt and stamped away, annoyed—not down the highway, but across the cornfield on one side. Kelder watched her go, wondering when she would be back—if ever. She was just as temperamental as Irith, though in a different way, and there was no prophecy assuring him that he would see her again.

Which was too bad; he did like Azraya, despite her temper.

Asha snuggled against him, and he looked down at her. Her blue tunic, the only garment she had, was wearing very thin—he wondered if Irith or Ezdral or Azraya could sew, an art he had never entirely mastered himself. They could buy fabric in Syndisha, though it would take a distressingly large portion of their money.

"Why didn't you want to ride?" he asked her.

She looked up at him. "Because I can't stand the way Ezdral looks at Irith when she's a horse," she said. "It makes me feel awful."

Kelder nodded.

"I can understand that," he said.

Together, they sat and waited.

CHAPTER 30

*A*zraya came back within a few minutes, and her next attempt to rouse Ezdral, a few minutes later, was successful. The four of them were on their way again shortly thereafter, and the sun was still only slightly past its zenith.

There were blue-uniformed guards at the Syndishan border, and without Irith along the party had no one they recognized; Kelder and Azraya had to make something called a "customs declaration," informing a scribe of all the magical articles they carried (none), how much gold they had (none), what livestock they were bringing into the kingdom (none), and whether they intended to settle down or were just passing through.

Ezdral was only semiconscious, so the officials informed Kelder that he was speaking for the Sot as well as himself. Asha being under age twelve, Azraya was arbitrarily chosen as her guardian and declared responsible for her actions as long as they were in Syndisha.

Azraya was not at all pleased about this, but tolerated it until one of the soldiers approached too closely. Then, suddenly, her belt knife was in her hand and she barked, "Don't touch me!"

The soldier in question spoke no Ethsharitic, but he got the message. After that, the officials quickly finished up and sent the party on its way.

They reached Syndisha Castle a little over an hour later, and as promised, Irith was waiting for them.

The castle was immense, incorporating the entire town; it was built in four concentric rings. Kelder could see that

much, and Irith confirmed it, while admitting that she might
have missed additional inner layers.

The outermost ring was a broad field between two stone
walls that served as the public market, where farmers wheeled
wagons of produce about, crying their wares, and various
groups stood about, discussing various business.

The next ring was the town itself, a single circular street
lined with inns and shops, with alleys branching off here and
there and a single broad cross-street that led from the market
gate across to the inner gate.

Irith said that the next layer in was where the wealthier
townsfolk lived, and the king's keep stood within that, but
Kelder never saw those for himself except for glimpses
through the gate.

"Why did they build it like this?" Kelder wondered aloud.

"Seems like good sense to me," Azraya said.

"Seems excessive to me," Kelder returned. "It must have
been expensive."

Irith shrugged. "This part of the Small Kingdoms has the
smallest and nastiest kingdoms of them all," she said. "I
mean, there's just one stupid little war after another, and it
seems as if half the princes go out and build castles and declare themselves kings. Maybe the Syndishans got thinking
about that and got a little carried away."

Attempts to locate a wizard turned up three warlocks, four
witches, and a theurgist, but no wizards. Since Irith's magic
was purely wizardry, that meant no chance of finding a countercharm in Syndisha.

On Irith's recommendation, they took lodgings at an inn
called the Broken Blade—and took two rooms. "If this
Azraya person is going to stay with us," Irith said, "we *have*
to. I mean, five people in one room is just too many!"

It didn't seem all that excessive to Kelder, who had seen
farmhands at harvest sleeping fifteen or twenty to a room, but
he didn't argue. Asha and Ezdral were in no shape to go any
farther, so the entire party was definitely staying the night in
Syndisha, and he wanted to keep things peaceful. Besides, di-

viding up three and two could mean that he would share a room with Irith.

It could, but it didn't.

Kelder was never quite sure just how the decision was made, but somehow the question never even came up; Irith, Asha, and Azraya took one room, and he and Ezdral got the other.

This did not suit him much—particularly since the dividing wall was thin enough that he could hear Irith and Azraya arguing, and later, when they had quieted and Ezdral was out cold, he found himself fantasizing that Irith might slip into the room in the middle of the night . . .

Or Azraya, for that matter, though he didn't really think she would.

Ezdral had gotten hold of *oushka* at dinner—he had had money somehow and had bought a bottle from the innkeeper. Kelder had tried to talk him out of it, but Ezdral was a free man and would do as he pleased, the lad had no authority over him.

Kelder had looked to Irith for support, knowing Ezdral would do whatever she told him, but she said, "Oh, let him drink it."

It was not a good night at all.

The next day's journey to Tuyoa wasn't any better; Asha and Ezdral seemed to be taking turns collapsing. Asha's falls were minor, and she recovered quickly, but Ezdral seemed to be deteriorating as Kelder watched. He stumbled all the time now, and his hands shook constantly. He spoke little and mumbled when he did. It took the entire day to get the five of them the twelve miles from Syndisha to Tuyoa.

This time it was Azraya who got fed up and marched on ahead, and Kelder feared he had seen the last of the short-tempered little Ethsharite, but when they reached Tuyoa she was leaning against the wall of a smithy, watching the village children chase a ball down the street.

Again, they took two rooms at an inn of Irith's choosing, and again divided the accommodations by sex. Kelder mentioned the sorry state of Asha's garb to Irith, who suggested they wait until they reached Ethshar.

"You can find some really good bargains there," she said. "You'd be surprised."

They had found no wizards in Syndisha, and they found none in Tuyoa. When they inquired, they were directed to two personable young men who turned out to be witches rather than wizards.

"I mean no offense," Irith said, turning away, "but it's not the same."

The following day was better; they reached Shesta Keep by noon and Castle Lamum well before dark. The road was veering westward again, toward the boundary between the Small Kingdoms and the Hegemony of Ethshar, and the landscape was changing from gently rolling hills to flat plain.

Lamum was blessed with two wizards, a sorcerer, and a warlock, but one of the wizards knew no counter for Fendel's Infatuous Love Spell, and the other was in the middle of a three-day ritual and could not be disturbed.

"Should we wait?" Irith asked.

Kelder looked at Ezdral, asleep on a bench in the town square, and said, "I don't think we should."

"It's two days to Ethshar yet," Irith said, "and *long* days, very long. Maybe we should rest here and see before we walk that far. Maybe it's the walking that's wearing Ezdral out."

Kelder considered that.

"I think we should wait," Asha said. "Walking is wearing *me* out."

Kelder looked for Azraya, but she was off window-shopping at a nearby bakery, out of earshot. "All right," he said, "we'll wait here, Ezdral and Asha and I—and Irith, you fly ahead, why don't you, and see what you can find, and then come back here."

"Fly to Ethshar, you mean?" she asked, startled.

"Well, yes, why not?"

"I don't know," she said. "Let me think about it."

She thought about it and decided she didn't like the idea. "It's a long way," she said, "and we'll get there soon enough.

What if I fly to some of the other kingdoms around here, instead? There's Thurion, to the north, and Porona to the east, and Thrullimion to the south."

Kelder had to admit that that was a perfectly sound idea, and so it was agreed. Irith would stay the night in Lamum and in the morning would start visiting the neighboring kingdoms, while the others waited.

At least, it was agreed among four of them. Asha wanted to rest; Ezdral did whatever Irith wanted; Irith and Kelder had arrived at this arrangement. Azraya, however, had other ideas.

"What, just sit here and fester?" she demanded.

"Or find work, if you like," Kelder answered mildly. "We don't have very much money left."

"Ha!" Azraya stamped off.

She made no mention of her plans that night, but in the morning she came down to the inn's breakfast with her shoulderbag packed, glaring belligerently at the others.

"You're going on without us?" Kelder asked, as they finished eating.

"You're damned right I am," she snarled.

"I wish you wouldn't," Kelder said, "but if you're going, good luck."

She stared at him for a moment, as if challenging him to say more, then said, "Good-bye, Kelder."

"Is there somewhere we can find you, when we get to Ethshar?" he called to her, as she turned toward the door.

She hesitated, then paused in the doorway and turned back. "If you really do ever get there," she said, "and if you really do want to find me, and it's not too late, come to the northeast corner of Shiphaven Market each morning. I've decided to take another try at finding a berth as a sailor, and that's the best place to look."

"Thank you," Kelder said, "I'll do that."

She almost smiled, then thought better of it. She turned and marched out.

"Well," Irith said when the door had closed, "we're well rid of *her*!"

"Oh, I don't know," Asha replied, "I sort of liked her."

Irith glared at the child, while Kelder said nothing, and Ezdral, as usual, simply stared blankly at Irith.

CHAPTER 31

There were no wizards in Thurion, simply by happenstance, and Klathoa, being ruled by witches, had outlawed all other forms of magic. In Ikala the three wizards had all learned their arts from the same master, who had disapproved of love spells on principle—an attitude that Kelder could appreciate, when Irith reported it.

That was the first day.

The King of Porona did not like his two wizards talking to foreigners, and Irith had to slip in through a window in bird shape in order to discover that neither of them knew a counter for Fendel's Infatuous Love Spell. The only wizard in Thrullimion was not home, and did not return home, although Irith waited most of the afternoon and well into the evening before giving up and making a moonlight flight back to Lamum.

That was the second day, and that evening Thellesh the Wondrous completed his ritual and began reading through the messages his apprentice had collected while he was occupied. When Irith awoke the next morning—which was rather late, since she had not gotten in until almost midnight—she found a message waiting for her in the innkeeper's care.

"It was delivered by a walking table," the innkeeper said, speaking in an awestruck whisper. Irith and Kelder looked at each other, not sure whether to believe this; then Irith unfolded the note and read it aloud.

Thellesh did not know the particular countercharm she was looking for, but would be delighted of a chance to discuss the matter with her.

Irith sent a reply, paying a girl from the village two bits to deliver it, thanking the wizard politely. Then she and Kelder and Asha sat down to consider.

They stayed one more day, resting; Irith paid a visit to Perelia, two kingdoms to the south, on the coast of the Gulf of the East, and found half a dozen wizards, all of them busy with something. One said he might have the counterspell, but would need to research it, which would cost three pieces in gold—he was not interested in trade of any sort, nor did he care who or what Irith was, that was his price.

Irith indignantly rejected it.

Two more were too busy to speak with her at all; two admitted they'd never heard of that particular spell; and the last one was incoherent, so that Irith was unable to figure out if she even spoke a recognizable language.

She was back in Lamum in time for supper, and they all went to bed early.

As Kelder had requested, the innkeeper roused them all an hour before dawn; they dressed, breakfasted, and packed, and by the time the sun had cleared the eastern horizon they were walking down the slight slope from Castle Lamum, toward the border post where soldiers in red kilts passed them into the Hegemony of Ethshar.

From there, they set out across the plain, into Ethshar.

The landscape was remarkably dull, Kelder thought—for mile after mile they walked between endless fields of wheat and corn, all of it still fresh and green. Tidy little farmhouses broke the monotony here and there, all of them whitewashed stone roofed with thatch. Noplace else along the Great Highway was so intensely cultivated; in fact, noplace Kelder had ever seen in his life was so thoroughly farmed. There were no side roads, no rocky patches, no trees or bushes, just fields, and small yards around the houses.

And it went on seemingly forever. The highway marched them onward to the southwest, sometimes straight enough to make a line to the horizon, sometimes curving gently and vanishing into the endless greenery ahead of them.

This was, beyond question, a vast plain; the prophecy was satisfied on that point.

The three-day rest in Lamum had them all in fairly high spirits, but Ezdral and Asha still moved more slowly than Kelder liked; the day wore on, and although they walked steadily, the landscape did not change. The only visible indication that they were making any progress was that Castle Lamum gradually shrank behind them and eventually vanished below the horizon. Other, faster travelers occasionally passed them going westward; none came *from* the west.

After they had been walking for hours, and the sun was high overhead, Kelder burst out, "This is *boring*!"

Irith nodded. "That's why I don't come here often," she said. "The Small Kingdoms are *much* more interesting."

"These fields go on forever!" Kelder said.

"It only seems like it," Irith said.

A moment later she added, "But it does seem like it."

They stopped for lunch at a spot that was just like all the others, and while they ate more westbound traffic passed them.

There was still nothing the other way. Kelder remarked on it.

"Of course not, silly," Irith said. "We aren't halfway yet, and nobody would stop for the night anywhere between Lamum and the bridge—the local farmers would probably kill you if you tried."

It was almost two hours past noon when they encountered their first eastbound traveler.

"Oh, may the gods help me," Kelder said, "you mean we're just now halfway?"

"Probably not," Irith said. "After all, they're probably faster than we are."

Asha whimpered at that and tried to walk faster.

The sun was setting, its parting magic turning the clouds to incredible shades of pink and lavender, and Kelder was becoming concerned that they would have no shelter for the night. He looked at the orange ball and suddenly came to two realizations.

First, the sun was off to the right rather than straight ahead; the road had turned until it was headed far more south than west. And second, the ground was no longer level, but sloping slightly downward. He looked down at the dirt beneath his feet, trying to convince himself that this was not merely an illusion.

Irith noticed what Kelder was doing, and her wings sprang forth; she rose straight up, flapping lazily, and peered ahead.

"I can see the river," she reported, "shining gold in the sunset. There's a bright line across it that must be Azrad's Bridge catching the sun, and a black line beside that that must be the bridge's shadow, and the inn is atop the ridge on the far side. Look closely, maybe you can see the smoke from the chimney."

Kelder stared and saw a line of smoke rising gently into the vast polychrome sky—but that by itself would have meant nothing, as many of the farmhouses had cookfires and chimneys.

"That's the inn?" he asked, pointing.

"That's it," Irith confirmed.

By the time they came within sight of the bridge, full night was upon them; the gods had washed the World in darkness and lit the stars anew. The lesser moon gleamed pink in the west, while the greater was nowhere to be seen. The fields to either side were black in the gloom, as was the road they walked upon.

And in truth, they could see almost nothing of the bridge itself, but the torches set along its rails blazed warm and inviting, beacons in the night. The sight gave Kelder and Asha renewed strength, and they hurried ahead.

Irith held back slightly, and Kelder turned, wondering.

Before he could speak, she said, "There's a toll."

"What?"

"They charge a fee to let you cross the bridge, just the way Caren wanted to charge tolls on the highway through Angarossa."

Kelder stopped. "How much?" he asked.

"A copper piece, it used to be—that was for each adult, no charge for children or livestock."

That meant three pieces—Irith, Ezdral, and himself. Asha would be free.

"I'll fly across," Irith said, "or maybe swim—I haven't been a fish in ages. And I'll meet you on the far side."

Two pieces, then; Kelder considered the contents of his purse and decided that was manageable, but he was not happy about it. "Maybe I should swim, too," he suggested.

"Are you a good swimmer?" Irith asked. "It's a long way to swim for a human, especially in the dark."

"I've never tried swimming at all," Kelder admitted. "There wasn't anywhere *to* swim, in the hills of Shulara."

"Then you can't swim, silly!" Irith told him. "It's something you need to *learn*! You'd just sink and probably drown!"

"Oh," Kelder replied, embarrassed.

"Come on!" Asha called; she had ignored the discussion and was waiting halfway down the slope.

Kelder came.

There were no guards on the bridge, so far as he could see, and he wondered if Irith's information might be out of date. He said as much as they stepped onto the first stones.

"I don't think so," Irith said. "I think they're at the other end. And even if they aren't, I'm going to swim, anyway—I haven't been a fish in *years*!" She leaned over, kissed Kelder on the cheek, then slipped away into the darkness beyond the bridge's torchlit rail.

He tried to watch her go, but outside the glow of the torches he could see nothing but the night. He sighed and led Asha and Ezdral onward.

Irith's information proved correct in every particular; by the time they were halfway across, Kelder could see and hear that four soldiers lounged at the far end of the bridge, chatting in Ethsharitic spoken in accents just like Azraya's, telling each other obscene anecdotes. When they spotted the travelers they broke off the conversation long enough to collect two coppers and then ignored the threesome thereafter.

Once aground again, Kelder hesitated; Irith was nowhere in sight, and although she had told him the inn was just the other side of the low ridge ahead, he could see nothing of it. It might be farther than he had hoped, and Ezdral was in a stupor and on the verge of total collapse. "You two go on ahead," he said, despite misgivings about sending a sick old drunkard and a child alone in the dark. "I'll wait here for Irith."

"I could wait," Asha offered.

Kelder considered; leaving a child alone in the dark wasn't any better, and might be worse.

Before he could answer, though, Irith called, "Here I am!"

Kelder turned to see her walking up a narrow path that descended from the bridge's entrance to the river. Even in the dim glow of the torches, he could see that she was soaked, her long hair hanging in ropes down her back, her white tunic drenched and clinging heavily to her body.

That was very interesting to look at, from Kelder's point of view, as the garment was almost transparent when wet, but he saw that it was also obviously cold and uncomfortable, and he helped her up the stone step that linked the path to the highway.

"What happened?" he asked. "I thought your clothes changed with you."

"They do," she said. "I feel dumb."

"Why?" Asha asked.

Irith snorted in annoyance, and Kelder felt her shivering.

"We can talk about it later," he said. "Let's get to the inn. Irith can dry off there, and we can all warm up."

Nobody argued, and the four of them trudged up the hill, drops of water pattering from Irith's clothes and hair. Kelder's sleeve was saturated as well, where he had put his arm around her.

The hill was longer than it had initially appeared—Kelder had assumed that it was covered with sprouting grain, as the other bank of the river was, though he could not see any in the dark; he had figured that into his estimates. In fact, the ridge was covered with meadows, which meant it was higher than Kelder had estimated. Furthermore, the inn was not at the top but at the foot of the other side.

They did reach it eventually, and found their way around to the entrance, which was on the opposite side. Ezdral was more alert on the way than he had been in hours, obviously seriously concerned about Irith. It was clearly all he could do to keep from wrapping protective arms about her.

"Don't you have a blanket, Kelder?" he asked, about half-way up the first slope.

Kelder cursed himself for his own stupidity and, without stopping, dug a blanket from his pack and wrapped it around the Flyer's shoulders.

When they reached the door it was closed; a torch blazed in a bracket above it, but there was no signboard or other indication that the place was open for business. Light spilled out through cracks in the shutters, so it was obviously not deserted, but Kelder hesitated.

"Are you sure it's an inn?" he asked.

"I'm sure," Irith said. Without bothering to knock, she opened the door and stepped in.

CHAPTER 32

Sound and light and warmth washed over Kelder as he followed Irith into the inn. He found himself in a large, comfortable room, standing on well-worn planking and facing several tables of assorted shapes and sizes. Half a dozen patrons were clustered about one of the larger tables, shouting encouragement to two burly men who sat facing each other, hands locked in an arm-wrestling match. The faces of the two competitors were red and strained with effort. Nobody seemed to be eating, but some of the spectators had mugs in their hands.

The walls were stone, but pierced with numerous doors and shuttered windows. At one end of the room a cheery blaze failed to come anywhere near filling a huge fireplace; a row of mugs stood on the mantel, and above them a scabbarded sword hung from wires set into the stonework.

Most of those present ignored the new arrivals, but a tall brown-haired man in an apron, apparently in his thirties or so, looked up and exclaimed, "Irith!"

"Valder!" Irith called back in Trader's Tongue. "How are you?"

"I'm fine," the man said in the same language, hurrying over. "What about you?"

"I'm freezing cold and dripping wet," Irith replied irritably, "but other than that I'm the same as ever."

"Well, come on over by the fire," Valder said, beckoning. "I'll get you something warm to drink. Thetta!"

A serving wench appeared through one of the doors and looked at the innkeeper questioningly. "Build up the fire a little, would you?" Valder told her. "And tell someone to bring some tea—the kettle's hot, isn't it?" Nor was he idle himself; as he spoke, he was shoving a table out of the way and setting a half-circle of chairs around the hearth.

Just then the arm-wrestling match ended, amid shouts and cheering.

"He got you good, Kelder!" someone called, and Kelder of Shulara growled to himself.

"Best two out of three?" another voice asked.

"That *was* two out of three!"

"Three out of five, then!"

"Done, for another copper."

"You're on." The huddle, which had shown signs of dispersing, coalesced anew. Thetta disappeared back into the kitchen, or whatever lay beyond that door; Valder turned, exasperated, then shrugged and gestured to the chairs.

Gratefully, the four travelers settled into the proffered seats, Irith in the center, Ezdral on her left, and Kelder on her right, with Asha on Kelder's right. They sat silently for a moment, warming hands and feet, while Valder poked at the fire and shouted for more wood.

Thetta reappeared with an armful of logs, and close behind her came a boy bearing a metal tray that held a teapot and half a dozen cups.

"You didn't say how many, sir," the boy said as he approached. "Is it enough?"

"It looks to be," Valder said, taking the tray from him. Thetta dumped the logs on the hearth and began placing them, one by one, onto the flames. Valder put the tray on the table he had moved aside, then poured tea, and distributed cups to the four new arrivals.

Ezdral didn't see his at first, and when it finally registered on his consciousness he glanced away from Irith long enough to look at it with mild distaste.

"You wouldn't happen to have anything stronger, would you, sir?" he asked. "A little *oushka* would warm me better than that, I'm sure."

Valder glanced at the others, and Kelder caught his eye.

The lad shook his head. "I'm terribly sorry," the innkeeper said, "but *these* drunken louts over here have cleaned me out." He waved at the party around the arm-wrestlers. "Not a drop of strong drink do I have until the next cartload comes."

Irith smiled over her tea at him.

Ezdral reluctantly accepted a teacup, just as Thetta dropped the last log into place and headed back toward the kitchens. Valder took a cup himself and pulled up a chair beside Asha, turned so that he was almost facing Irith and Ezdral.

"Now, Irith," he said, "tell me how it is that you came in here soaking wet, when it hasn't rained for a sixnight."

"Yes, Irith," Asha said, "how'd you get all wet?"

"I turned into a fish," she said.

"But when you turned back," Kelder began, "isn't this an awful lot of water? . . ."

"I did something silly," Irith said, giggling slightly at herself; the hot tea and warm fire had done a great deal toward improving her mood. "I turned into a fish to swim the river, so I wouldn't have to pay the toll, right?"

Valder and Kelder nodded.

"Well, I got into the water just fine; dove in and changed in midair, so I was a fish when I landed. And I swam right across, following the bridge piers—it's *dark* down there in the river, and fish eyes aren't any better than human in the dark!"

"I hadn't thought of that," Kelder said.

"That's all right," Irith told him. "Neither had I, and I'd been a fish before, and *you* never were."

"Go on," Valder said. "It was dark . . ."

"Right, it was dark," Irith agreed, "but I found my way across by following the bridge and just by sense of direction—fish can feel the currents, and even when there aren't any currents you can sort of tell directions. It's hard to explain, it's just something fish do."

Kelder could believe that. Everyone said that different animals had different senses.

"And I got to the other side," Irith continued, "and suddenly remembered why I hadn't been a fish for a hundred years."

She paused, relishing the suspense she had created.

"Oh, come on, Irith, tell us!" Asha begged.

"Fish can't get out of the water," Irith said.

For a moment the others all sat, thunderstruck; then Valder burst out laughing uproariously. Kelder and Asha joined in; Ezdral simply stared at Irith.

The shapeshifter smiled at the amusement to her right, then turned left and noticed Ezdral. She stared back at him, annoyed.

"So you were sitting there in the river?" Valder asked, distracting her. "You had to turn back under water?"

"Not *sitting*," Irith said, regaining her good humor. "When I turn from fish to human I come out lying facedown. So there I was, lying in a foot of cold water, fully dressed."

Kelder stopping laughing to listen.

"So I got up, half drowned, and I waded ashore, and there these three were wondering what had happened to me," she said. "And would *you* have said, 'Oh, I forgot fish can't climb out of the water, so I spent ten minutes trying to figure out how to do it'?"

Asha giggled hysterically, and Kelder chuckled.

"Listen," Valder said when the laughter had subsided, "you aren't much bigger than Thetta; why don't you see if she has some dry clothes you can wear, and we'll hang yours by the fire?"

"Oh, please," Irith said, "that would be wonderful."

"Fine," Valder said. *"Thetta!"*

While they waited for the servant to appear, Valder asked, "Have you folks eaten?"

"No," the younger three chorused.

"We'll take care of that as soon as Irith's back, then," he said. Thetta emerged, and he called to her, "Tell someone to bring dinner for four, and while that's fixing, take Irith here upstairs and find her some dry clothes, all right?"

Thetta turned and leaned through the door, calling something to someone else, then came and waited.

Irith rose, put her tea on the table, and said, "Lead the way."

A shout rose from the arm-wrestlers once again, as the other Kelder was defeated for the third and final time, and this time the group began to disperse. A couple of the men eyed Irith with interest as she passed, but no one did more than look.

Once the two girls were gone, Ezdral announced, "I think I . . . I think I'll go see if I can help with supper." He rose and shambled toward the kitchen.

Valder looked questioningly at Kelder, who sighed and shrugged. "He's looking for liquor," Kelder said, "but I don't know how to stop him, short of locking him in somewhere."

Valder sighed. "Let him go, then."

That left three of them, Asha, Kelder, and Valder, sitting in front of the fire.

"Tell me," Valder asked, "who are you people, and how do you come to be traveling with Irith?"

Kelder had been made so comfortable so quickly that he had forgotten that Valder had no idea who he was. "I'm Kelder of Shulara," he said. "That's Asha of Amramion, and the man cadging *oushka* from your kitchen help is Ezdral the Sot. I met Irith on the Great Highway, and we just decided to travel together. We bumped into Asha in Angarossa, after she ran away from her father and her brother got killed, and we found Ezdral in Shan on the Desert."

Valder considered that. "You seem pleasant enough, and I can see why Irith's traveling with you," he said. "And I suppose she felt sorry for the girl." He nodded politely at Asha, who smiled. "But why in the World would Irith put up with the old man, or he with her?"

"She enchanted him," Kelder explained. "A long time ago, when he wasn't much older than I am now. She put a love spell on him, and then didn't know how to take it off."

"And she didn't just fly off and forget about him?" Valder asked, startled.

Kelder was equally startled by accuracy of the innkeeper's guess. "Well, actually," he said, "she did, but then we ran into him in Shan, and he followed us, and when I found out why

I said we should try to find a cure for him, not just leave him there."

"That speaks well of you, lad," Valder said. "Most people would have just left him to rot."

"Oh, I don't think so," Kelder said, embarrassed.

"*I* would have," Asha said. "Why didn't he find his *own* countercharm *years* ago?"

"I don't think he even knew it was a spell," Kelder told her.

"*I* didn't know Irith had any love spells," Valder remarked.

"Well, she doesn't use it much," Kelder said. "It causes trouble. Like turning into a fish."

Valder smiled. "I can see how it might," he said. "So you're looking for a countercharm?"

Kelder nodded. "I thought we could probably find one in Ethshar," he said.

"You may not need to go that far," Valder said. "Do you know the spell's name?"

"Are you a wizard?" Asha asked suspiciously.

"No," Valder replied, "but my wife is."

"It's called Fendel's Infatuous Love Spell," Kelder said, wondering why a wizard would ever have married an innkeeper.

"Oh," said Valder, grinning cheerfully, "that should be no problem, then—Iridith knows just about all Fendel's spells. Fendel was in here just about five years ago, and the two of them traded recipes."

This was too much for Kelder; his jaw dropped, then snapped shut.

"You're teasing," he accused.

"No, I'm not," Valder said.

"Fendel the Great is dead, isn't he?"

"Well, he wasn't the last time I saw him," Valder said, "but I don't know for certain whether he is now. It seems unlikely; he's been around for a very long time."

Over his initial shock, Kelder remembered that Perina had said Fendel *was* rumored to still be alive. He moved on.

"Iridith," he said, "do you mean the famous wizard, Iridith of Ethshar?"

"I mean my wife, Iridith," Valder said, "and she's a wizard, and a good one, but I didn't think she was particularly famous, and she's from Ethshar, but I didn't think she *had* a cognomen. She's just Iridith."

"But there are other people named Iridith . . ."

"And I suppose you're the only Kelder from Shulara?"

Kelder decided that argument wasn't going anywhere. "You're trying to tell me," he said, "that you're married to a powerful wizard and that Fendel the Great is a friend of yours? Why in the World would a wizard marry an ordinary innkeeper, and why would Fendel associate with one?"

"I like to think," Valder said, with both amusement and sarcasm in his tone, "that Iridith married me because she likes me. And Fendel isn't so much a friend as a business acquaintance; we met during the War."

"What war?" Kelder asked, afraid he already knew.

"The *Great* War, of course," Valder said. "How do you think Irith and I came to be friends? Those of us who live longer than normal—I wouldn't go so far as to call us immortals, you understand, but on the other hand, I don't have any intention of dying any time soon—anyway, those of us who live more than a century or two tend to run into each other eventually."

Asha was staring wide-eyed at the innkeeper.

"You're telling me," Kelder said, eyes narrowed, "that *you're* hundreds of years old?"

"About two hundred and fifty," Valder replied. "I'm under a curse, you see—Fendel made a mistake in a spell he put on my sword when I was in the army." He pointed at the sword that hung above the fireplace. "I can't die until it kills me, and it can't kill me until it's killed a few other men first, and the war's over, which means I could get in trouble if I went around lopping off heads. Besides, I'm in no hurry to die."

"Oh," Kelder said, not sure he believed this.

"I don't usually tell people this," Valder added, "but if you dragged Ezdral here all the way from Shan on the Desert, at least your *intentions* are good."

"So you . . . you met Fendel the Great during the war, because he was enchanting swords?" Kelder asked. "And he still comes to visit? And was it during the war that you met Iridith? And Irith?"

"No," Valder said, "I met Fendel accidentally, when I stumbled across his hiding place, and he enchanted my sword to get rid of me. I've only seen him once since then, when he stopped at the inn on his way somewhere and talked shop with Iridith. As for my wife, I met Iridith after the war, when I was looking for a wizard who could fix the spell on the sword. And I met Irith about fifty years after *that*, when she turned up here at the inn, and since you don't meet very many girls with wings, I got interested and found out her story." He paused, then asked, "You do know who she is, don't you, and how she got that way?"

"She's told me," Kelder said warily.

Valder smiled wryly. "I don't know what she told you or didn't," he said, "but it probably wasn't the entire truth. Did she say why she used Javan's Second Augmentation?"

"Yes," Kelder said. "She was bored . . ."

"She was scared green," Valder interrupted.

"She said there was a scare that the Northerners were going to invade . . ."

"There might have been," Valder conceded, "but mostly she wanted to get out of serving her term."

"Serving? . . ."

"Sure," Valder said. "There was a war on, and every journeyman wizard was required to serve a five-year term in the military—sometimes more. And Irith wasn't about to do that."

"Oh," Kelder said.

"And did she tell you about the glamour?"

"The what?"

"The beauty spell," Valder explained. "She was pretty to begin with, but come on, do you think a face like that could be natural? She used a glamour, a spell that enhances appearance, makes you more attractive—it was one of the set she put in there, but somehow she never happens to mention it—does she?"

"No," Kelder admitted, "she didn't."

"And she probably told you about the eternal youth," Valder continued, "since she wouldn't have put a love spell on an old man, so she must have done it while he was young, and you'd have figured that out."

"She told me about that," Kelder said a little defensively.

"Did she tell you *all* about it?" Valder insisted.

"What do you mean?"

"I mean, did she tell you that not only can't she grow old, she can't grow *up*? She'll be fifteen forever, not just physically, but mentally."

"She said she was fifteen," Kelder agreed warily.

"She meant it," Valder said. "She's fifteen in every way, except chronologically. She can't ever change, can't mature. She'll *always* be flighty and spoiled and selfish."

"Well . . ." Kelder began.

That didn't sound possible, somehow. He turned to see what Asha thought, only to discover that the child had fallen asleep in her chair.

Then Irith called from the stairs, and the kitchen door opened for the delivery of their dinner, and Kelder decided to worry about it later.

CHAPTER 33

*Valder, in a generous gesture that Kelder found him-*self not really appreciating, gave Ezdral, Irith, and Kelder separate rooms, at no charge; Asha he put in Thetta's room.

The dinner, too, was on the house—except for the wine. That he charged for. Ezdral didn't seem to mind, however, having obtained *oushka* somewhere. Valder had to carry the old man to his room.

Asha had woken up long enough to stuff bread and cheese in her mouth and had then dozed off again, and been turned over to Thetta for the night.

When Valder returned from hauling the unconscious Ezdral upstairs, he took a place at the table and said seriously, "We need to get that spell off him."

"I know," Kelder said. Irith looked down at her plate.

"Iridith should be back in a couple of days," Valder went on, "and I'm sure she knows what to do—it's probably something very simple, really."

"She's not here?" Irith looked up.

"No, she's up at the other inn," Valder replied.

"What other inn?" the Flyer asked.

"Oh, didn't I tell you?"

Irith shook her head.

"We bought another inn, up in Sardiron, in The Passes," Valder explained. "The man who built it was getting old and wanted to retire to his grandson's farm. It's called the Crimson Wolf, and it's in a really good location, on the road from the Tazmor mines to Sardiron of the Waters. I figure that every so often I'll move up there, and then my son can come back and run this place a few years later."

"Your son?" Kelder asked.

"He doesn't have a son, silly," Irith explained. "That's how he keeps people from realizing he's two hundred years old."

This confirmation that Valder really was ancient, and that he and Irith apparently did share a good many secrets with one another, was reassuring. It meant the innkeeper was neither lying nor mad. "I see," Kelder said.

"I guess we'll just have to put up with him until she gets back," Irith said.

Kelder nodded agreement.

"Well, you're welcome to stay until then," Valder said. "You may have to double up if it gets busy, though—I don't *usually* have three empty rooms."

"That would be fine," Kelder said, "but we don't have much money . . ."

"Don't worry about that," Valder said. "I never charge Irith or her friends."

"Oh," Kelder said, "if you're sure . . ."

"I'm sure."

"Well, thank you."

"And I'll do what I can to keep liquor away from the old man," Valder continued. "But it probably won't do any good."

"I know," Kelder said. "Thank you anyway."

Valder waved his gratitude aside. "That takes care of *him*, then," he said. "But I don't think he was the *only* problem you brought with you. What about the little girl?"

Kelder and Irith looked at each other, then back at Valder. "Her father beat her," Irith said, "so she ran away from home. She was going to stay with her brother, who had joined a party of bandits in Angarossa, but they tried to rob a caravan that had hired a demonologist as a guard." She shuddered delicately. "The merchants are getting *mean* about Angarossa now."

"The brother's dead?" Valder asked.

"Oh, yes," Kelder said. "We built his pyre ourselves."

"Any other sibs? Or her mother?"

"Her mother's dead," Kelder replied, "and there weren't any other sibs."

"She's very stubborn," Irith remarked.

"Tough, too," Kelder said. "I think that if she just had a roof over her head and steady meals, she could take care of herself just fine."

"Do you want to keep her with you?" Valder asked him.

Kelder hesitated, then said, "The problem is, *I* don't have a roof over my head, or steady meals."

"Do you have a home somewhere?"

"Well, my parents are back in Shulara," Kelder explained, "but I don't think they'd take Asha in. Or maybe they would—I don't really know." He hadn't really considered it. He had planned on taking Irith back to Shulara as his wife, but the idea of taking *Asha* there had simply never occurred to him.

"Can she work?" Valder asked.

Kelder and Irith looked at each other again.

"I don't know," Kelder answered.

"If she can," Valder said, "and if she wants to, she can stay here. I'm not short-handed right now, but Thetta keeps talking about leaving, and Semder wants to leave and find an apprenticeship now that he's old enough, so I probably *will* be short-handed soon enough. The work's not hard, really."

"You'll have to ask her," Kelder said, "but it sounds good to me."

"Me, too," Irith agreed.

"Well, then," Valder said, rising, "I guess that's everything."

"I suppose so," Irith said, also rising. "And I'm going to bed—I'm *tired*, and I've been using the bloodstone spell too much lately."

"I'll be up in a few minutes," Kelder said. He sat where he was and watched Irith walk gracefully up the stairs. She was wearing a plain woolen tunic of Thetta's, simple and unadorned dark blue, with a black wool skirt, and neither garment was particularly attractive; even so, she was astonishingly beautiful.

Valder watched, too, and then looked at Kelder. He sat down again.

"You're in love with her, too, aren't you?" he asked.

Reluctantly Kelder admitted, "I think so." He started to say more, to tell Valder about Zindré's prophecies, then stopped. The innkeeper seemed like a trustworthy sort, the kind of person one wants to confide in, but really, Kelder thought, it wasn't any of his business.

"Do you think she might have used the spell on you, too?"

Kelder considered that, but shook his head. "I don't *think* so," he said. "I'm certainly not as obsessed with her as Ezdral is. And Irith says that if she *had* used it on me, I wouldn't argue with her so much."

"*Do* you argue with her?"

"Sometimes."

"Then you're right, you're probably not enchanted."

It was a relief to hear that from a knowledgeable third party. "Thank you," Kelder said. "*She* is, though," he added a moment later.

"Is what?"

"Enchanted," Kelder explained. "I'd like to break that, too."

Valder's eyes widened. "There isn't any love spell on *her*," he said, "is there? I didn't think that was possible—she's supposed to be immune to magic."

Kelder shook his head. "I didn't mean a love spell," he said. "I meant Javan's whatever-it-is."

"Oh, *that*," Valder said. "She doesn't *want* to break that, though."

"Are you sure?"

"Well," Valder said slowly, "Iridith offered to try to break the spell, years ago, and Irith wasn't interested."

"She might be now, though," Kelder said.

Valder shrugged.

"She might," he said.

That night, lying in bed alone, Kelder thought long and hard about his future.

He had had his fill of traveling. The towns along the Great Highway were all very well, but he had no place in them, and he had no great urge to spend his life wandering from one to the next, working odd jobs and living in inns. He was ready to settle down again, at least for a while.

But did he really want to go home to Shulara?

Zindré had said he would go back, so he had taken it for granted, but did he *want* to go back? Back to the rolling green hills, the hard, boring work on the farm, his oh-so-superior older sisters? Returning covered in glory might be fun, but living there again—somehow, after all his traveling, Shulara seemed smaller and duller than ever in retrospect. The Great Highway hadn't been lined with magicians and minstrels, he hadn't seen a single dice game or bedded any serving wenches; the World was not the bright roaring carnival he had hoped for. It was, instead, larger and more complicated than he had imagined.

Going back to Shulara—he didn't think it would work.

But if he didn't want to go on wandering, and didn't want to go back, what was left?

He could settle somewhere else, of course—find a home, a steady income. Friends, maybe.

He remembered Azraya, who intended to become a sailor, and thought that might be the best of both paths, in a way— your ship was your home, your crewmates your friends, yet you traveled the World, seeing its wonders.

That might be worth trying.

He couldn't sign onto a ship here on the river, though—at least, not so far as he knew. From here, he had two routes he could take.

Ethshar lay one long day's march to the south—Ethshar of the Spices, the largest city in the World, which the bolder storytellers claimed was home to a million people; Ethshar, the greatest port in the World, whence ships sailed to the far- thest lands of north, south, and west; Ethshar, home to the in- vincible army of the city's overlord, to all the greatest magicians, the wisest scholars; Ethshar, where it was said that absolutely anything could be had for a price.

He could be there in a day, once Irith's spells were all broken. And he could find work there, even if it was just soldiering in the city guard.

Or he could go back home to Shulara, to the farm and family.

There wasn't really anywhere else he wanted to go in the Small Kingdoms; none of the towns he had passed through stood out as a good place to settle. If not back to Shulara, then on to Ethshar.

But should he go home? That was what the prophecy had said.

But it had not said *when*, and it had implied he would see Ethshar first. If Iridith could break the spells on Ezdral and Irith right here, there was no more need to go to Ethshar—but there was no reason he couldn't. He could always change his mind and go back later.

And if he went home, he could leave again, couldn't he?

Well, perhaps not, not if he had crops and children to worry about. Better, then, to see Ethshar first, then go home.

And then there was Irith to consider. He did not think she would accept a marriage proposal just yet; *maybe* she would, but he wasn't ready to try it.

But would she be more likely to accept if he was going on to Ethshar, or if he was going home to Shulara?

He tried to imagine Irith living with him in the hills of Shulara, tending the house and crops, trading at the market. The image wouldn't come; every time he thought of her he saw her spreading her wings and soaring upward, away from anything so mundane as farm and family.

If her spells were broken, though, she would have no wings.

He remembered once, as a boy, he had watched the princess ants emerging from their nest, swarming upward into the sky on their transparent, shining wings. His father had explained how each one would find a new place, a new nest, where she would settle in. Her wings would fall off, and she would become a queen, staying safe underground and laying her eggs while her offspring tended to her.

Irith was like that; she had fled her old home, where there was no safe place for her, and had flittered about the World.

Sooner or later, though, came a time to shed the wings and settle in.

Kelder had been away from home less than a month, and he felt *he* was ready to settle—if it was with Irith.

But somehow, he knew she would never settle while she had her magic. She might try, but he would age, and she would not; he would mature, and she would not; and one day she would get bored and fly away.

But he was sure she would agree to give up her magic. After all, after two hundred years, she must be tired of it all, must be ready to grow up and settle down.

It might take her a while to realize it, but surely she would.

He rolled over and went to sleep.

CHAPTER 34

Iridith returned to the Inn at the Bridge some three days after Irith and her companions had arrived; she flew up to the door around midafternoon of the third day, startling Kelder considerably. He had never seen anyone fly without wings before.

That three days had been pleasant enough; Asha had been delighted at the suggestion that she might stay at the inn permanently and had immediately set out to learn her way around the kitchen, yard, and stable. Ezdral had remained much the same, drinking surreptitiously, staring at Irith, following her and muttering incoherently when awake, and spending most of his time asleep, or at any rate unconscious.

Kelder and Irith had wandered about the area, admiring the broad river, the vast open sky of the plain, the impressive engineering of Azrad's Bridge—and each other.

Kelder was surprised, the morning of the first day, to see that the inn was built at a fork; the Great Highway split here, running in three directions, rather than two.

The northern route led back across the bridge to the Small Kingdoms; the southern to Ethshar of the Spices; and the third road went westward, to Ethshar of the Sands and all the northern lands.

When Iridith arrived Asha was washing plates, Ezdral was snoring by the hearth, and Irith was off somewhere fluttering about in the shape of a rainbow-hued bird, while Kelder sat out front and contemplated the three roads, thinking about nothing in particular. Thus only Kelder saw the wizard descend gracefully out of the sky and land gently on her feet.

"You must be Iridith," he said in Trader's Tongue, as she stepped up to the door.

"I suppose I must," she said in Ethsharitic.

Kelder switched languages, apologized for his rudeness, and introduced himself as he opened the door for her and then followed her inside.

He stood quietly not watching as she and Valder greeted each other enthusiastically. When the two were no longer touching, he broached the subject of countercharms.

"The love spell is easy," the wizard said, once the situation had been explained. "A drop of the spell-caster's blood in each of the victim's eyes will clear that right up."

"The spell-caster?" Kelder asked.

"In this case," Iridith said, "that would be Irith."

"We need her blood?"

"Certainly. Just two drops; a pinprick will do fine."

Kelder was unsure just how willing Irith would be—but after all, it was just two drops, and it would cure Ezdral.

On the more serious question of how Javan's Second Augmentation could be ended, Iridith hesitated. "You know," she said, "I've had ideas of how to do it before, and Irith has always refused."

"I don't think she will this time," Kelder said. "I think she's finally growing up."

Valder and Iridith looked at one another silently, then back at Kelder.

"Kelder," Iridith said gently, "she *can't* grow up. Ever. At all. Not until the spell is broken."

"I think she has," he insisted. "Just a little."

"Well," Iridith said reluctantly, "we can ask her."

They did ask her, an hour later, in the main room of the inn.

"Kelder," she said, staring at him, "are you *crazy*? Give up my magic? Let myself grow old and ugly, and die someday? Spend all my time in one shape, so I can't get away if someone bothers me? Give up *flying*?"

"But, Irith . . ." he began.

"Are you *crazy*?" she repeated. "Of *course* I won't give it up!"

"I was thinking you could come back to Shulara with me . . ." Kelder began.

"To *Shulara*? What, and be a farmer? Just sit in one place until I *rot*?" She stared at him in disbelief. "You *are* crazy! Kelder, why would I want to live like *that*? I'm famous and free! I'm *special* the way I am!"

And then, as if to emphasize her point, she vanished. A moment later Kelder heard the beating of wings outside; he stepped to the door and saw her appear again, rising into the air on gleaming white pinions.

He watched her go with his gut hard and tight with disappointment.

"I should have known," he muttered to himself.

Valder and Iridith said nothing.

Irith returned during supper, and the subject was never mentioned again; instead, Iridith explained how to remove the spell on Ezdral.

"That's all?" Irith asked. "Two drops of blood? I could have done that *years* ago!"

"Yes," Iridith agreed, "if you'd known, you could have."

Irith frowned. "Well, *next* time," she said, "I'll know what to do."

"Next . . ." Kelder stopped himself before another word could escape, but the knot of dismay in his belly grew larger and heavier.

"Shall we take the blood now?" Iridith asked, drawing the silver dagger from her belt.

Irith eyed the blade unhappily, then glanced at Ezdral, still asleep on a bench by the hearth. "There isn't any hurry, is there?" she said. "I mean, Ezdral won't care if we wait a few days."

That was the pebble that sank the barge. Kelder grabbed Irith by the arm and shoved his face close to hers.

"Listen," he said, "you are going over to Ezdral right now, and I'm going to prick your finger, and we're going to put a drop of your blood under each eyelid, just the way Iridith said, whether he's asleep or not. He's been under your damnable spell for forty years too long already!"

"All *right*," she said, pulling away, "you don't need to *shout*!"

She turned and looked at the drunkard with distaste, but when Kelder reached for her again she rose quickly and crossed to him. She knelt beside him and held out her left hand.

"Here," she said.

While Iridith watched silently, Kelder used the point of his own knife to draw blood from Irith's left little finger. He dabbed up a drop on his own little finger, then peeled back one of Ezdral's eyelids with his other hand and carefully pressed the drop onto the eye beneath.

Ezdral snorted, but did not stir.

Kelder repeated the operation with the other eye, then sat back on his haunches and waited.

Nothing happened, except that Irith said, "*Hai*, that hurts! Has someone got a bandage, or some water? Iridith, do you know healing spells?"

The two of them ate their supper that night in resentful silence. At the next table, where Valder and Iridith were bringing each other up to date, Asha made a point of bringing Iridith her meal, to impress her new mistress with her enthusiasm and ability. Whenever the girl looked away Iridith grinned with delight. When Asha was watching, of course, the wizard kept her face serious, accepting the overattentive service in the spirit in which it was meant.

Afterward, Kelder decided that something had to be done. He suspected that Irith, in terror of being coerced out of her magic, was on the verge of fleeing. That would not do. If she fled this time, somehow, he was less certain than ever before that he would ever see her again. Zindré's predictions seemed a tenuous thread to bind her with; he could no longer trust only in the prophecy. He wanted to speak to Irith in private, to explain, to tell her he loved her and ask her to marry him.

After all, why should he keep the prophecy secret any longer? If she was to be his wife they had to trust each other.

And even with her magic, even with her refusal to consider a life in Shulara, he still wanted her. They could live in Ethshar, if she wanted, or somewhere else; there was no hurry about going back to Shulara, and he didn't really care if he *ever* went back—except that Zindré had said he would, and it was her promise that made him dare to ask Irith for her hand.

After all, how could an ordinary farmboy have the audacity to try to wed a legendary creature like Irith, without some magical support of his own?

He needed to tell her all that. He needed to talk to her alone, but with the inn full of customers, with servants hurrying hither and yon, finding a suitable place was a challenge.

Finally, in a moment of inspiration, he borrowed a lantern from Valder and suggested to Irith, "Come out to the hilltop with me and let's look at the river in the moonlight. Both moons are up; it should be especially pretty."

She considered him for a long moment before saying "All right."

Together they walked up to the top of the ridge behind the inn, not speaking yet, and together they settled onto the grass of the meadow. The night air was cool, but not cold— certainly warmer than it had been on previous evenings. The river was a constantly changing band of rose and gold sparkles in the light of the two moons, and for a long moment they watched it in silence.

"Thank you," Kelder said at last, "for curing Ezdral."

"Well, it wasn't his fault," Irith said.

Kelder was still trying to puzzle out exactly what she meant by that when a blood-curdling shriek split the night. Both of them started; the crickets fell silent for a moment before resuming their interrupted chirping.

"What was *that*?" Irith asked.

"I don't know," Kelder said. "I think it came from the inn." He turned to look.

"Where is she?" screamed the voice. *"Where is that bitch?"*

"That's Ezdral," Irith whispered. Kelder turned in surprise, and she added, "He's really mad at me."

Kelder had not thought about how Ezdral might react, once the spell was removed. Now that it was thrust under his nose, though, he realized that naturally, the man would be furious. The love spell had protected *itself*, in a way, by making it impossible for Ezdral to think ill of Irith; now that the spell was gone, forty-four years of frustration and anger could pour out all at once.

And Irith was its obvious target.

Kelder stood and looked back toward the inn.

He could see a shadowy figure, barely visible in the distant light of the torch over the door—a man, standing unsteadily in the road. The figure shook a fist in the air. *"Irith!"* Ezdral bellowed. "I'll hunt you down and kill you, you stupid little monster!"

"What should we do?" Irith asked, holding Kelder's leg.

"I don't know," Kelder said, frozen with indecision.

The figure by the inn was turning, turning and scanning the dark landscape, and now his gaze climbed the ridge, and Kelder suddenly realized that he must be silhouetted in the moonlight, and that Ezdral might well blame *him*, as well as Irith, for all his misfortunes—however unfair that might be.

Ezdral spotted him.

"Irith!" the old man bellowed again.

Kelder had not even considered the possibility of mistaken identity.

"Come on," he said, "let's get out of here." He pulled Irith up and began running down the slope toward the river—not with any particular goal in mind, but simply because it was away from the raging Ezdral.

Ezdral, his mind still fogged with drink and fury, saw the figure atop the ridge fleeing and knew unthinkingly and beyond question that it was Irith, that his vengeance was at hand if he could catch up with her. He charged up the slope, yelling.

"I wasted my *entire life* hunting for you, you stinking little idiot," he shouted, "and by all the gods, I'm going to *catch* you, finally!"

Kelder and Irith stumbled down the northern slope, toward

the bridge and the river, in a panic; Kelder kept a firm grip on
Irith's arm. The four soldiers, the toll collectors, turned to see
what the commotion was, and in response Kelder instinctively
steered away from the bridge, not realizing that that left nothing but the steep bank of the river.

"Kelder," Irith gasped, "Kelder, let go of me!"

Kelder stumbled on dew-moistened grass, and Irith pulled
free. She turned and saw Ezdral, with incredible speed for a
man in his battered condition, charging down at her.

She squealed in terror and froze for a few seconds. Then,
as Ezdral neared, she vanished, and a frightened bird fluttered
upward into the night.

An instant later the enraged Ezdral, unable to stop on the
steep, slippery slope, lunged through the spot where Irith had
stood and went tumbling over the verge and into the river.

He struck with a tremendous splash; a few drops spattered
Kelder's breeches. And then, to Kelder's horror, the waters
closed over the old man and began to calm.

Ezdral did not reappear.

"Irith!" Kelder screamed. "Save him!"

Irith transformed herself in midair, from bird to winged
girl, and called back, "Are you joking? He tried to kill me!
Besides, I'd get soaked."

"But he'll drown!"

"He's an icky old drunkard," Irith replied. "*Let* him
drown!"

Words failed him, and Kelder, desperate, dove over the
bank and into the river.

He struck the water unevenly, arms and legs flailing, and
was astonished at how much the impact *hurt*—he hadn't
thought water was that solid. Then he was in the water—and
under it, as he quickly discovered that Irith was right, swimming *is* something one needs to learn, it does not happen by
instinct.

He thrashed wildly, trying to get his head above water, but
to no avail; the air rushed from his lungs, and the water
closed over his head. He floundered, reaching for the bottom
with his feet and not finding it. He tried to call for help, and

the water flooded his mouth and nose, choking him. His chest felt as if it were about to burst.

Everything went black, and he waited to die—but death did not come.

Instead, strong arms took hold of him, twisted him around until his face was out of the water. He couldn't see his rescuer as he felt himself dragged through the current, as firm hands clasped his arms and hauled him up onto the bank.

The pressure on Kelder's chest became unbearable; his mouth opened, and he vomited what felt like the entire river out onto the grass.

And with that out of the way, he fainted.

CHAPTER 35

When he awoke Kelder needed a long moment to figure out where he was. The ceiling was whitewashed and featureless, with morning sun streaked across it, and at first that was all he could see. He was in a bed, he knew that by the feel of the mattress and bedclothes, but which bed he could not tell.

It gradually sank in that he was in his bed at Valder's inn.

He turned his head and found Valder's serving maid, Thetta, sitting beside him, reading something from a small stack of papers. He tried to speak, to ask her what was happening, but all that came out was a croak.

That was enough; she looked up from the papers and said, surprised, "You're awake!"

Kelder was unsure just how to respond to so obvious a statement, but since his voice didn't seem to be working yet, that didn't matter much. He croaked again in confirmation of her observation.

"Just a minute," Thetta said, giving him a comforting pat on the shoulder, "I'll go get Valder." She rose and hurried out the door.

Kelder used the time until her return to see if he could get his voice working, and when Valder and Thetta entered he was able to ask, still in a croak but intelligibly, "What happened?"

"The soldiers pulled you out," Valder said. "Ezdral, too. They heard the splashing, and Irith yelling, and they came and got you."

That made sense, Kelder saw. "Is Ezdral all right?" he asked.

Valder grimaced. "More or less," he said. "He didn't drown, if that's what you mean, and he didn't swallow as much water as you did, or breathe any in—Kelder, don't you know *anything* about being in the water?"

Kelder shook his head.

"Well," Valder told him, "you did just about everything wrong it's possible to do."

Kelder shrugged and smiled wryly. That much he could do; it was only things involving breathing or his throat that were painful.

"Anyway," Valder went on, "Ezdral didn't drown, but he came out of the river still screaming at Irith, and mad at you, and me, and Asha, and just about everybody else. Not that I blame him." He sighed. "I had the soldiers keep him, and they took him back to Ethshar when their relief arrived—they're well on the way by now; that was hours ago."

Kelder blinked. "What . . ." he began, and found he didn't have the breath to continue. He tried again. "What will happen to . . ." Again, his wind gave out.

"What will happen to him there?" Valder guessed, and Kelder nodded. "I don't know," Valder admitted. "I asked them to try to find him a job, maybe clerking for one of the guard captains, but I don't know if that'll work. If not, I suppose he'll wind up in the Hundred-Foot Field—but that's better than the back market in Shan, I'm sure."

Kelder swallowed carefully, readying his throat, and asked, "What *is* the Hundred-Foot Field?" He had wondered that ever since Azraya had first mentioned it.

"Oh, don't you know?" Valder smiled. "Well, Ethshar is a walled city," he explained, "and it was built during the Great War, when the walls and defenses were serious business, so it has what is probably the biggest, fanciest city wall ever built. It goes around three sides of the city, and the fourth side is the waterfront. There's an entire army camp built into it on the east side—they call the area near there Camptown, as a result. Even so, though, if there was a real war, and the city was under assault, or siege, the wall isn't big enough to move all the troops and equipment you might need from one spot to another, and it's *too* big to man and equip the whole thing constantly. So there's a strip of land just inside the wall that Azrad the Great declared had to always be kept clear to allow troop movements, a strip extending one hundred feet in from the inner side of the wall. The inner edge is a street, naturally—Wall Street—but nobody needs a hundred-foot-wide street, especially when you can only build on one side of it, so the rest is an open field. That's the Hundred-Foot Field. The penalty for building anything permanent there, even just a few bricks stacked up, is death."

Kelder still looked puzzled, and Valder added, "And since it's the only place inside the wall where nothing can be built, including fences, and since it goes all the way around the city, it's where all the beggars and thieves live. It's a sort of labor pool, too—anyone who hasn't got a place will wind up there, and some of them aren't thieves, just down on their luck, so when someone needs workers and isn't too particular, he can just go to the Field and give a shout, and usually get half a dozen. I used men from the Hundred-Foot Field when I built this inn, two hundred years ago." He smiled reassuringly. "Ezdral could do worse than winding up in the Field, believe me."

Azraya had not been so sanguine about it, and she had actually lived there, while Valder presumably had not. "It doesn't sound any better than Shan," Kelder said bitterly.

Valder shrugged. "Well, you can't save someone who doesn't want to be saved," he said. "And at least you got the spell off him, so he has a chance now, once he calms down. Besides, Shan on the Desert is dying, it's been declining for a century—nobody wants to go all the way out to the end of the World, and now there are other places to get most of what Shan sells. The Great Highway isn't all that great anymore; it used to carry three times the traffic it does now. Most of my customers here are bound to Sardiron or one of the Ethshars; those are all healthy and growing."

Kelder was mollified, but not entirely convinced. He had

wanted to do better in his role as champion of the downtrodden. He had found Asha a place, here at the inn; he had wanted to do the same for everyone he had traveled with.

Of course, Azraya had gone on ahead, and he had no way of knowing what had become of her. And now Ezdral was gone, as well.

That left Irith—and himself, of course.

"Where's Irith?" he asked.

"Downstairs," Valder said. "Would you like to see her?"

Kelder nodded, and Valder left.

A moment later Irith peeked around the door, a worried expression on her face. "Kelder?" she asked. "Are you all right?"

"I'm fine," he said. His voice cracked.

The shapeshifter slipped into the room and took the chair Thetta had used. "You're really all right?" she asked.

Kelder nodded.

"Oh, *good!*" Irith said, smiling. "You were so *silly*, jumping in after Ezdral, when you *know* you can't swim! I mean, I didn't realize it was that *important*, that you were going to try to save him *yourself* if I didn't. I mean, *really*, Kelder, that was *dumb!*" She giggled nervously, a laugh like a bird's song.

Kelder stared at her.

Not that important? A man's life, not that important?

"Well, he's all taken care of *now*, of course," Irith went on. "The soldiers took him to Ethshar, and good riddance, I say. And Asha's happy here with Valder, so that just leaves the two of us, and of course we don't want to go to Ethshar *now*, because it's a big city and all that, but we might run into Ezdral there, and besides, there isn't any *reason* to go, now that we aren't looking for a good wizard." She giggled again. "And I *told* you we might meet Iridith! She travels a lot, and once she and Valder had a spat that lasted almost two years and she stayed away the entire time, so I wasn't *sure* she would be here, and besides, she doesn't usually like people to know that Iridith the wizard and Iridith the innkeeper's wife are the same *person*. I mean, you can see how that would be inconvenient, can't you?"

Kelder looked at her blankly.

"Oh, of course you can, I'm being foolish," Irith said, waving a hand airily. "I don't know how she stands it sometimes, a great wizard living with an ordinary person, I really don't know why she does it, but then, Valder's an old dear, and she keeps him young with her magic anyway. I wish *I* could do that!"

She looked anxiously at Kelder for a second, then resumed her good humor and her babbling.

"*Anyway*," she said, "I thought that we could head east again, along the highway, because after all, you didn't really get to see much of Shan on the Desert, I mean, did you ever even see it by daylight at all, really? And if you want, we could make a side trip to Shulara, and I could meet your family, but of course I wouldn't stay, I mean, what would *I* do on a farm? Turn into a cat and catch the mice in your barn? I *hate* mice—I mean, they taste good, but I think you have to grow up a cat to really like catching the little things and eating them, especially raw."

Kelder stared at her. She was beautiful, very beautiful indeed; her hair caught the light spilling in through the window and blazed golden, and every curve of her face was soft and perfect, but somehow that didn't matter as much as Kelder had thought.

"*You* wouldn't stay there, either, would you?" she asked worriedly. "I mean, just go back to your farm to live?"

He shook his head. "No," he said. Zindré had never said he would *stay*, merely that he would return safely, and he supposed that someday he might.

Just now, though, he did not particularly care whether he ever saw Shulara again—and what's more, he didn't care whether Zindré had been absolutely omniscient or a lying old thief.

"Good!" she said. "Well, then, we'll go on to Shan, and you can see it properly, without worrying about nasty old drunks or stealing severed heads or troublesome little children, and we'll have a *wonderful* time, won't we?"

"No," he said again.

She stared at him. "But, Kelder, why *not*?" she asked, baffled.

"I'm going to Ethshar," he said. "To stay, I think."

"You're still confused," she said, patting his arm. "I'll talk to you again when you're feeling better, and we'll decide what to do." She stood. "Good-bye, Kelder," she said.

Then she turned and left the room.

He watched her go, her white and gold tunic draping splendidly over her curves, and he realized that she hadn't changed at all; she was just as she had been the day they met.

And after all, why shouldn't she be? That was less than a month ago, a month out of more than two centuries, for her. Brief as the time was, though, he knew *he* had changed. So had Asha. So had Ezdral.

And Irith hadn't.

And she never would.

And really, destined or not, how could he marry a child like that?

CHAPTER 36

*K*elder hefted the pack onto his shoulder and looked up.

Irith waved a final farewell, then swooped eastward, her wings gleaming brightly in the morning sun. She dwindled in the distance.

He wondered if he would ever see her again. If he did, he suspected she wouldn't recognize him, or would pretend not to. And he would not presume on old friendship, he promised himself.

Valder and Asha were busy inside, he knew, but he waved a farewell to them, as well, just in case they happened to be looking out the window. Then he set his foot firmly on the highway and set out toward Ethshar.

He was looking forward to seeing it, to finding himself a place in the city—and perhaps even finding Azraya there.

He had never heard Azraya laugh; perhaps she, too, had a laugh like birdsong. Any number of women might have such a laugh.

And Zindré might have been just a charlatan; it really didn't matter anymore whether the prophecy was absolute truth or nothing but lies. He would live out his life as he saw fit, taking it one step at a time, and not worrying about whether it fit any predictions.

He rather hoped he would meet Azraya again, when he got to Ethshar. Maybe, he thought, they could find a place together.

270

He smiled at his own eagerness and shook his head. Maybe they could.

Or maybe not.

AUTHOR'S NOTE: *Linguistics*

Some scholars may wonder how the people of the Small Kingdoms are able to learn foreign languages as quickly as they do.

It must be remembered that all of the two hundred languages spoken in the World in the fifty-third century of human speech diverged from a single mother tongue within the last five hundred years—and that that mother tongue, Ethsharitic, is still alive and flourishing.

For a Dwomorite to learn Quorulian is not equivalent to an American learning Japanese, but to an Italian learning Spanish. Many of the so-called languages are in fact merely different dialects. The difference between, say, Krithimionese and Ethsharitic is no greater than the difference between English as spoken in York and New York—perhaps less.

Trader's Tongue is a simplified version of Ethsharitic with various borrowings, an altered accent, and a certain bantering tone suited to haggling added in.

The greatest linguistic disparity in all the World, between Semmat and the island dialect of Tintallionese, is roughly the same as the difference between English and German.

ABOUT THE AUTHOR

Lawrence Watt-Evans was born and raised in eastern Massachusetts, the fourth of six children in a house full of books. Both parents were inveterate readers, and both enjoyed science fiction; he grew up reading anything handy, including a wide variety of speculative fiction. His first attempts at writing SF were made at the age of seven.

Being qualified for no other enjoyable work—he had discovered selling door-to-door and working in ladder factories, supermarkets, or fast-food restaurants to be something less than enjoyable—he took to writing, with no great success until the completion of a fantasy novel, *The Lure of the Basilisk*, which sold to Del Rey Books and began his career as a full-time writer.

Taking Flight is fifth in the Ethshar fantasy series, following *The Misenchanted Sword*, *With a Single Spell*, *The Unwilling Warlord*, and *The Blood of a Dragon*.

He has also authored science fiction and horror novels, and has written more than thirty published short stories, including the Hugo-winning "Why I Left Harry's All-Night Hamburgers."

He married in 1977, has two children, and lives in the Maryland suburbs of Washington, D.C.